The Story Tree

The Story Tree

David Spangler

The Lorian Association Press
PO BOX 1368
Issaquah, WA 98027
www.lorian.org

The Story Tree

Edited by Susan Sherman and Julia Spangler

Cover art and interior illustrations by Deva Berg

Published by The Lorian Association
PO Box 1368
Issaquah, WA 98027

ISBN 0-936878-04-5

Library of Congress Cataloging available

Spangler, David
The Story Tree / David Spangler

Library of Congress Control Number: 2003113863

First Edition: December 2003

Printed in the United States of America

0 9 8 7 6 5 4 3 2 1

www.lorian.org

ACKNOWLEDGEMENTS

When a book happily sees the light of day and the hands and eyes of a reader, it is usually due to the efforts of many talented people. This is certainly true in this case. Without the indefatigable work of Jeremy Berg and Freya Secrest, this book would never have been produced. My wife Julie provided invaluable editing and story suggestions. Because of her keen eye and good story sense, these tales are better than they would have been. Susan Sherman added her editing skills as well to ensure that the words you read are polished and not raw. Valorie Fanger brought her experience and skills in book layout and artistry to make this collection of tales a delight to the eye, and Deva Berg contributed the wonderful, delightful illustrations that do so much to bring each story alive.

I want to thank as well my good friend and fellow writer John Matthews, both for his encouragement to publish my stories and for his permission to reprint here the Grail story which first saw publication in a book of Celtic tales titled *Within the Hollow Hills*, a most excellent book which he edited and which was published by Floris Books/Lindisfarne Books.

Finally, I want to acknowledge and appreciate all the friends and family who have been the recipients of these stories every Christmas season and who by their enthusiasm encouraged me to keep writing and to create this anthology. Thank you, one and all!

DEDICATION

To my family
Julie, John-Michael, Aidan, Kaity, and Maryn,
My live-in audience for whom these stories
have been written.

THE STORY TREE

Table of Contents

Introduction - 1

Santa's Gift - 5

Tannenbaum - 19

Second Verse - 47

The Grail - 57

The Magic of Christmas - 87

The Story Tree - 109

The Glitch that Stole Christmas - 147

Mr. Thompkins' Window - 161

The Visitors - 179

INTRODUCTION

When I was a child, my favorite thing at Christmas was the tree with its colorful ornaments and bright lights. I loved to turn all the other lights in the living room off and just look at the tree glowing in the dark. It was always a thing of wonder, and wonderment was what Christmas was all about.

The idea of having a tree in the house was itself too marvelous for words. It transformed the entire room into a magical place. I felt as if it came to us accompanied by the spirits of all the Christmas trees that had ever been, so it seemed as if our living room played host to an ancient forest.

And the ornaments! Each of them seemed to tell a story. They weren't elaborate as many of today's ornaments are, but they were evocative. There was the Christ child. What a mystery he is! And there is Santa with his reindeer. How magical! Every part of the tree appeared wreathed in imagination. It seemed to stand in the corner of the living room like a guardian of strange new worlds and wondrous adventures, if only I knew how to enter them.

The Christmas tree was a tree filled with stories to me. When I grew older, as I recount later in this book, I actually had a separate tree during the Christmas season that I called my Story Tree, which held all those theme ornaments from TV shows and movies that are so popular these days. But eventually I gave that second tree up; it just couldn't match the mystery and wonder of the real thing.

Whatever else it may be and signify in our hearts and souls, Christmas for me is a celebration of imagination and stories. Perhaps that is why I love Santa so much; he reminds me of the magic and wonder that exist in our world and in ourselves if we only open our hearts and minds to see them. To me, Santa Claus is a very real spiritual being who comes once a year to remind us of that magic and of the love that is at the heart of Christmas.

To honor this celebration of imagination and wonder, every year for the past dozen or more years I have written a Christmas story as a gift to all our family and friends. The stories reflect my interests: wonderment, fantasy, science fiction, Santa Claus, the mystery and magic of Christmas. I wrote them for my kids and for the kid in myself, as well as for friends and family.

When writing them, publication was the farthest thing in my mind. But now that the opportunity has come to share them with a wider audience through this book, I feel this is a special gift in its own right, both for the stories and for me.

So from my Story Tree to yours, may these tales of wonder and magic brighten your spirit and bring a smile to your lips. Merry Christmas, everyone!

Ho Ho Ho!

Santa's Gift

As in many households, we put out milk and cookies for Santa every Christmas Eve. Usually it is the children who do this, but one year I ended up as the one responsible. This got me thinking about Santa as the eternal gift-giver, and I wondered, "Who gives Santa a gift? What kind of gift would he appreciate?"

I have been planning to write a novel about Santa Claus for children. To that end, I have done a great deal of research into the origins of Santa and some of his mythic antecedents in the dark ancient forests of northern Europe. Thinking of how our image of this magical, spiritual being has changed through the centuries and yet still retained certain essential characteristics, I suddenly had an idea as I stood by our hearth with a plate of cookies in one hand and a glass of milk in the other of just what a gift to Santa might be like. The following year, this story was the result.

SANTA'S GIFT

Santa pulled on the reins, and the reindeer landed on the roof of the diner. The sleigh bounced once, then came to a stop. It was not the most graceful landing they had made that night. Santa knew exactly what was on their minds: warm stalls, tasty hay, and a chance to sleep. Why stop at a building where no children lived and there were no presents to deliver? The reins jerked as Dancer and Prancer shuffled forward, testing to see if perhaps they couldn't take off again right away.

"Whoa, there," said Santa. "I know you boys are tired and want to get home. Well, I'm tired, too, but I've got one more stop to make. It's important, understand? So hold your hooves and settle down!"

Comet snorted, but they all did as Santa asked. He was, after all, the Boss.

Santa climbed out of the sleigh and looked over the roof. A couple of ventilation pipes and heat ducts rose out of the tarpapered surface. *Well*, he thought, *with my powers, I could go down one of those. It would be the traditional thing to do.*

He thumped the side of the sleigh. "Hang tradition!" he said out loud. "I've gone through enough dirty, smelly chimneys for one night. I'm going through the front door!"

He laid a finger beside his nose, then disappeared in a cloud of twinkling dust, only to reappear in an identical cloud on the sidewalk below in front of the diner's only entrance. He sneezed. "I hate magic dust," he muttered, fanning it away with a black-gloved hand. "Dratted stuff always gets up my nose!" He sneezed again.

He looked about. It was a run-down part of town, with trash in the gutters, graffiti on the buildings, and the occasional abandoned car on the street. Old apartment buildings lined one side of the street, while small mom-and-pop shops were on the other. The diner sat alone on the corner in the middle of a parking lot, remnant of a much better day.

Except for the streetlights, everything was dark, as it should be in the wee hours of Christmas morning. *Everyone should be in bed, dreaming of sugarplums*, Santa thought. Somewhere in the distance, a siren began to wail. "Well, almost everyone," he sighed.

Above the diner, the neon sign proclaiming this building as "Dick's Diner" was dark. The little sign on the door said "Closed." Inside, he could see the long counter and stools in front of the long serving window opening onto the kitchen, a few tables, and booths by the windows. They all looked like pale ghosts in the glare from the streetlight. There was no moon tonight.

He turned the doorknob, and the door opened.

Santa stepped into the silent, dim room and closed the door behind him. At the far end of the room a small Christmas tree stood on the end of the counter. On its top, a painted wooden Angel leaned to one side, an ornament obviously too heavy for the stem of the small tree. Lights and colored globes and ribbons of popcorn hung here and there in a cheerful disorder upon the branches, as if the tree had been decorated in haste and then left.

A faint, lingering odor of coffee and cabbage filled the room, confirmed by a handwritten note on a small blackboard on the wall proclaiming "Stuffed Cabbage—Original Recipe" as the previous evening's special.

Santa sneezed again.

He looked once more at the Angel on the top of the tree. It was painted white, with a suggestion of white wings and a gold halo shimmering above a smiling, cherubic face. Some of the gold on the halo had flaked off, and the white dress or whatever it was had become more gray over the years. Then he ambled up to one of the stools in front of the counter, heaved his bulk up onto it, and said, "Well, I haven't got all night! My reindeer are restless." As if on cue, the sound of hooves pawing on the roof echoed through the dim interior.

A steaming cup of coffee appeared before him. He looked at it appreciatively. "Ahhh," he said. "Smells fresh!"

"Should be," said a sharp, woman's voice from the air on the other side of the counter. There was a hint of a New Jersey accent. An Angel appeared in front of him, holding a coffee pot. "I just brewed it. Jamaica Blue Mountain."

She looked like she had been the model for the wooden Angel on the tree, same white dress, same white wings and golden halo, same cherubic smiling face with slightly chubby cheeks. Right now she was frowning. "How is it?"

8

Santa took a sip. "Wonderful!" he said. "My favorite!"

"I know." She beamed at him.

"Say, you wouldn't have a sandwich hidden away somewhere, would you?" Santa looked around, noting as he did that the wooden Angel was no longer on top of the Christmas tree.

The Angel made a gesture with her free hand, and a plate appeared on the counter with little triangular slices of white bread with green things in between them.

"Cucumber?" asked Santa in disbelief.

The sandwiches blurred on the plate, then reappeared as roast beef and cheese between thick slices of dark rye with the tangy odor of horseradish. "Sorry, love. Last year you said you were going on a diet."

"And I did." He patted his ample belly. "Can't you tell?"

He picked up the sandwich and took a bite. "Ahhh, heavenly, as always," he said. The Angel floated comfortably in front of him. He closed his eyes and took another bite.

"Who'm I kidding?" he said, when he was done chewing. "I really did go on that diet, but it makes no difference. I stay the same every year. In fact, I think I'm actually getting fatter. It's how everyone thinks of me now, you know. Not like the old days." A wistful look passed over his face.

"Yes, I know," the Angel said. "You are plump and jolly, merry and bouncy. That makes you..."

"A beach ball!"

The Angel tut-tutted. "Didn't your mother tell you not to interrupt?" She grinned. "I was going to say, that makes you more approachable and lovable for children."

"I suppose you're right, though I notice Michael Jordon's tall and thin and kids still seem to like him." Santa finished his sandwich, then took another long sip of coffee. He sighed and closed his eyes in contentment.

"Tired?" the Angel asked, putting down the coffee pot and leaning forward to take his black-gloved hand in her own golden one.

"A little." Santa agreed, his eyes still closed. Soon, he knew, it would be time for him to leave, to return to his icy home and begin preparations for the next year's journey. But for now it was nice just to relax and let the Angel hold his hand in hers. After all, how often did he see an Angel?

Actually, if he wanted, he could see them more often than he did, but his days were busy and time passed quickly. Seemed like no sooner was he hanging up the sleigh bells and harnesses than he was taking them down again. That was the problem with being a legend. You never got a vacation.

Santa looked at the Angel. "I'm thinking of retiring."

She raised an eyebrow. "Retiring? You can't retire."

"Of course I can. I can just stay home on Christmas Eve. For that matter, I can go to Jamaica on Christmas Eve. Float in the Caribbean like all the other beach balls."

The Angel poured more coffee into his cup. On his plate another roast beef sandwich on rye appeared. The Angel looked at him. "Don't be a sourpuss. You can no more quit than I can."

"Umph," replied Santa, his mouth full.

"I mean, think of the children!"

Santa laughed. "They'd never miss me. There are Santa Clauses on every street corner and in every department store. And parents buy most of the gifts now. No one would know I'm gone."

"But you would miss them."

Santa brushed bread crumbs out of his beard. "Yes, you have a point there. I would miss them."

"And who would spread the magic around? That's what you do, you know. Spread the magic." She held up her fingers and counted. "The magic of imagination, the magic of wonder, the magic of love, the magic of giving, the magic of hope…"

"Oh, yes…let's not forget spreading the magic…" Santa turned and looked out the diner's window. Outside, just wandering into the glow of the streetlight, a man weaved up the street. His overcoat was threadbare and dirty, his trousers had holes in the knees, but he was wearing expensive shoes, although without socks. A gray stubble on his face showed he had not shaven for a while, and his hair was wild under a New York Yankees baseball cap.

"Wait here," said Santa.

He went to the door of the diner and opened it. Stepping out, he stood in front of the man, who blinked at him, his eyes bleary.

10

"He...hey, Santa," the man said, peering at him. "Mer...Merry Christmas!" He belched, and Santa was immersed in bad breath and alcoholic fumes. "Out kinda late, ain'tcha?"

"Just finishing my rounds, my good man. And Merry Christmas to you, too!"

"Just finishing.... My gawd, those rott'n slave drivers at the store sure kept you late! And..." he hiccoughed. "And on Christmas Eve, too!" He got a crafty look in his eyes. "Say, you wouldn't have a twenny on you, would you, or maybe a fiver? You know, for the spirits of the season!" He cackled at his own joke, sending more fumes in Santa's direction.

"No, I have no money to give you. Would you like some magic? I'm told I have lots of magic to give."

"Magic?" The man frowned. "What magic? Say, you puttin' me on or somethin'?" he asked, his tone belligerent. "Unless..." he cackled again, "unless your magic comes in a bottle!" He stumbled forward, his arms falling around Santa's shoulders to keep himself upright. Santa reeled backward at the strength of the man's breath. "Y'got any bottles in your bag, Santa?"

Abruptly the man disappeared. Santa looked around, and saw the Angel standing just inside the front door of the diner. "Really, Santa," she said. "Badgering that poor man."

"I wasn't badgering him," Santa said, stepping back into the diner himself. The door closed behind him. "I just wondered if he wanted magic, since it seems that's all I have to give."

"Self-pity doesn't become jolly fat men whose bellies shake like jelly!" said the Angel, sitting down in one of the booths.

Santa sat down across from her. "Where'd he go?"

"Oh, you know, just a small Christmas miracle. He'll wake up sober with no headache tomorrow in that shelter three blocks over."

Santa humphed. "Well, I think I made my point. What use is magic these days? There's MTV, video games, computers, the Internet. Ask any kid. Ask him, 'Hey, kid, want some magic of imagination or magic of wonder?' You know what he'll say? He'll say, 'Sure Santa! Will it play on my X-Box?' And those are the *good* kids. You can imagine what the naughty ones would say!"

The Angel looked through the grimy window at the city beyond. "Sometimes magic is all that keeps this place going. Especially the magic of hope."

Santa didn't respond. Against the wall just under the window sill was a small juke box with a coin slot and a little sign that said "50 Cents a Song." He idly fingered the tabs that turned the pages. "I don't suppose they have "White Christmas" on here?"

"They don't work. They're just for show. Dick's been meaning to get them repaired, but…"

"It doesn't matter. I got tired of hearing that song a long time ago! Rather listen to Elvis."

The Angel faced Santa. "Santa, we've been meeting like this for five years, and I've never seen you in a funk like this! You're not getting burned out, are you?"

For a moment, Santa flashed back to a Christmas Eve five years ago. He had finished and was heading back to the North Pole when he'd spied a neon light in the city that was blinking on and off, "Need coffee, Santa?" Intrigued, he'd flown down to see what it was and saw the Angel standing outside the diner, holding up a coffee pot. Naturally, he'd had to stop. They'd been friends ever since. Stopping at the diner was now part of his routine.

Coming back to the present moment, Santa laughed. "Burnt out? Ha! I passed burnt out in the Eighties! Ask the reindeers!"

"You've never shown it before."

"Because I'm a jolly old elf! Emphasis on 'jolly.' Ho Ho Ho Hum!"

"You *do* need a vacation!"

"I need to lose a hundred pounds at least and find a new profession! Maybe shave my beard off and dye my hair orange."

"No!" the Angel recoiled, her hands going up to her mouth. "It would clash with your red suit and rosy cheeks!"

Santa looked at her, his mouth open, then laughed at the sight of her eyes bugging out. She laughed, too, her face resuming its normal cherubic look.

"So, Red Guy, what's really bothering you?"

Santa pointed to a poster up above the window into the kitchen. It was an advertisement for Coca Cola, the one with Santa holding up a coke bottle. "That! That's what's bothering me!"

"What? That you're appearing on an advertisement?"

"Well, that too. Far too many people are using me to sell things these days. But no, that's not what I meant. I used to be tall, thin, distinguished looking, more like a saint or a wizard than a beach ball. I was Father Christmas or Saint Nicholas. Then that company began advertising that wretched drink making me look like that! And that became my new look. I became cute! Harmless! Roly-Poly! Cuddly. I wasn't meant to be cute! Friendly, yes. Cute, no!"

She raised her eyebrows. "You're not the only one with something to complain about, you know, if we're talking body image here. Look at me! Halos, wings, fluffy dresses, this chubby face that's always smiling. Do you know what you get when you're always smiling? Sore jaws!"

She scowled at Santa, and somewhere in the distance he heard thunder roll across the sky. "You think I look like *this*?" She wiggled the wings on her back. "I look like some wimpy fairy princess!"

Taken aback, Santa said, "I've known some pretty powerful fairy princesses…"

"They're not Angels, though! They don't wield cosmic powers!" Thunder sounded louder in the distance. She gestured at the counter and the coffee pot floated over to her along with a mug. She poured herself some coffee and downed it in a single gulp. "But that's the way it is with legends. We look like what the public thinks we look like or wants us to look like." She glowered at him in a most un-Angel like way. "So don't talk to me about *cute*!"

"Well, maybe you should quit, too! They can always place a star on top of their trees."

The Angel looked sad for a moment. "You think we've got it bad. Those Christmas stars are Angels, too. Imagine having to spend every year all pointy like that!"

"I never realized…"

"And this year, my tree is too small, so I spend all my time leaning over and bobbing about. Good thing I don't get seasick. Besides, you

13

just imagine spending the whole Christmas Season with a tree stuck up your—"

"I get your point. So I say again, let's quit!"

"But I can't quit. I am what I am. A Christmas Angel. And you are what you are. Santa Claus!"

"But that's just it. I wasn't always Santa Claus. I didn't always look like this. I've had better days. I used to run with stags and wolves and wrestle the sunlight away from the powers of darkness."

"Wolves?" asked the Angel.

"Yes." Santa's eyes seemed to look into the very long ago and the very far away. "Ah, the wolves. I loved my wolves. Wonderful creatures. Friendly, polite, but fierce and proud. You wouldn't see them selling Coca Cola! Or anything else!" He sighed. "I wish I had them with me again. I wouldn't be so cute!"

The Angel laughed. "I like them, too, but reindeer are better for children. Less intimidating."

Santa looked askance at the Angel. "Oh?" he said. "Seen any children lately? They can be pretty wolf-like, if you ask me!"

"My kind watch over children everyday." The Angel paused. "Hmm," she said, "I see your point." She grinned. "But they're angels, too!"

Santa chuckled. "I knew you'd say that. You just haven't had that many sitting on your lap! Anyway, I was once a protector of nature, and the gifts I brought were the promise of a new year and the return of the light." He thumped his chest, making his belly roll. "I was like the Terminator! I terminated the darkness and brought back the gifts of spring!"

A clatter came from the roof. Santa looked up, then slid out of the booth. "It's been a long night. The reindeer are restless, anxious to get home. I don't blame them. For me, it's been too many treats of milk and cookies! I can't tell you how tasty your coffee and sandwiches have been. They should call this place 'Angel's Diner.'"

"Ah, Dick's an angel, too. After all, he puts up a little tree every year with me on it for his customers."

The Angel floated over to Santa and gave him a hug. "So, did our conversation go anywhere? Will I see you next year?"

Santa grimaced. "Maybe. Maybe not. I'm forgetting my past, Angel. I can't let it all slip away until I become just a fat, happy symbol for merchants to use and for children not to believe in. You talk about my magic. My magic is in my roots, and I'm losing them."

The Angel held up her hand. Santa stopped at the doorway. The peace in the room deepened. The Angel seemed to listen, then nodded.

"What is it?" Santa asked.

"Why," the Angel grinned, "it seems *my* Boss has a gift for *you!*"

"A gift? For me...?"

"Well, we can't have you losing your magic, can we?" She gestured broadly, and suddenly Santa found himself caught up in a spinning whirlwind of rainbow colors, colors which shifted, darkened and deepened into the dark black of rich soil and the green of ancient, virgin pine forests. In the midst of this, he heard words. "Remember and be renewed! Remember and renew My world!"

Then the colors were gone, as was the short, plump, roly-poly, jolly, red-garbed, bewhiskered Santa. In his place stood a tall, imposing figure, dressed entirely in green, with a long, broad green cloak and hood around him. His head was crowned with a circlet of twigs and leaves entwined together. A thick staff was in one hand, wrapped around with mistletoe and holly. A wide black belt encircled a muscular waist, and from it hung little bells that jingled softly as he moved. Also at his belt hung a pouch in which embers magically burned without consuming the leather.

The only thing he had in common with the Santa Claus who had vanished was the thick, white beard and hair, but now they wreathed a rugged face in which one eye burned an ice-bright blue and the other glowed with the green of young grass and new leaves, for legend said he had the double Sight and could see into the realm of Faerie and Spirit as well as the world of humans and nature.

He was the Winter King, guardian of the land, bringer of the gift of new light and new life after the long nights of winter, symbol of the love that renewed the world even in its seemingly darkest hours. He was the champion who ventured into the blackest darkness to wrest the sun free and bring it back to the earth.

He felt the vigor of a wind-swept mountain fill him, and he let out a mighty shout. It was a shout that shook the dreams of all the sleepers in the city around him and turned them from visions of sugarplums into dreams of raging, singing rivers cracking through ice and racing down the slopes in torrents of freedom. It was no "Ho, Ho, Ho," but a release of the fierce joy and exaltation of all things green and growing.

"Well, Santa, you seem to have changed," the Angel said.

The figure turned and beamed at the Angel, his face aglow as if he were standing in front of an open furnace. "Yes! Yes! I'm the Winter King again! I'm what I once was. Not the sitter-in-malls or the hawker of wares, not the funny red clown nor the jolly old elf. I'm not the bringer of toys that break or clothes that are never worn. I do not bring what is not wanted or give what is not needed. No!" He swung his staff about and down as if striking a foe, and the Angel ducked. "No! I do not bring trinkets. I bring the great gifts, the ancient gifts. I bring the dark mysteries of the forest and the bright clarity of mountains! I bring the wonder of starry nights and the promise of long, sun-filled days! I bring expectation and delight!" He shook the glowing pouch at his belt. "I bring the fire that never dies, the light that always returns!"

He began to tap his staff on the floor and dance about, his little bells jingling as he did so. A wind seemed to spring up about him, a wind sweet and warm, bracing and chill. "I bring fierce promise and sweet hope," he shouted. "I bring strength and honor and all that uplifts life!"

He stopped and faced the Angel. He exhaled with a great puff of breath. "Thank you, my friend!" he said. "It is good to remember!" He laughed, and it was like the earth rumbling deep in its belly. When she heard it, it was for the Angel like drinking the sweetest of wines. "Remembering is even better than your sandwiches!"

"Enjoy it. Have a vacation! Run with your wolves and stags! You'll become red and round and jolly again soon enough, for the world has come to know you that way now. But if you remember who you truly are, Winter's King and Spring's Champion, then others will, as well. They will appreciate what your gifts really are and what is real about your gifts."

16

Somewhere, a wolf howled. The Winter King raised his head. "My wolves...." he said.

"Yes," said the Angel. "I sent the reindeer home. It seemed the thing to do. I thought the wolves might make them nervous."

The Winter King pulled the hood of his cloak over his head and raised his staff. "I must go!"

"I know." The Angel gestured and the wall of the diner disappeared. Beyond it stood a snow-clad forest, dark and wondrous, while overhead uncountable stars burned and twinkled in the night sky like a river of light flowing around a bright, full moon. From out of the trees, a pack of sleek, gray wolves appeared. With a bound, the green clad figure sprang out into the snow and ran to them. They gathered about him, leaping and cavorting like pups. He touched each of them, then turned back to the Angel. He raised his staff. "To life and the Light!" he shouted. Then he and the wolves ran disappearing into the forest.

The Angel watched him go. "Enjoy your vacation!"

The wall of the diner reappeared. She turned and walked over to the tree, shrinking and changing as she did until once more she sat on the top, leaning over slightly because she was too heavy and the tree too small. "Maybe next year," she thought, as she settled in, "I'll give him corned beef on pumpernickel..."

Tannenbaum

I love science fiction stories. When I was a child, I wanted nothing more than to be a spaceman, exploring among the stars. The universe has always seemed to me a place of fabulous wonder and mystery, a lot like Christmas in that way.

When I began writing Christmas stories every year as gifts, I knew that one of the stories would have to take place in space. Originally, I thought of a story of what a Christmas celebration might be like for people on a generation ship, a vast starship that was their home, not just their transportation from one planet to another. What kinds of myths and legends would such a star-faring culture create? If they had anything like Christmas, what would it be like?

Unfortunately, that story I have yet to tell. The pieces would not fall into place when I tried to write it. For me, stories unfold. They tell themselves. I don't tell them. So when those voyagers were not ready to talk to me, I ended up letting them be for another time. But they did leave me with another image, perhaps of a place they had seen in their journeys, of a planet whose trees looked like Christmas trees with bright fruits like ornaments. From that image, Tannenbaum emerged.

TANNENBAUM

Standing by his landing craft, he removed his facemask and took a deep breath of the air on this alien world.

It was, he knew, a stupid, possibly fatal, thing to do. He held his breath for a moment, then slowly let it out. The air was fresh and invigorating, with a faint minty tang. He took another breath, held it, then once more let it out in a long exhalation, his eyes closed in satisfaction. This atmosphere felt right. The whole world felt right, in fact. Gravity, atmospheric density, mean temperature, axial inclination, ratio of water to land, distance from the local star, rotation, albedo... All were incredibly within ninety-seven percent of earth normal. If Earth had a twin in the universe, this planet was it.

"Are you all right, Jason?" The soft female voice arose from the air next to his left ear, projected from the communication patch attached to his collar.

"Yes, Angel, I'm fine. I...I took off my mask, and I'm breathing unfiltered planetary air."

There was a moment's silence. "That was foolish of you, Jason."

"Angel, your scans already indicated this atmosphere is so much like Earth's I might as well be there instead of thirty light years away."

"My sensors are not sufficiently refined to insure complete safety at the microbiotic level."

"Perhaps not, but it's done now. The air is wonderful! And I feel fine."

"A subjective evaluation, Jason. The deleterious effects of many atmospherically borne toxins or biota do not show up immediately, as you know. You have been irresponsible."

"Well, it's too late now. If there are any little critters floating about waiting to get me, I've given them their chance. But I'll die happy breathing something other than ship's air."

Although he knew the scout ship's artificial intelligence couldn't do so, it sounded as if it sniffed. "You will need a complete bioscan for foreign microorganisms when you return on board. In addition, you will be quarantined when you return to the *Odyssey*."

"I understand." He took another breath. "All right. Let's make this official down here. Please record that on December 24th, Christmas Eve day, Jason Stewart of the colony ship *Odyssey* first stepped onto a new world. Considering the date, let's hope this planet is our Christmas gift!"

"A hopeful sentiment, Jason. May it prove to be so."

Jason took another deep breath and looked around. "Angel, it looks incredible down here! I think this may really be our new home."

"If you would wear your minivid, I could see what you are seeing."

"I'm sorry. I was in a hurry to get outside and didn't take time to put it on. I will in a moment, but first let me tell you what I'm seeing. I am standing on a slight rise. Off to the south the ground slopes gradually down towards the plain. It is covered in what looks like tall, golden grass, almost like wheat. It is about knee high on me. The lander is to the west of me. As I turn north, I see that the ground continues to rise towards the mountains beyond. It is in that direction that the anomaly we detected from orbit should be. There are clumps of green trees to the north as well, and off to my right, to the east, I see a forest. At this distance the trees resemble earthly conifers. They look like pine trees, Angel."

"Are they glowing?"

He squinted at the trees in the distance. He thought he saw faint colors, but he couldn't be sure. "It's hard to tell in this light. It's pretty bright down here right now. I would say it's about local noon or a little before." He bent down and looked at the vegetation at his feet. It reminded him of grass, but each blade was rounded like a thin tube. Within the tubes he could see movement, like tiny sparks moving up and down barely visible channels. "There's a faint bioluminescence within the grass-analog. I imagine that's what we saw in the forests."

When he had approached the planet in the scout ship, he had come in from the sunlight side, awestruck at the uncanny similarity between this new world and the old one from which he had come on the colony ship *Odyssey*. Angel had inserted them into orbit. However, as they passed over the terminator between night and day, he had been dismayed to discover that there were patches of glowing light on the darkened land masses, with narrow lines of light running out from them. Even the darker areas seemed to have a faint shimmer.

His first thought had been that he was looking at cities and roads. His heart had sunk, for he knew that the presence of sentient life would greatly reduce the chances that the humans could set up a colony on this world. In their crippled colony ship, time was running out, and if this world proved unsuitable, they had very few options left.

But Angel had quickly determined that the glow was not artificial. Rather it seemed to have some natural, non-radioactive origin, though what it might be, the AI could not tell from orbit with the instruments available to it. While not exclusively so, the glowing patches turned out mainly to be forests.

Jason turned back to the lander and went inside. The control seat dominated the cabin, leaving barely enough room to stand up and move around. In back was a locker that he opened and from which he began to remove various devices. "Angel, I'm going to go take a look at the anomaly, and I'll look at the trees on the way. How much time do I have?"

"I estimate nine hours until local nightfall. In fifteen hours you must depart and rendezvous with me if we are to return to the *Odyssey* on schedule."

"Great. That should be more than enough time to do a quick recon and return." He attached the minivid to his right shoulder, strapped on a backpack with sample bags and various tools, along with emergency food, water, and medical supplies, and hooked his datacorder onto his belt, along with a canteen. He then took a pulse rifle down from its rack. One of the oddities of this world was that Angel had been unable to detect any signs of animal life, but the scans had necessarily been incomplete in the time they had had and did not seem able to penetrate the thick tree cover. Though nothing seemed to live in the grasslands, something could dwell in the trees. For that matter, animal life here might be subterranean.

He exited the ship and electronically locked the door behind him. "Distance to the anomaly?" he asked.

With hardly a pause, Angel answered from geosynchronous orbit above him. "Eight point three kilometers to the northeast." Jason

23

turned in that direction. It was uphill, towards a clump of trees. "No problem," he said confidently. "I can be there and back before dark, and study some of the trees on the way." He looped the strap of the pulse rifle onto his shoulder and headed off, the sunlight glinting off the reflective material of his flight suit.

Walking up the gently sloping hill, the sun warm on his back, a gentle breeze stirring his hair, Jason found it easy to pretend that he was walking in the Cascade foothills near his home on Puget Sound in northwestern North America back on Earth. Yet, it was indeed an alien world, one that apparently had once had its own civilization. On their third orbit, Angel had initiated mineral scans. The planet proved to have rich mineral deposits, but scattered here and there around the three major land masses were exceptional concentrations of minerals, including artificial alloys. "I estimate a ninety-eight percent probability those are buried cities. There was a civilization here once," Angel had commented.

Jason remembered how his hopes had dropped as he thought again that there might be an indigenous culture. "Or there still is. Those could be underground dwellings..."

"I don't think so, Jason," Angel had replied. "I detect no energy readings at all, no electromagnetic or radioactive emanations of any kind. Furthermore, the scans suggest these concentrations of artificial minerals are mixed in with normal soil. They are not in tunnels or caves. I suggest they are buried ruins."

"Buried ruins? Perhaps there was a war...that might explain the lack of animal life. Cities destroyed. Life wiped out. But since then, the planet has healed. The forests have taken over again."

"A romantic projection, Jason, based on the possibilities in your own culture's history," Angel had replied. "There is not enough data here to make any suppositions at all."

They had left it at that. But then, on the fifth orbit, which had taken them over a mountain range in the northern part of the largest continent, Angel had found the anomaly.

Jason stopped to adjust the minivid where it was chafing on his shoulder.

24

"Anything wrong, Jason?" Angel queried.

"No, you're just getting heavy on my shoulder."

"Do you wish to rest? You are well within your time parameters."

"No, it's OK. I just had to adjust the camera." He took a swallow of water from his canteen. "Angel, any more readings on the anomaly?"

"Nothing new. It still registers as a concentration of organic and inorganic materials in a pattern that is unknown to me. Are you sure you wish to continue? I would advise against it."

It was an argument they had been having ever since the anomaly had been detected. At that time Angel had announced that it had found something unknown which it had been unable to analyze. "It registers as organic, but it does not appear to be a life form," Angel had said. "It is large and also has high concentrations of artificial alloys. It is definitely an artifact of some sort."

Jason's interest had immediately been piqued. "Any visuals?" he had asked, excited.

"No, it is in a small canyon, and it is nighttime there."

"How long until dawn?"

"Five point six earth standard hours."

"Fine, we'll complete this orbital scan, then I want you to go into geosync over that site. I'm going to take the lander down there once it's light."

"A landing is not part of your mission, Jason. You are simply to determine if this is a suitable planet for colonization and then return to the *Odyssey*."

"A landing is an option within my orders if I deem it necessary, and I do so deem it. I need to put my feet on this planet, Angel, and experience it firsthand before I can give a full report. I need to know more than your electronic eyes and ears can tell me. In some ways this planet seems too good to be true. I need to touch it before I'll really believe it. Seeing this artifact will be a bonus."

Actually, Angel had been right, he thought, as he continued trekking overland towards the hills and the small canyon they concealed, breathing the air of an alien world that nevertheless increasingly felt like home. Landing wasn't part of his orders. And he did have enough

25

information from Angel's orbital scans to take back to the *Odyssey* without taking the risk of a landing.

But there was the wonder of it all and the chance of discovering something new. That was important to him. How had that old television show put it a hundred years ago? Something about boldly going to find new worlds and new civilizations? Well, that was what he was doing. He was boldly going, and while he hoped he wouldn't find a new civilization—at least not now and not here—he was certainly finding a new world.

Besides, overhead an electronic guardian angel watched over him, though Jason knew if he got into trouble there would be very little the AI could do to help him out. It could, however, return to the colony ship and bring them here.

The colony ship. *Odyssey.* Five thousand humans living in a hollowed out asteroid to which had been affixed two B-drives. They were Earth's first effort at seeding humans on another world. By entering Bohm Space, they could transcend the lightspeed barrier and accomplish in months what otherwise would take years. But a disaster so familiar to science fiction writers as to be a cliché had overtaken them midway through their voyage. Somehow the Bohm Drives had become misaligned, setting up a tidal force that had destroyed one of them, crippled the second, and had dropped the ship back into normal space. Now they were lost in space, facing the eventual loss of life-support, light-years from where they were supposed to be. They had repaired the crippled B-Drive enough to make one final jump through B-Space, but their range was limited to three light years. Where should they go? Where could they go?

Telescopic sensors had identified three potential planetary systems within jump range of the *Odyssey's* position. They had four one-man Bohm-drive scout ships. They could send recon missions to the three systems and back, but the colony ship itself could only make one last jump. They had to choose right the first time.

One scout had gone out to the closest system, half a light year distant, but it had returned saying the planets were too inhospitable. Then, a second pilot had gone out to the second system, but he had failed to return. Jason had drawn the third possibility, nearly three light years distant from the colony ship, almost at the limit of its jump capability. He had left while they were still debating risking their fourth scout ship to see what had happened to the second, and he had hit paydirt. He had found Earth's twin.

"Angel," he said.

"Yes, Jason?"

"If anything should happen to me, you know you must return to the *Odyssey* and tell them about this place."

"I know, Jason."

"All right. Not that I expect anything to happen. This place seems as peaceful as a park. In fact, the whole planet seems like a park just prepared for colonists like us."

"I know, Jason. And that troubles me."

"You're programmed to be suspicious, Angel. You know what they say about never looking a gift horse in the mouth."

"I know, Jason, but what if it is a Trojan horse?"

An hour after he left the lander, Jason approached a large grove of trees. He could have made it in a shorter time, but he had stopped at several points to fill bags with soil and "grass" samples. In spite of his exertions and though he had been walking uphill the whole time on legs that had not experienced full planetary gravity for months, he felt invigorated. Something in the air or the land seemed to give him energy, so that he felt better even than when he had started.

He walked over to one of the trees. From a distance it had resembled a fir tree. Up close, however, the resemblance ended. The tree was seven meters tall. Its trunk and branches were a smooth material that seemed almost like plastic but which was warm and soft to the touch. And though like an earthly fir tree it seemed covered with tiny needles, in this case the "needles" were small tubes and blunt on the end. And like the tubular grass, he could see faint sparks moving up and down through the needles.

What was most different, however, from any earthly conifer were the various small, multi-colored globes that hung from the branches like fruits. They, too, were warm to the touch and squishy, as if filled with liquid.

"Tannenbaum." Angel's voice startled him.

"What?"

27

"Tannenbaum. Christmas tree. Those trees look like Christmas trees. It is an image in keeping with the day."

Jason stared at the tree. Standing back, he could see what Angel meant. With the different colored fruits on it, the tree did look as if it were hung with ornaments. The effect, he thought, must be even more striking at night, when the bioluminescence would be more visible.

He looked around him. He could see other groves of the trees off in the distance, and to his east, a forest of them. He thought of the whole planet covered with such trees.

"Angel, I think you've just named this world. Tannenbaum, the planet of Christmas trees!"

"Fanciful, but appropriate, Jason."

He grinned, delighted with the image. "All right, Angel! How does it feel to know you've named a new world?"

"I am satisfied if it pleases you, Jason."

"Well, it does please me." He drew his scanner from his belt and checked its connection with the datacorder. He pointed it at one of the fruits. "Angel, this is fascinating. According to the readings, this fruit or whatever it is, is extremely rich in amino acids and proteins, and they appear to be compatible with human biochemistry."

"I hope you are not thinking of eating one, Jason, just to be sure."

Actually, the thought had passed his mind, but he knew that would be pushing his luck too far. "No, Angel, I'll wait until they've undergone the full treatment back at the *Odyssey*'s labs. Still, it's a wonderful thought. Imagine a Christmas tree with edible ornaments! I think I'll call them sugarplums."

He put his scanner away and took out a couple of sample bags. With his knife, he cut off a couple of the fruits and bagged them. Then he began cutting at a small branch. Suddenly, there was a bright flash and he felt something hot and hard slam into his chest. His muscles jerked spasmodically as what felt like an electric current pulsed through him. Then all went black.

"Jason! Jason! Wake up! Please respond!"

Angel's voice seemed to come from a long distance, pulling him reluctantly back from whatever warm and dark place he had been. He opened his eyes. He was lying on his back. Above him he saw a blue sky. There was a bitter, burnt odor around him, and every muscle ached throughout his body. He had no idea where he was. Then memory rushed back in.

"Jason! Please respond!"

Painfully, he turned over, fighting down a wave of nausea that cramped his belly. "I...I'm here, Angel. What happened?"

"You were subjected to an electric shock. You have been unconscious for three point two five minutes."

Jason sat up, holding his head to stop the sudden spinning. He looked around. On the ground next to him lay his pulse rifle where it had fallen from his back, and a sample bag filled with the sugarplums. His knife lay on the ground as well. The burnt odor was coming from the front of his flight jacket, which had been burned in an uneven pattern over its surface. Above him towered the tree, now not seeming so Christmas-like or friendly.

He brushed at the charred surface of his jacket. "An electric shock? But how..."

"I think from the tree. As you were starting to cut off the branch, I detected a sudden surge of bioelectric energy in the tree. There was a flash, and I have been looking at the sky ever since."

Jason stood up. He felt wobbly but basically unhurt. Realization struck him. "It was defending itself, Angel. These trees must be like electric eels on Earth." He picked up his knife and the sample bags and put them in his backpack. "Well, I'll let someone else get samples from the trees, then!"

"How are you feeling, Jason?"

"Sore, but otherwise all right. No damage seems to have been done. I am puzzled, though. We have an organism here that produces fruits with a high nutrient value and that has a sophisticated defense mechanism. But what eats the fruits? And what does the tree defend itself against? There has been no sign of animal life."

"None that we've been able to detect, anyway. Are you planning to continue? My recommendation would be to return to the lander."

Jason stretched and jumped up and down a couple of times. "I feel OK, Angel. I want to go on and see the anomaly. I'll just take care not to run into any more trees!" He picked up his pulse rifle, which now felt very good in his arms. Backing away from the tree, he headed off towards the rise of hills to the northeast.

He lay on the edge of a precipice, speechless with wonder. Below him stretched the canyon in which Angel had detected the anomaly. He estimated it was two kilometers from where he was to the opposite rim. The whole canyon wall opposite him, lit by the early afternoon sun, was carved into a vast cavern filled with terraces covered with trees and structures. Or he assumed they were structures; they could have been sculptures or a giant bas relief. The shapes were strange, alien, but they had a grace and beauty to them that took his breath away.

Looking down, he could see that the canyon wall below him had also been similarly carved. His eye followed the curves and lines out onto the canyon floor where more terraces descending from both walls led to a river flowing through the center of what was more recognizably a collection of buildings.

There was an air of immense age about these structures, but there was no sign of decay. They gleamed with color in the sunlight as if fashioned from gold and silver, sapphire and ruby, emerald and obsidian, opal and jade, and mother-of-pearl. It was the colors that took his breath away. He felt transported, as if he were a fantasy hero in some holodrama who had stumbled upon a mythical fairy kingdom.

About ten meters directly below him was a flat, opalescent platform, apparently the roof of a building carved into the canyon wall. The wall beneath him was as sheer as glass and blacker than space itself. Curious, he ran his hand over it. To his astonishment, his hand penetrated part way into the wall. Startled, he tried to pull it back, but the wall held him as if his hand had been plunged into black tar. He pulled harder, and with a popping sound, his hand came free.

Sitting back, he examined his hand closely. It looked none the worse for its experience. He reached down and put his hand on the black substance again. Once more it penetrated into the wall. There was no sensation at all other than the feeling of being gripped. He pulled his hand out.

Turning around, he swung his legs over the edge and lowered himself down. Then he jammed his feet into the wall. Like his hands, they penetrated part way, giving him the feeling of standing on a narrow ledge. Not looking down, he brought his left hand down and stuck it into the wall. Then he followed with his right hand.

He was spread-eagled against the wall, like a fly climbing a piece of obsidian. Then, slowly at first but with gathering momentum, he felt himself sliding down, as if the wall had turned into a viscous liquid that was now flowing downward. He panicked for a moment, but his hands and feet remained securely gripped by the black material.

When his boots touched the top of the platform, the flowing stopped. He pulled his right hand, and it came free from the wall with a whispery popping. He then pulled his feet free followed by his left hand and stepped back.

Curious, he reattached himself to the wall. This time the wall flowed upward, carrying him back to the top of the canyon rim.

"Interesting," said Angel's voice in his ear. "The wall is a transportation device of some nature. Your point of entry probably determines whether it flows up or down."

"Any idea what this stuff is?"

"My sensors suggest it has biological characteristics, but beyond that I cannot say."

"You mean, it's alive?"

"Insufficient data to form a conclusion like that, but it seems organic. However, after your experience with the tree, I would advise against attempting to take a sample of it."

"I agree." He looked down, wondering what he needed to do now to get the wall to carry him back down into the alien city. "Down, please," he said out loud, pushing slightly with his feet, and the wall obligingly began to flow downward again. "Amazing!" he said. "The lab techs will have a field day figuring this out."

Once he reached the platform, he pulled away from the wall and stepped backwards a few steps. The surface of the platform was opalescent, faintly sparkling and yielding to his step. He knelt down and touched it. It was warm under his fingers. He wondered if it, too, were organic in nature. In fact, it dawned on him that the whole city might be alive in some alien way.

This thought ought to be disturbing, he knew. If he were truly trespassing upon the body of some unknown and unimaginable organism, he could be in very real danger. Instead, he felt strangely

31

comforted. He had a flash of memory of crawling into his mother's lap on stormy nights, her warmth and soft voice comforting him with the conviction of being completely safe.

Standing up, he walked over to the edge of the platform. Below him was another drop of five or six meters, but unlike where he was, the surface below was covered with trees, their fruits—what he thought of as sugarplums—faintly glowing in the early afternoon light. Off to one side, he could see a flight of what appeared to be ordinary stairs leading down from where he was.

"You are thinking of going down those stairs, aren't you, Jason?"

"Yes, Angel, I'm just going to go down for a quick look."

"My past experiences with you tell me I will not be successful in persuading you to return to the lander, so I will instead advise caution. You are entering into unknown territory."

"I'm fully aware of the risks. However, I feel good about this place. It feels safe."

"A purely subjective evaluation not necessarily in accord with the facts."

"Are you picking up anything I should know about? Any life forms?"

"Negative, but the organic properties of the city itself may mask any other life form readings that may be present."

"OK, I'll be careful. Besides, I might find a present for me under one of those Christmas trees down there. After all it is Christmas Eve!"

"I would not trust any alien Santas, Jason; they might have claws..."

"Very funny," Jason chuckled. "Since when were you programmed for puns?"

He stepped cautiously onto the stairway and waited in case it suddenly started to move. After a moment in which nothing happened, he concluded that it was just an ordinary stairway, and he began to descend. He knew Angel was right. He was taking a risk going deeper into the alien city. But he felt so good here. He couldn't explain it, but he felt warm and excited, like a kid on Christmas morning, rushing downstairs to see what Santa had left under the tree.

He stepped off the stairs into a grove of alien trees, their fruits glowing more brightly in the shadow cast by the canyon walls. Walking to the edge of the platform, he saw another set of stairs leading downward to a similar platform with still more trees. Without consulting Angel, and with no word from the AI, he stepped down.

He descended two more levels, each platform or terrace like the one above it. The next level down was different. Here a large pyramidal structure rose amidst the trees. As he approached, the side began to glow and in the air in front of him, shapes began to appear. There were graceful, multi-colored pictograms and curving, wavy lines punctuated with triangles and dots.

"We appear to have triggered a message, Angel. What do you think it says? Eat at Joe's Diner? Don't pick the sugarplums?"

"How about, 'Keep Out—Alien Trespassers will be Shot!'?"

"Angel, you have the most lurid imagination, but I agree we'd better assume that it could be a warning of some sort. Better safe than sorry, right?"

"Would you repeat that, Jason? My processors can't believe you just said that!"

Jason chuckled. Stepping closer to the images suspended in the air, he put his hand up to touch one. His hand passed right through it. "Holographic," he said.

He looked up at the pyramid, which was roughly twice his height. "Wish I knew what this was," he muttered. Suddenly, a series of musical tones rang out. "What was that?" he asked, looking around.

"Jason, my sensors detect an energy emission of some nature coming from that structure. It is much stronger than anything I have registered before. I recommend you leave this vicinity immediately."

"All right, Angel," Jason said. "I'm outta here. We'll leave this to the tech boys when we return in the *Odyssey*."

Before he could move, the pyramid's wall glowed again, and this time, a large opalescent sphere with a smaller sphere on top of it emerged through the side of the structure. To Jason's startled amazement, it looked like an unfinished snowman, perfectly proportioned but lacking eyes, nose, and mouth.

With a faint pop, the apparition separated from the pyramid's wall and floated towards him. He heard Angel's voice begin to speak, then a green beam shot out from the thing and enveloped him. At first it felt warm, but then his body seemed to catch fire, as if every nerve ending was being burned, and he screamed. As he did so, the intensity of the fire seemed to lessen. Reflexively, he unslung his pulse gun from his shoulder and in a single motion fired at the alien object. As the beam from the gun hit it, it exploded in a cloud of crystalline dust.

Freed from the green beam, Jason fell to his knees, his body shuddering in memory of the pain.

"Jason!" Angel's voice was urgent. "The structure is emitting even more energy than before. I suspect more of those creatures are about to appear. You must get away!"

"Right," Jason muttered, shaking off the effects of the alien beam and getting to his feet. Holding his rifle at ready, he backed toward the stairway, then turned and raced up it. But just as he neared the top, one of the snowmen figures materialized from the surface of the platform above him.

He raised his gun to fire, but before he had a chance, another beam shot out, this one a deep ruby red. His world exploded in fire. He felt himself toppling backward into space, falling, falling, his body blazing. Then there was merciful unconsciousness.

He awoke in darkness and in pain. He opened his eyes. He was lying on his side. Ahead of him he could see Christmas trees, covered with glowing ornaments, sparkling with winking stars of white light. Of course, he thought, remembering as if from another life, it's Christmas Eve night.

Christmas! He wondered what Santa had brought him. He tried to remember what he had wanted. He tried hard, but all he could remember was standing with his father in the snow, looking up at the stars. His father was telling him something about wonder....

He saw snowmen appear from around the Christmas trees, their white bodies reflecting the bright colors of the ornaments. They were like the snowmen he had built as a boy, but they were unfinished. They lacked eyes or noses or mouths. Perhaps they were waiting for him to finish them. But he couldn't move. He wanted to move, but his body would not obey him.

As he watched, one of the snowmen came closer. He couldn't see how it moved; it seemed to float. But it didn't matter. Snowmen were magical anyway, he thought. Just think of Frosty. But where was the magic hat?

The snowman stopped next to him. Nothing happened that he could see, but he could feel something come out from the creature and touch him, like an invisible hand. It seemed to be probing him deep inside. He flinched, but the touch was not painful. In fact, where it touched him, the pain in his body went away. He began to feel warm and good all over, and he drifted into sleep. After all, if you didn't sleep, Santa wouldn't come....

He awoke to find himself standing alone in a vast featureless plain. It was lit as if by moonlight, but looking up, he could see neither moon nor stars. The sky might as well have been a reflection of the land about him, or vice versa.

Without warning, a voice spoke to him in his head. *You are a human Your name is Jason. You are a scout from a stranded spaceship.*

His mind grappled with this information. *A spaceship? No, that was wrong. He was just a boy, having Christmas with his parents...*

The plain shifted and swirled around him, and he was standing in thick snow outside a mountain cabin. The winter night was crisp and cold, and a bright moon shown down on the snow-covered pine forest around him.

He heard the door open behind him, and a shaft of golden light speared across the white snowdrifts. He turned around. His father was coming out of the cabin, closing the door and putting on thick, warm gloves. His breath was steaming out around his face, like fog around a mountain crag.

"Come on, Son," his father said, "let's go look at the stars while Mom fixes the hot cocoa."

But that was wrong, he thought. His father was dead, killed by a landslide while climbing on the slopes of Mt. Olympus on Mars. And he was a soldier in the Northwest Bioregional Militia....

The cabin vanished. There was still a forest, though a different one, and snow covered everything. However, the dark woods did not seem magical at all. They were deadly, places where the enemy could hide in shadow, places where traps could be laid.

35

He was lying in a hole that he and his buddies had spent much of the afternoon digging. It had been a lousy way to spend Christmas Eve day. Word was, though, that the New Constitutionalist raiders would be coming through those woods tonight, heading down to the rich, plague-free cities along Puget Sound. If so, they would find that the NBM had prepared a warm Christmas reception for them. He patted his M-01 pulse rifle. Yes, he thought, we would be ready for them.

But this was wrong, too. He was not a soldier. He was an astronomer, an explorer. He was on the *Odyssey* colony ship heading for a world seventy light years from Earth.

He sat in a reclined chair in a small domed room. A dozen other pilot/scientists sat around him in similar chairs. The ceiling above him blazed with stars, a simulation of what he would be seeing if he were outside on the surface of the asteroid, but in the middle of the display a holographic replica of the Captain's head was speaking to them. He stared at the unfamiliar groupings and constellations of stars while listening to the briefing. They were lost, with only the capacity for one last, minimum range jump through B Space. They needed scouts to go out and find a world that could receive them. The Captain was asking for volunteers.   Jason's finger pressed the button that would log his name in as a volunteer, but his eyes kept roaming through the starfield, looking, wondering, where would be their new home....

But he had left the ship. He had found a world, a wonderful world. He remembered landing on it, his first breath of planetary air, his delight in how beautiful and peaceful it had all seemed, the walk to the alien city.

He remembered the snowman and the burst of green fire that had enveloped him.

That was a mobile sensor. The voice spoke again in his mind.

He whirled around, but there was no one to be seen. He was back on the featureless plain. "What?" he said. "Who's there? Who's speaking? And where am I?"

You are in a place I have fashioned for our conversation. I am the Giver. You need not fear.

"But you shot me!"

No. My sensor was scanning you, investigating your nature.

"It hurt."

My tree was hurt when you cut it.

"What? But I wasn't going to kill the tree! I just wanted a small sample."

Why?

"To study. To learn from, to understand the nature of the tree."

I wanted to sample you as well, to understand the nature of the being who had invaded my world. I wasn't trying to kill you, either. However, I miscalculated the strength of the scan, and it brought you pain. Then you destroyed my sensor. I sought to scan you in a different way, but I did not anticipate that you would fall and be injured.

Jason looked himself over. "I remember the pain and not being able to move, but now I seem fine."

You are enfolded within me, but your body lies injured within my physical matrix you call the anomaly.

"Am I dead?"

No. You live, but your body is beyond my power to repair without greater knowledge of your kind. I have placed it into beyond time and have drawn your essence into me. The plain vanished, and Jason found himself hovering above the terrace with the grove of alien trees and the pyramid. At the base of the stairway, he saw his body sprawled out on its side, looking like a broken toy cast aside by some giant child. Next to it stood one of the creatures he thought of as a snowman.

"But where are you? Who are you? What did you mean you are the Giver?"

I am in this place you call the anomaly, but I also exist in the multidimensional reality you call Bohm-Space, which allows me to be everywhere upon this world at once. As to our communication, your mind is inhabiting my own within this larger reality. We are sharing thoughts. I have learned about you and your mission, and your language, by absorbing the information contained in the artificial intelligence controlling your scout ship.

"You mean Angel?"

That is correct.

"What have you done to her?"

Nothing. It is intact, only dormant so it may not contact your mother ship until I have made decisions about you. It is interesting to me, though, that you refer to this artificial intelligence as if it were alive and a person like yourself. I am pleased you have concern for its...her....welfare.

37

"I....She just seems very real to me. Anyway, what did you mean about making decisions about me?"

Like this artificial intelligence you call Angel, I am a construct, made by beings who could manipulate both physical and multidimensional reality. Like your Angel, I also was made with a task to perform, one that springs from the remorse and penance of my makers.

"Your makers?"

They were a great race that built a mighty empire among the stars and then left this universe to explore the infinite realms of multidimensional reality. In their youth as a race, however, when they first left their home world, they were a warrior people who delighted in conquest and destruction. This planet was one of their victims, its own civilization wiped out and its cities left in rubble.

"I was right, then!" Jason exclaimed. "The ruins we detected were the results of a great war."

Yes. Over millenia, my makers matured as a species, and their warrior ways changed to peaceful and spiritual pursuits. They regretted the worlds they had ravaged and the civilizations they had destroyed. They could not bring back the Destroyed Ones, but as penance, they restored their victims' planets, turning them into worlds that would be ideal as a home for a new species. Beings such as myself were created to guard them.

"But why did they do this?"

In order to be gifts from my makers to other races who could honor the Destroyed Ones by enabling these worlds to flower once more with a growing civilization. It is my task to protect this world until I can give it to a suitable people to be a new home. That is why I am the Giver.

Suddenly, Jason saw images of strange ships orbiting this world and even stranger beings descending to its surface. *There have been races who have come to this world seeking to make it their own, but they have all been warrior races such as my makers once were. These are not suitable for the gift.* Jason saw the ships and beings disappear in bursts of light.

"You killed them?"

I translated them into the multidimensional realm and sent them away. They were unharmed but no longer part of your dimension.

"Is this what you will do to me and my people?"

Yes, if you are not suitable for the gift.

"Giver, we need this world. What can I do to prove we are suitable?"

Tell me why you are here.

"You already know that. We will die if we do not find a suitable world on which to land."

That is because of an accident. It tells me nothing. Had all gone as you had planned, you would not have come to this world. What interests me is why you left your home world and traveled into space in the first place.

"My race is outgrowing our world. We are looking for new places to settle, new resources.

The voice of the Giver interrupted him. *The simple need to expand is not enough to deserve the gift. Tell me, why are you here?*

Jason felt despair. What did he need to say or what could he do to convince this being that humans were worthy?

He gazed out over the infinite plain, trying to imagine what to say. He thought about this world and what it could mean to his people, perhaps in time to all humanity. He thought of the forests of trees with their sugar plum fruits glowing in the dark, and as he did so, a memory bubbled up out of his unconscious, a memory of lights and wonderment.

You remember...Let your memory tell me more....

As the memory surfaced, the plain rippled and faded, and then he was there....

The Christmas tree filled the living room with its glowing presence. He was unable to take his eyes off it, even as he put on his warm woolen jacket and cinched tight his snow boots. He was mesmerized by the beauty of the lights and ornaments, a cascade of colors that flowed around the tree like a river of reds, greens, blues, golds, purples, and silvers. Some ornaments had miniature computer chips that generated holographic scenes. Those were his favorite, each one a little world in which some holiday theme played itself out: Santa flying over the world in a magical sleigh or elves holding snow ball fights at the North Pole. One ornament even had tiny people acting out the entire story of *T'was the Night Before Christmas*, while another depicted the story of the Nativity. The whole effect of the tree reminded him of a galaxy spinning in space, filled with little worlds of color and life.

Finally he turned away and went out through the front door onto the porch, feeling the painful but refreshing bite of the cold night air. He crunched down into the snow. A bright moon shown down on the whitened pine forest around him. Through the window, the colorful light of the Christmas tree spilled outward onto the nearby woods, reflecting and sparkling off snow-covered branches, making the forest seem enchanted, like some magical fairyland.

He heard the door open behind him, and a shaft of golden light speared across the white snowdrifts. He turned around. His father was coming out of the cabin, closing the door and putting on thick, warm gloves. His breath was steaming out around his face, like fog around a mountain crag.

"Come on, Son," his father said, "let's go look at the stars while Mom fixes the hot cocoa."

The snow crunched and crumbled under their feet like a thin crust of crystallized sugar over meringue as they walked to a platform at the top of a small hill. A telescope with an attached holographic viewer was mounted on the platform, protected under a transparent dome.

For a time, they just stood and looked at the blazing galaxy above them, and to Jason, it was as if their Christmas tree had been transported magically from their living room into the heavens. Then his father opened the top of the dome, adjusted the telescope so that it pointed to Saturn and turned on the holoviewer. The ringed planet appeared in the air in front of them, looking like a miniature Christmas ornament. "Just think, Jason. Right now a dozen men and women are on a spaceship heading towards the moons of Saturn. Isn't that exciting! Who knows what they will discover?" His father squeezed his shoulder. "Someday you may be out there, too, traveling between the stars."

They stood in silence for a time, just watching the great ringed planet float in the air before them. Then they heard his mother's voice calling to them that the cocoa was ready. His father switched off the holoviewer and closed the dome. They trudged through the snow back to the cabin.

Later, when the hot chocolate was gone and the fire had collapsed into hot embers, Jason and his father sat in the darkened living room and watched the glowing tree, his mother having gone off to bed. "Early morning tomorrow," she had said, smiling at Jason. "Just try to sleep at least till five, OK, Kiddo?"

He snuggled up to his father. "I love this part!" he said.

"Which part is that?" his dad asked.

"Just sitting in the dark and watching the tree all lit up. It's so...." he groped for the word he wanted, "exciting!"

"Thinking of what Santa will bring?" his father chuckled.

"Oh, the presents are exciting, too, but that's not what I meant. I don't know....It's just that all the lights and stuff...it seems...it seems just like when we were out on the hill looking up at the stars, Dad. It's like looking at Saturn or Mars.... Do you know what I mean?"

"Why, yes," his Dad replied. "I do. I feel that way, too. It's the wonder of it. Who knows what presents you'll find under the tree in the morning? Who knows what wonderful and exciting discoveries we'll find out in space? It's the same thing. It's a feeling of promise, of something new to discover. It's a feeling that has led to the best that humanity has created."

His dad picked up the old brass poker, blackened from rummaging around in many fires, and stirred the embers in the fire place. A small flame obligingly shot up, as if saying 'hello' and acknowledging his efforts, only to sink back into its comfortable and satiated sleep amongst the coals.

"You know, Jason," his dad continued, "the tree has always been a symbol of life. The Christmas tree just reminds us that in life there are mysteries to be unwrapped and new delights waiting to be found. It reminds us of what is best about life, the light of discovery and promise at the heart of everything."

Jason thought about what his father was saying, and it seemed just right to him. It was what he felt. When he looked at the Christmas tree all lit up, it was like looking at a gateway into a universe of worlds to explore. That was exactly what he felt.

"Yes, Dad, that's it!" he exclaimed, finding words for his feeling. "It's wonder, isn't it? It's the wonder of the unknown!"

"Exactly! Why, we're just starting to explore the solar system, and if my colleagues in the Institute are right, by the time you're a young man, we will have a working faster-than-light engine that will enable us to travel to the stars. And when we do, you'll hear lot's of talk about

41

finding new worlds to colonize and resources to mine, as if it were all economics, but what will really take us to the stars is just what you said: wonder. It is the excitement of exploring the unknown and discovering who knows what." His father sighed. "Ah, I wish I could be one of those who will make that journey, Son, but I think you could be, if you want to."

"I do want to, Dad!"

His father looked at his watch. "Well, then, as a future star traveler, you'll need your rest, so it's time to go to bed." His father picked up a small jolly, red-garbed figure in a sleigh pulled by eight tiny reindeer. Sensing the warmth of his hand, animations began, with Santa cracking a whip and calling out in a small voice, "On, Dasher! On, Dancer! Merry Christmas to all!" Jason's father smiled. "Besides, how can Santa come if we sit here hogging the tree?"

The scene began to fade, and nine-year old Jason suddenly transformed into the Jason who really was a star traveler, the Jason whose body lay broken on a strange world but whose spirit was caught up in the presence of an alien mind.

I see, the Giver said. *This is very interesting. You are drawn by wonderment. Do all your people feel this way?*

"No, but many do. On my ship, I would say most do."

I must investigate this. But before I do, I have a question.

"What is it?"

Something I saw in your memory. The red figure in the vehicle drawn by animals that could fly...

"You mean Santa Claus."

Yes. He seemed important to the weave of the memory, part of the wonder. Who is this?

"He is a mythic figure who magically brings toys and gifts to all the children of the world and leaves them under their trees on Christmas night."

He is a Giver, like myself?

"Yes, I suppose you could say that."

And you celebrate him?

"Yes."

Interesting. The Giver was silent for a long time. In fact, where there had been a sense of presence, now there was an emptiness, as if the alien had turned its attention elsewhere. Then, abruptly the presence was back. *I have examined your people on your ship,* it said, *and it is as you say. There is an appreciation for wonder in their souls.*

"You've been to the *Odyssey?*"

It is not a long journey for me. I had to see for myself. You see, the civilization that once lived on this world also valued wonder, which my creators at first did not. My makers thought it a useless trait that made their victims weak. However, in time, they came to value wonder, too, because they learned how it gave them new possibilities and enabled them to see what they had not seen before. By learning to follow their wonder, they matured to become a great people.

My makers would have appreciated the wonder that brings you here, Jason of Earth, Jason of the Christmas tree. I think your people show promise. I have decided to bring your ship here and give this world to you. Together, I believe we can fulfill the promise this planet once had.

Jason felt a wave of relief and exultation sweep over him, but before he could say anything, the Giver continued. *In keeping with your Christmas, I shall be like Santa, your Giver, and give you a present. I have learned how to fix your body. Before visiting your people, that is what I shall do first.*

Three light years away, the *Odyssey* floated in space, its sensors alert to the return of its children, the scout ships that had gone forth in search of hope. On the bridge, the Captain sat in her chair and waited.

"Isn't it about time that Jason Stewart should be returning?" she asked her second-in-command.

"Yes, Captain, all going well, his estimated time of return should have been thirty minutes ago."

The Captain sighed, stretching her back to relieve some of the tension in her body from sitting too many hours in the command chair. However, she swore she would not leave the bridge until all the scouts had returned. Jason was the only one left out there. All the others had brought back bad news. They had found nothing. Would that be Jason's report, too? She pondered those three words: *all going well....* Not much had gone well for them recently.

Suddenly, the Communications officer said in a quiet voice that nevertheless only barely masked his excitement, "Captain, we are picking up the signs of an approaching vessel."

"Is it the scout ship?"

There was a pause. "Negative, Captain. It's like nothing I've seen before."

The Captain stood up. Now what? "Can you give me a visual display?"

"Yes, coming up."

In front of the bridge crew, a large monitor sprang into life. At first, the Captain couldn't make out what she was seeing. Then, with disbelief, the vision came into focus.

"What th...!" exclaimed her second-in-command.

Outside, the object approached the *Odyssey*, a tiny mite circling a giant boulder. But as sensors and holovision cameras focused in upon it, the Captain and her crew could see it very well.

It was Santa Claus riding a bright red and gold sleigh, being pulled by eight reindeer across the vacuum of space. And sitting next to Santa, grinning as if his face would split, was Jason!

"Science, what is that?" the Captain exclaimed. "Is it real?"

"It looks like Santa Claus, Captain," her Science officer replied, gazing at an array of monitors, "and it's a real artifact, but it's encased in some kind of B-Space force field that I've never seen before."

The communication speakers crackled, startling them, and a loud voice came booming into the bridge. "HO HO HO!" it said. "MERRY CHRISTMAS!"

A shudder ran through the asteroid that was the ship. The Captain, unable to take her eyes off the monitor, called out, "What was that?"

"The Bohm drives have started up by themselves, Captain," replied her second-in-command. "We are preparing to make a jump through B-Space!"

Before the Captain could reply, Jason's voice came over the speakers. "Don't worry! It's all right. I've met an alien called the Giver, and this is his way of saying 'hello!' And believe me, has he got a Christmas present for us!"

"HO HO HO," boomed the voice. "ON, DASHER! ON, DANCER! ON PRANCER AND VIXEN..." the Santa figure yelled, shaking the reins in its hands. The sleigh turned and took off and the Odyssey shuddered again and began to move.

"Jason..." called the Captain. "What is going on?" But whatever reply Jason might have given was drowned out as the Giver began singing in a loud, deep voice, "O TANNENBAUM, O TANNENBAUM...." and sleigh and ship disappeared into the infinities of Bohm-Space en route to their new home.

Second Verse

To me, the greatest Christmas story of all time, aside from the Nativity tale itself, is Charles Dickens' A Christmas Carol. *I have nearly every movie version of it, from the classic 1951 film with Alastair Sim to the Disney cartoon with Mickey Mouse and Uncle Scrooge. I even have one wonderfully warped version in which the three ghosts turn a lovable, generous kindhearted Scrooge into a miserable old miser!*

Every Christmas season, part of my holiday ritual is to watch every one of these movies, some more than once, and I always cry at the end. I really enjoy transformations! The rest of my family is not so obsessive, but they will join me for some of the viewings. Two of our particular favorites are the musical Scrooge *with Albert Finny and the* Muppet Christmas Carol *with Michael Caine.*

I think of this story as a second verse to the Carol, *with apologies to Dickens. I loved writing it. It flowed out like honey from a hive. All my stories should come so easily! I cried at the end of it, too!*

The Second Verse

In the end, he was penniless. Even a fortune as great as his had been could not last forever, not with all the charities he supported, the good works he sponsored, and the gifts he gave. Tonight, after ordering the last of his gifts to be delivered, he had had just enough money left for the soup he had eaten and for the small candle that now burned on the nightstand beside his bed, casting flickering shadows but little heat in the wintry cold of his room.

He would not have had it any other way. He was content. Though he had nothing left except the old, drafty house in which he lay abed, he felt richer than he ever had when he had been surrounded by his coppers and his gold, a frigid old miser, unloving and unloved. He had wonderful memories now that filled him with satisfaction and joy, and he had countless friends.

Indeed, he knew that if he but let be known the severity of his impoverished state, he would be the recipient of many offers to render assistance, not least from his nephew and his lovely wife.

But he would not let it be known. His reticence was not due to pride. He had long ago lost that particular burden, though not his dignity. No, never his dignity. It was simply that he knew, in the way that it is sometimes given us to know, that his time on earth would come to an end that very night.

For many of us, knowledge of our immanent demise would be dismaying, as it had been for him many years before on this very night when the ghosts had first appeared. But since then, the knowledge of his mortality had troubled him not at all. There is nothing like hobnobbing with spirits to take the sting away from death.

He leaned over and blew out the candle. The illumination in the room hardly changed, for it was only a tiny candle, a ha'penny's worth, and the light of a full moon was flooding through the window. He had lit it out of habit as much as out of need. He lay back against his pillow and closed his eyes. He would die in his sleep, he thought, in his own bed, happy and at peace. A man could hardly ask for a greater gift. That he was alone bothered him not at all, for he had had a habit of being alone all his life, and he felt the solitude as an old and trusted

49

friend. If he had any regret, it was only that there were other men in the world like he had been, tight of heart and purse. He knew that for all his work, he had not reduced their number.

He slept.

Then he awoke. Everything was bright and still. He wondered if he had crossed over the last threshold, but then he realized he was in his own bed, the covers snuggled up to his neck, the moonlight filling the room with a silvery glow. He was still alive, and he felt a momentary pang of disappointment. What had awakened him?

He suddenly realized the old clock in the sitting room had just struck the first hour of the day. The hour of the first ghost, he thought, and then wondered why he had thought of that.

He raised up his head and peered into his room. Surely, it was too bright just to be moonlight? As he sat up, he realized it was even getting brighter. Perhaps his clock was wrong and the dawn was breaking?

Then he saw them, three indistinct shapes merging into the moonlight. No, he corrected himself, they were emerging out of the moonlight. As he looked more closely, even while his hand fumbled on the nightstand for his spectacles, he realized it was only one figure emerging.

As it had done years before, the spirit stood by his bed and beckoned to him. He sat up even more, pushed back the covers, and swung his legs around to put his feet on the floor. A breeze slid up under his nightshirt, wafting across his boney knees, but instead of being winter cold as it should have been, it was summer warm and soothing. He looked up at the shimmering form and trembled nonetheless.

"Though it has been many years, I know thee, spirit. You are the Ghost of Christmas Past, first harbinger of my present happiness. But why, O specter, have you come to me now? Have I left something yet undone? Have you more to show me?"

"Take my hand, Mortal," the spirit said. He did as he was told. This time, instead of finding himself drawn into the world of his own memories as he had been once before, he saw a collage of uncounted images, all bright and glowing, all shifting and sliding around each other like the shards of colored glass in his nephew's kaleidoscope. Confused, he raised his free hand to cover his eyes.

50

"Spirit!" he cried out. "What mystery is this? What is this phantasmagoria such as a madman might see?"

The spirit's voice was calm. "Look again. Look closely."

He lowered his hand and looked again. This time to his relief the images moved more slowly. He could see that each was a scene, some outdoors, some indoors, in which people stood or moved about. "Why," he exclaimed in recognition, "there is Bob Cratchit and his son, Tiny Tim! And there is my nephew! And over there, the fishmonger who stands on the corner of old Threadneedle Street! And there, the fruitseller and Old Martha from whom I bought my soup tonight! And there are others, many others I know..." He looked more closely. "But many of these people are strangers to me."

"They are all those whose lives have been touched by your generosity which has rippled out like a Christmas tide even to those who are unknown to you," the spirit explained. "Their Christmases past have been brighter than they would have been otherwise, and I am now brighter because of it. You have done well."

The spirit released his hand. The visions disappeared. His sight was still dazzled, though, so he missed the approach of the second specter whose massive presence bid fair to fill the room. When he could see again, his eyes widened in happy recognition of this apparition, and he smiled broadly.

"And you, fair spirit, can be none other than the Ghost of Christmas Present. But you have grown mightily in girth and stature since last I saw one of your brothers!"

The booming voice filled the room like an avalanche of merriment. "That is because my brothers and I have been well fed since then. Joy and compassion are our meat and loving kindness our drink. You have supplied us with both in hearty measure all these years. You have done well!" With that, the great spirit patted him on the shoulder, making him glad he was still sitting, for he surely would have toppled over had he been on his feet.

A third figure approached, robed and hooded as he remembered him but no longer a figure of dread. The Ghost of Christmas Future held no terrors for him now. "And you, good spirit, who showed me the dark future I might have had and thus saved me from it, what have you to show me tonight that I do not already know?"

51

The head within the hood was unseen, but he had a feeling it had bowed toward him. Then the spirit opened its robe, and he saw a snow-filled graveyard. A fresh tombstone stood there, as yet bare of snow, and he didn't need to see the name carved upon it to know that it was his. But what drew his attention were the people crowded around, some singing softly, many weeping, filling the cemetery in all the directions he could see.

"So many people," he said in wonder. "For me?" Again he had the impression the figure nodded. Then the picture disappeared and in its place was simply light, a light so inviting, so lovely, so embracing that he ached to leap into it.

"If this is my future," he said, "then this time let it be as it is shown. I am ready."

"We know," said the Ghost of Christmas Present. "That is why we have come, to take you on to your destiny. But first, we would ask if there is any boon we might grant in gratitude before you leave this mortal coil?"

He thought for a moment, then he grinned. "Why, yes," he said, "now that you mention it, there is."

He found Marley floating in limbo, much as he had last seen him on the Christmas Eve he had been reborn. The chains were still wrapped about him, the coin boxes still attached. "Hello, old friend," he said, flying up to him.

"It's you!" the ghost exclaimed. "But how come you here? I had heard you had changed."

The man laughed. "And I did, thanks to you. Do you see any chains on me?"

Marley stared. "Nary a one."

"Then you must let me help you with yours." With that, the man took hold of Marley's chains and began to loop them around himself.

"But this is not allowed! These are chains I forged myself. They are my weight to bear throughout eternity!"

"No, my friend, only until one loves you enough willingly to bear them with you. And in the name of the One who was born to free us from all our chains, I do love you, Marley. You made possible my salvation, and now I return the favor." He pulled more of the chains onto himself, hardly feeling any weight at all from them, and as he did, they slid off his old partner and onto him.

"I am free!" Marley said in wonderment.

"Yes, my friend. So be on your way and find the heaven you have longed for."

Marley began to fade as limbo lost its hold on him. "But what of my chains? What will you do with them?"

The man laughed long and heartily. "Oh, I think I shall find some use for them, not having any of my own."

The clock on the desk struck two. The big, black-bearded man sighed and set aside the contract he had been working on, his eyes scowling under bushy brows. Tomorrow, he thought, tomorrow Fothringhall will sign this contract, or I shall have his business. Then he remembered that tomorrow was Christmas, and the scowl became deeper. "Humbug!" he muttered, rising from his chair and blowing out the light from the single candle on his desk. It would have to wait.

The man let himself out from his office, his clerks long gone. Probably out getting drunk, he said darkly, his beard quivering with indignation. He locked the door with a heavy key and started down the quiet, snow-filled street toward his home.

As he walked, he thought he saw a beggar sitting in the shadows of a building. He frowned fiercely in the man's direction so that he would know not to approach. Where were the police? What was becoming of London that beggars were allowed to accost honest, hard-working men? They should all be swept up and hauled out of the city like the refuse they were. He would write a letter to the *Times* about this tomorrow, Christmas or no Christmas.

Finally, he came to the front door of his house. It was an old house with an old door. No one seeing it would know that a man of wealth and property lived within, and that was how he liked it. He took out another heavy key, inserted it in the lock, and reached for the handle of the door. As he grasped it and pulled the door part way open, he was startled to see the old brass doorknocker begin to flow as if made of melting wax. Transfixed, he watched with growing horror and amazement as the metal transformed itself into the head of a man. A familiar man. Who was it, anyway?

The face looked at him and winked, and he suddenly knew. It was that old man who kept badgering him about giving to the poor. It was...

"Good Heavens!" he exclaimed, "It's Ebenezer Scrooge!"

And from the dark depths of his house, he thought he heard a dry chuckle and the clinking whisper of old chains being dragged across his floor.

The Grail

One of my best friends is the English scholar and writer John Matthews. A most wonderful fellow, he is a treasure house of knowledge and wisdom concerning the history of the Grail and all things pertaining to the legends of King Arthur. John was visiting us late one November, and the Grail had been much in our conversations. So when I set about to write that year's Christmas story, I found myself in the world of Camelot, Arthur, Merlin, the Round Table, and the knights questing for the Grail. In particular, I found myself with Hodge, a young man who had a very special tale to tell. It has nothing to do with Christmas, yet it has everything to do with Christmas and with the spirit of the one whose birth we celebrate.

This story was originally published in a wonderful book of Celtic tales, Within the Hollow Hills. *John Matthews was the editor, and it was published by Lindisfarne. I reprint it here in a slightly different form acknowledging their generosity and permission in allowing me to do so. If you enjoy this story, buy the book in which it originally appeared. You won't be disappointed.*

THE GRAIL

"Out of my way, boy!" shouted Sir Kay, pushing Hodge roughly to one side as the knight strode quickly down the castle corridor. He was followed by two squires, young boys hardly older than Hodge himself. The smallest of the two was almost running to keep up with the knight's long stride. The larger paused by Hodge, looking at him with a smirk of superiority. "Yes," he said, imitating his master's tone, "out of our way, kitchen boy!" With that he gave Hodge another shove, and the younger boy stumbled against the damp wall of the corridor and fell down. The squire laughed and ran to catch up with Sir Kay.

Hodge's face burned with embarrassment. Most of the squires were good-hearted lads who did not put on airs, but Sir Kay's squires were like their master, arrogant and rough. Once again, Hodge wondered how Sir Kay had ever become one of the Fellowship. If Kay had not been the King's foster brother, Hodge was sure he would never have qualified to sit at the Round Table.

Hodge picked himself up, only to flatten himself again against the wall as he saw another knight come running up the corridor towards him. It was Lancelot, he noted with awe, whom rumor said was the greatest of all the knights. Other less complimentary things were also whispered in the kitchens about him and the Queen, but Hodge felt it disloyal to listen to such tales and so paid them no attention.

Running fast, the great knight passed Hodge with hardly a glance in his direction. Hodge sighed. That was his life. He was either in the way or invisible.

Looking down the corridor as the running figure disappeared around a corner, he failed to see another figure coming toward him. Turning, he walked right into a hard-muscled frame and once again was knocked down, his cap falling over his eyes.

"Ho, there, little one," a firm voice said, "you must watch where you're going!" A hand was thrust down to him, and Hodge grabbed it. He was pulled to his feet, and a gentle hand rearranged his cap. He found himself looking into the laughing brown eyes and bearded face of Sir Bors, one of his favorite knights, a man of simple origins like Hodge himself who never put on airs and who was always kind to the castle help .

"Sor...sorry, my lord," Hodge stammered, once more embarrassed. It was his secret hope to one day be accepted by Sir Bors as a squire, and he did not want this man to think he was clumsy and unaware of his surroundings.

"It's all right...hmmm, Hodge, isn't it? ...but if I were you, I would not be wandering these corridors just now. There has been a most holy and miraculous event in the Great Hall, and it has stirred this place up like a bear's paw in a beehive. Knights and squires are running all over the place, as you have seen, getting ready for a quest."

"A quest?" the boy blurted out.

"Aye, Hodge, a most holy quest. Only a short time ago, while we were at meat around the table, the cup of Christ appeared in the air above us. Like the disciples at Pentecost, we were all filled with a holy fire. We looked upon each other and saw things no mortal man should know about another. But rather than fear, we felt love and a great wonder. Then the Grail disappeared, leaving us with a longing like nothing I have felt before, not even when I met my wife, comely as she was."

Sir Bors closed his eyes for a moment, remembering. Then he looked at Hodge, his eyes bright with wonder. Hodge was filled with wonder, too, not only at the story but that this knight was taking the time to tell it to him. Obviously, Sir Bors needed to talk about what had happened.

"We all sat stunned, when Sir Gawain jumped to his feet and pledged that he would go on quest to find the answer to the mystery we had seen. Then others joined him, pledging themselves to find the Holy Grail on behalf of Arthur and the realm. Even I, who, as you know, am not much given to quests, found myself on my feet, shouting with the rest. Then the King stood up and formally charged the Fellowship to find the cup of Christ, though if truth be told, he seemed sad as he did so. Indeed, Lancelot, who sits closer to Arthur than I, mentioned the King had leaned to him and said that this quest might be the end of the Fellowship itself."

Perhaps, Hodge thought wildly for a moment, catching the knight's excitement, he has noticed me and wants me to accompany him on this quest! That hope, however, was dashed in the next moment, as

Sir Bors patted him on the head and said, "I think, Hodge, this is not a good night to be roaming the corridors. If I were you, I would go to the kitchens and work there where you won't be run over by knights and squires rushing about to be the first to leave and find the Holy Grail As for me, I go to spend some time with my family before I shall set off like the others." With that, the knight gave the disappointed boy a friendly squeeze on his shoulder and continued down the corridor himself.

Following Sir Bors' advice, Hodge made his way through the castle to the kitchens where he spent the rest of the evening washing dishes and listening to all the rumors that raced through the room faster than the knights were running about themselves. A new knight had arrived, it seemed, a youth in shining armor accompanied by an old man, who might have been the missing Merlin himself. Hodge listened astonished as one of the serving maids swore she had been told by one of the squires that this new knight, Sir Galahad by name, had actually sat in the Siege Perilous, the seat at the Table that no one ever sat in lest he be blasted by supernatural forces. Yet, the youth had sat there unharmed, much to everyone's amazement. Then the mystical cup had appeared in the air above them, and the old man had exclaimed, "There is the Cup of Christ!"

It was very late that night when Hodge was finally released from his work to go to bed. There had been one demand after another as squires and knights prepared their gear and packed food for the journeys ahead. Yet, the excitement in the castle was so contagious that no one felt tired. Everyone talked about the wonders that had taken place or that would take place, and with each telling, with each new rumor, with each whispered "I have a friend who has a friend who says..." the stories grew more wondrous indeed.

So it was that when Hodge was done, he was too excited to sleep. Instead, he found his feet carrying him to the Great Hall where the Round Table stood, the place where the Grail had appeared only hours before. He didn't know why he went there. He rarely came to this part of the castle, and he was sure that someone would stop him before he arrived. Commoners like him were rarely allowed in this Hall unless they had business with the Fellowship or the King, and there were almost always guards at the door. But in the still early morning hours past midnight, the corridors were empty, and he saw no one. Strangely, even the guards were gone.

The Great Hall was lit only by the dim glow from a fire dying in the hearth. The Round Table was a huge presence in the room, and as always, Hodge felt a deep reverence and awe when he saw it. Like nearly every other servant boy in the castle, it was his dream to one day sit at this table, to be part of the Fellowship, to ride forth and do great deeds for God, King, and Realm. At the moment, the way such a dream might be fulfilled seemed as dark to him as the shadows that lay heavy everywhere within the room.

Hodge crept warily through those shadows and up to the Table itself. Hesitantly, he put his hand out and touched it. Its rough wood had been carefully polished, and it was warm to the touch, as if deep within it, a faint fire burned, but as he rubbed his hand over its surface, he realized with a shock that it felt no different from the tables he cleaned in the kitchen or in the common dining rooms where the squires ate. In fact, as he looked more closely, he thought he saw a stain upon it.

Squinting in the dim light from the fire, Hodge saw that someone had spilled gravy onto the table and it had never been cleaned up! He felt a wave of indignation at the thought. He knew the knights took their meat and drink at this table, as well as debating the affairs of state, but somehow, it had never occurred to him that some of them might spill their food like a common workman or that the Round Table might be stained like any common board upon which a poor man took his food.

Without thinking, Hodge took the edge of his sleeve and began rubbing fiercely at the stain. He thought he was cleaning it off, but the growing shadows as the fire sank deeper into its own ashes made it difficult for him to see. Yet, somehow, it seemed very important to him that this stain be removed. He rubbed even harder.

All at once, there was a light about him, as if a torch had been lit. Startled and frightened that someone had found him rubbing on the great Table and that punishment would surely now befall him, he jumped back. As he did so, his foot caught in the leg of one of the chairs drawn up to the table, and he fell backwards, landing ungracefully upon his backside.

It was then that he saw the glowing object in the air above him. It was a simple cup, not all that different from one he might use himself in the kitchen, but it shone like molten steel from the blacksmith's forge. It gave off no heat, yet in its light, Hodge felt a warmth like nothing he had ever known before. It was not as if his body were warm but as if something much deeper and somehow more real was being warmed and awakened within him.

He realized in an instant that this cup was what had appeared to the assembled knights, that it was what the old man had proclaimed the cup of Christ, the Holy Grail. But that was all he knew. All other emotion, save awe and an overpowering sense of being loved, were swept from him in the light of this apparition. He did not even know that he had scrambled to his feet and was standing by the Table again, unable to take his gaze from the glory of the vessel hovering in the air above him.

Then, as suddenly as it had come, the cup disappeared, its light lingering for a moment in the room like the memory of a dawn. Then all was dark again. Hodge felt himself coming back as if from a very far place. Shuddering, he drew a breath.

"So, you saw it, too, eh, lad?"

The deep voice coming from the shadows made him jump and whirl around in fright. Who had spoken?

From the shadows near one of the tall pillars that lined the Great Hall, a hooded figure stepped. Frightened, Hodge made ready to bolt from the room, sure that he would be punished severely for daring to look upon so holy an object as the Grail. However, the voice spoke again, and something in it held him rooted to the spot as if he had become a pillar himself.

"Don't be afraid, boy! I will not hurt you." The figure came closer, and Hodge saw it was an old man dressed in a monk's habit. The figure unceremoniously pulled out one of the chairs by the table and sat down. An old and weathered hand reached out from under the sleeve of the robe and took his arm. The touch, while firm, was nonetheless gentle, and Hodge felt all his fear drain away.

"You see, boy? I will not hurt you. How could I hurt one to whom the Grail has shown itself?" Now Hodge could see the man's face. It was in fact an old and wrinkled face, but the eyes were alive and fierce like those of a hawk on its first hunting flight.

"Tell me, boy, and hold nothing back. Who are you and what are you doing here?"

To his amazement, Hodge heard his voice pouring forth his life's story, how his father had been a farmer tending a landhold not far from Camelot, how the farm had been raided one day, how his father had fought the raiders but had been killed in the end, and how, when all had seemed lost and their house was burning, one of the knights of the Fellowship—Sir Gawain, it had been—had arrived on the scene and had killed the raiders and rescued him and his mother. He told how they had been brought to the castle, where he had become a kitchen boy, and how his mother had died the last winter from fever, leaving him alone.

The old man's eyes were encouraging. Hodge found himself telling him how his deepest longing was to be a knight himself, who could protect the weak and helpless and rescue people as he had been rescued. He told him of his desire to battle monsters and evil-doers in the name of the King and the Land. He told all these things and more, without emotion, like telling the story of a figure in a dream with whom he felt little connection. From time to time, the old man would interrupt and ask him a question, but for the most part he listened in silence.

Finally, Hodge had told all there was to tell, and his voice stopped, not as if he had willed it to do so, but as if it had simply come to the edge of a cliff and had stepped off into the silence below. The old man continued to hold onto his arm, and the fierce eyes continued their hawk's survey of his soul.

Then, like a soft wind from the farthest corners of the earth, the old man sighed and released him. For a moment those eyes closed, and Hodge felt like a mouse must feel who has reached the safety of his den. Then, the eyes snapped open once more, and he realized that that den was in fact nowhere around.

"Boy...Hodge...listen to me. It is given only to a few to see the Grail. No man can make it come or go, not the holiest saint nor the most powerful magician. It goes where and when it will, and no King or Queen can gainsay it. That it came to this company here tonight was an act of its own, not mine, not anyone's, and now we will see what results."

The old man sighed again. "The King, the Queen, the Fellowship, Camelot, all of us are called to a new undertaking but whether it is one of questing or not, I cannot say. We are poised in time. In this moment

64

a new world could be born or an old world die. Perhaps it is both. I only know we will all never be the same. Our prayers must be that whatever emerges from this moment, from what occurred in this room, will be for the good."

"But how could it be otherwise, if what we saw was the cup of Christ...?" Hodge blurted out, and then was shocked at his impudence. What did the likes of him know of holy cups and heavenly visions? The old man smiled, and Hodge sensed it was not a smile of mirth. "Ah, that is a mystery, Hodge. The coming of the Grail does not foretell how men will receive it or interpret its presence. Its light is a flint that can set fire to wisdom or to folly. From it one can drink insight or madness. Which will you drink from it, boy?"

"I...I...don't understand..." He was beginning to feel fear again beneath this stranger's penetrating gaze and hearing such strange words. Then, the eyes softened, and the fear fell away.

"I know you don't. I do not expect you to understand me, nor am I sure I understand all that has occurred. I only want you to listen to me as I have listened to you. For the Grail chose you, Hodge, as one of those to whom it would reveal itself. It was no accident you were here this night. There is a reason you were shown the same vision as those of the Fellowship."

At these words, Hodge's heart leapt and burned with an excitement as if a new Grail had just appeared before him. "Does this mean I can be a knight and go on quest with the others, Sir?"

The old man looked at him without answering. Hodge felt abashed and embarrassed by his outburst. Still, he *had* seen the Grail, and even this old man had said that was important and special.

"Hodge, knighthood and the quest are not yours, I am afraid. I can see that your life weaves a different thread. But I tell you this, knighthood comes in many forms and many ways, and not all knights wear armor and ride horses or are chosen by a king. Anyone who cherishes compassion in his heart and strives to do right for others and is a true servant can be a knight of a deeper order. There are many more fellowships than that created by Arthur."

At these words, Hodge's heart sank. He did not know of any other fellowships and could not understand this strange old man's words. How could a man be a knight if he were not invested by the king? What was a knight without his horse or armor? And why would he have seen the Grail if he were not to be a knight?

"I do not know why the Grail showed itself to you, Hodge," the old man said, as if reading his mind, "but I know it had a reason. You may not have a quest but you have a task to perform. Who knows, boy, it may be more important than all the quests put together. Only time will tell."

The old man stood up. "I must go now. There is still much to do, and time is short. And you, Hodge, should go to bed."

"Yes, Sir," Hodge replied, but he felt unable to take a single step. The old man began to walk away, then turned. "By the way, boy," he asked. "I saw you rubbing on the Table as if you would set it on fire. What were you doing?"

Hodge felt all the indignation he had felt earlier rise up in him. "It was gravy, Sir! A stain on the Table! Someone had spilled and had not cleaned up. I was trying to clean it!"

The old man looked at him for a moment, then threw back his head and laughed, a rich, deep laugh. "Gravy! By the Gods!" Then the laughter cut off, and the hawk eyes fixed themselves on Hodge so fiercely that the boy felt more like a trapped mouse than ever. "That is it, boy! That is what you must do! Clean the Table!"

Hodge felt a jolt pass through him. "Clean...clean the Table?"

"CLEAN THE TABLE!" The old man did not raise his voice, but to Hodge, it sounded as if he had shouted at the top of his lungs. Then the hawk eyes flashed as if bolts of lightning were sparking from them, and the man pointed at Hodge. "And now, GO TO BED!"

Hodge flew from the room, down the corridors, down the stairs, down more corridors and more stairs and finally flung himself into his room far down in the bowels of the castle, onto the straw-filled mat he called his bed, and into a darkness of dreams in which cups glowing like molten gold floated over the land and a god-like voice said over and over, "CLEAN THE TABLE!"

It was late morning when Hodge awoke. He was astonished that no one had come to wake him, since usually his day began before the sun came up. With trepidation, he ran from his room and made his way to the kitchens. He hoped there was some food left and that he wouldn't have to begin work right away. His stomach felt as if a badger had burrowed a long hole in it and now lay growling at the bottom.

When he arrived at the kitchens, he was astonished to find it empty except for the wise woman who supervised the collection and drying of herbs. He was glad to see her, for after his mother had died, she had taken a liking to him and had begun to teach him a little of her herbal lore.

As he ran into the room, the woman said without looking up from what she was doing, "You are late, Hodge."

"I'm sorry, Marta. I overslept. But why did no one fetch me? And where is everyone?"

"Everyone is off at the church watching all the Fellowship receive the blessing of the King and Queen and Bishop before they go off to find the cup of Christ. I did not think they would welcome someone who practices the old religion. Besides," she spat onto the floor, "we have our own cup already, and need not go traveling the land and leaving King and kingdom behind like some addle-headed swain in pursuit of the latest comely wench he sees."

Hodge knew she was speaking of those like her who followed the old ways. His mother had been a Christian, but she had not lived long enough to give him much instruction. He had found himself intrigued and drawn to what Marta had to say about the land and its powers. But he had little time or energy to think about religious things, so he did not bother himself with them. At least not until last night.

"There's some porridge in a bowl by the window for you and some bread there as well."

"Thank you, Marta!" Hodge said gratefully and ran over to the window to fetch his breakfast.

After he had eaten, he found he had little to do—a rare occasion in his life. Marta seemed occupied and unwilling to be bothered, so he wandered outside and climbed up a tree that grew by the wall of the keep. From there he could see down into the village square, where throngs of people were gathered outside the church. The sound of voices singing drifted up from down below and mixed in a pleasant way with the bird song he heard around him. The sun's warmth worked its way into his bones, and his eyelids drooped.

67

He slept without knowing it. In his dreams, he was part of a brilliant company, each of whose members were garbed in armor that seemed struck from the colors of the rainbow. He could recognize Gawain, Bors, Lancelot, and all the others. Even Sir Kay looked different, resplendent in a new way, his harsh and arrogant face softened. Around them a great light gleamed as the sun dashed itself upon their shiningness and sprayed out as golden foam. Looking down he saw his own body encased in a shining white armor which seemed to weigh nothing at all, sitting astride a great warhorse. Ahead of them stood three figures. One he knew to be Arthur, his great sword Excalibur raised above his head. The other was the old man he had met in the Great Hall the night before, and the third was unknown to him, a man of middle age with a trim black beard and hair, a brightly colored feathered cloak around his shoulders, and a harp in his hand.

Beyond them stood another figure, this one wrapped in pure light. As Hodge watched, he raised his hands and held up a simple cup, but he might as well have been holding up the sun, for it rivaled in its splendor the fiery orb high in the sky. As he did so, a great shout rang out from all the assembled company and...

Hodge suddenly felt himself falling, and flailed wildly about him, grabbing hold of a branch just as he started to plunge towards the ground. He wrapped his legs around another branch and held on tightly. He had fallen asleep in the tree and had been dreaming. There had been a great shout...

He realized that he was hearing such a shout that went on and on, and that it had not been in his dream. Settling himself back in the tree, he realized the shouting was coming from the village down below. Looking down, he saw that the knights were emerging from the church, their armor gleaming just as in his dream. As the people cheered, the knights made their way down the street, their warhorses cantering and prancing. Even Sir Bors was among them, not having spent as much time with his family as he had hoped.

For a moment, Hodge felt wholly disoriented. Had he not just been in that company? Where was his horse, his armor? Why was he not down there with them, heading forth on the quest of all quests?

Then he realized it had just been a dream. He was not a knight, not one of the Fellowship, not going forth on quest. He was just Hodge, a kitchen boy who would always be a kitchen boy. Yes, he had seen the Grail, but why? It seemed like a cruel joke by a cruel god. He felt a pain as keen as if a sword had twisted in his entrails. Tears swelled in his eyes as he watched the last of the knights ride out of the village towards the forest beyond, and a bitter taste rose in this throat. He was no knight. He was only Hodge, and the only quest he would ever know was to find enough soap to clean the pots and pans.

That evening, as things began to return to normal, Hodge was called before Gedron, the headman of the kitchen. He was a big, bluff man, given to petty tyranny at times over those who worked for him, but given to bursts of generosity as well. He had beaten Hodge in the past for minor infractions of rules or for jobs not done to his satisfaction, but he had also given him extra helpings of food and had even presented him with a new woolen blanket—a true luxury—the week after his mother had died. Hodge suspected that some of the man's favors came because he was afraid of Marta and knew that the wise woman had taken the boy under her protection.

"Hodge," Gedron said gruffly, "the King himself has just asked for you and wants you to see him by the Round Table in the Great Hall."

"The King? He wants to see me?" Hodge could not imagine why the King would want to see him.

"I have just now received the message." The headman looked at him suspiciously. "What have you been doing that I don't know about, Hodge?"

"I...I don't know, Sir. Nothing...I have done nothing!"

"Hmmm," the man said, obviously not believing him. "Well, perhaps it is nothing, then, but you must get along. And wash your face and hands first! And mind your manners! I would not have you shame me before the King himself."

"I will, Sir! I won't, Sir!" Hodge stammered, as he ran to a bucket of water and threw cold water over his face and hands. He dried himself off on his sleeve as he ran out of the kitchen and up the stairs and down the corridors to the Great Hall. He had told Gedron he did not know why Arthur wanted to see him, but he was sure it was because of what had happened last night. Whoever the old man had been, he

69

must have told the King that one of his kitchen help had seen the Grail. Hodge didn't know whether to feel excited or afraid, so he felt both.

He slowed to what he hoped was a dignified walk as he approached the Great Hall where the Table was. Two men-at-arms stood at guard by the door.

"Well, look what we have here!" smirked one of the guards, towering over Hodge. "Have you come to scrub the floors? Where is your bucket and mop, kitchen whelp?"

Hodge felt anger rising through his fear and excitement. He had done nothing to be mocked. These men had not seen the Grail, he was sure, so who were they to mock him?

"The King has sent for me," he said. "I am Hodge."

"'I am Hodge,'" the guard mimicked. "You sound like a knight. Who are you to put on such airs? You should feel the flat of my blade on your rump, kitchen whelp."

"Stop it, Pudge," the second guard said. "The boy is right. The King did send for him. Perhaps he wants his privy cleaned."

The two guards laughed while Hodge turned a bright red with anger and embarrassment. The first guard stood aside. "Go on in, Sir Hodge! The privy quest awaits you!"

Hodge darted past them as they laughed, then slowed to a walk as he again entered the Great Hall. But he could feel his face still burning and his eyes were brimming with tears, which made him all the more angry and discomfited.

At first he thought he was alone in the Hall again, which was unusual as there were almost always people in it who had business with the King. However, now it was as empty as it had been—or at least had seemed—last night. As he walked towards the Table, he cast his eyes about, expecting to see the monkish old man standing by one of the pillars. But the room was empty.

As he walked up to the Table, he heard a door open somewhere. Then, from behind the King's chair stepped Arthur himself. He was no longer in his golden armor. He was dressed in a plain brown tunic and trousers, with a woolen cloak about his shoulders. He wore no crown upon his head. His red hair was tousled, as if he had just been rubbing his hands through it. Blue eyes sparkled above a rugged face softened by his red beard.

Hodge fell to his knees and bowed his head, gazing at the wooden floor below him. Two feet clothed in soft leather slippers appeared in his range of vision and a hand touched him on the shoulder.

"Arise, Hodge," Arthur said. Hodge was surprised to hear how soft Arthur's voice was, for he had always heard how the King could bellow like a bull. Hodge got to his feet, but still kept his head lowered and his eyes on the floor.

"Look at me, Hodge. Is your liege too ugly for you to look upon?"

"Oh, no, my lord," Hodge stammered, looking up at the King. "You are the handsomest of all men!"

Arthur chuckled. "Well, I won't argue, but there are some who might disagree." A puzzled, wistful expression crossed the King's face so quickly that Hodge was not sure he had seen it at all. The King's eyes, blue like a summer sky, caught and held Hodge's own. "That is better, boy. Eyes that have seen the Grail have no reason not to see the world unafraid and with honor." Then Arthur looked more closely. "You have been crying, Hodge. What is the matter?"

Hodge began to blush again, but the King's question had been so solicitous that his shame vanished. "It is nothing, my lord."

"Well, perhaps, but my guess is that my guards were teasing you. They are not my regular guards, but two men called up from the barracks while my own men are attending to a matter elsewhere. With all the turmoil and changes around here today, I did not have time to be too choosy. Be assured, they will not bother you again."

"My lord," said Hodge, aghast at the thought that something he had said or done might cause trouble for the guards, for though he had been angry at them, he still thought of them as something special for being the King's guards. "I would not cause any trouble for anyone."

"Nor have you. Yet, in my realm, the King is the servant of all the people. That is the basis of the Fellowship and of the Table Round, and I will not have any of my subjects, no matter how lowly, treated with anything but the utmost respect by those who represent me."

The King went over to his throne, beckoning Hodge to follow. He sat down and then indicated that Hodge should sit on the Queen's throne. "Gwenny won't mind," he said, "and besides, if the Father deems you worthy enough to be shown the holy cup that held the blood of his Son, then you are surely worthy to sit on one of these chairs!"

Hodge, head spinning with what was happening, gingerly sat on the edge of the Queen's throne, prepared to leap off in a minute should thunder roll or lightning flash in the sky.

Arthur leaned back, suggesting by his example that Hodge should feel relaxed as well. "Well, Hodge, Merlin told me all about you and your experience last night." So, thought Hodge, the old man *was* the fabled magician after all. But where had he been for so long? "It must have been a shock for one so young. It was a shock for me and my knights when the Cup appeared. So naturally, I wanted to meet you. Merlin said you wished to become one of my knights."

Hodge sat up straight. "Oh yes, Sire, more than anything!"

"Well, Hodge, perhaps one day I shall set you upon the path to knighthood, though you must understand that it is not the King who makes a knight."

"It isn't? But who, then? I mean, I thought..."

"Oh, I formally proclaim a man a knight, but only when the man has already become a knight in his heart first. Do you understand what I mean?"

Hodge thought. Then he remembered Sir Bors once telling him and other boys about the trials and tests a man needed to go through before he could become a knight. "Yes, my lord, I believe so."

"Good. For it is important you understand there are many routes to knighthood, but they all are paths of service. A knight is simply another kind of servant, just like you."

"But not one who works in a kitchen, Sire," Hodge blurted.

Arthur laughed. "That may be so, but imagine, Hodge, how useful would a knight be if he were always hungry because no one cooked his food or cleaned plates for him to use or kept the castle in good repair?"

Hodge thought, then grinned back at the King. "I suppose we do all have our uses, Sire."

"Good, Hodge. Yes, that is what I want you to say, for a knight cannot always choose the kind of service required of him, nor where it will take him, nor what it may cost him. And a knight, pledged to service, may be called upon to do many things he does not like or would not choose otherwise. Do you understand?"

"Yes, Sire."

"Wonderful. Then, Hodge, you will not be disappointed if I say I wish you to serve me just as my knights do."

"Oh no, Sire!" Hodge's heart began to beat with excitement. He was going to become a knight, in spite of what Merlin had said.

"Fine, Hodge. Then here is what I want you to do. From henceforth, you will be one of my personal servants with one task and one task alone."

"And what is that, my lord?"

"You are to clean the Round Table. You are to keep it in good repair, in good polish, clean and shining. You will be the servant of the Round Table itself."

Hodge looked at the King blankly for a moment, for all he could hear roaring in his ears was the voice of Merlin and the words, "CLEAN THE TABLE!" Then he felt a wave of bitterness and disappointment, for obviously the old magician had put this idea into the King's head. For having seen the Grail, the King would have made him a knight if it hadn't been for that meddling old man.

Arthur looked at the boy. "Hodge, this is an honor I am offering you. It is a path of service, and perhaps it is the path that will take you to the knighthood you wish. You are not disappointed, are you? You would not refuse the King's gift, would you?"

Hodge shivered and threw off his feelings. "Oh, no, my lord. To serve you is my greatest wish, and if it is to be as the one who cleans your Table, then that is what I shall do!" And in that moment, Hodge knew he really meant it. He would clean that Round Table as it had never been cleaned before.

"I am glad, Hodge. Merlin told me it is the right task for you— your quest, if you wish—and I have never known Merlin to be wrong. However, I must correct one thing you said. It is not *my* table you clean and serve, but the Round Table, which is its own thing in a way. No one owns it, you see, except perhaps the Land itself or the Son of God. I do not always understand it, but I know magic when I see it. That knowing comes from being raised by Merlin." Arthur leaned forward and gave the Table an affectionate thump with his fist. "And this, Hodge, is magic!"

As if in response to his blow, a squire wearing the King's colors magically appeared from around the back of the throne. The King stood up, and Hodge did as well. "Hodge, you will now become one of my squires and wear my colors. I will have tutors teach you, for it is not meet that someone who has been graced with the vision of the Grail should not know his letters. You shall be one of my household, with all the honors there attending. And," his eyes flashed, reminding Hodge for a moment of Merlin, "everyday you shall clean this Table!"

And so it came to pass that Hodge became the servant of the Round Table. And while each day, somewhere in the Realm, a knight of the Fellowship would unlimber spear and sword to meet some adventure upon the quest for the Holy Grail, Hodge would each day come to the Table with bucket and sponge, soap and polish, and face the depredations of wine and gravy, oil and grease.

Of course, since all the knights were away, the Round Table was not used much. Now and then a knight or two would return to tell of their adventures, only to leave soon thereafter. Sometimes after such a visit, Hodge had some real cleaning to do, but not always. Occasionally, the King and Queen would dine at the table, but they were not messy eaters. Mostly they ate in their chambers, though increasingly, Hodge noted, the King dined alone.

So, as it turned out, there actually wasn't all that much for Hodge to do. Some days, a simple rinse with the sponge and a swipe with the polish was all it took. Then he was free to roam about the castle or the village or even the lands nearby when he was not being tutored. He still visited Marta, and she would take him into the woods and show him different herbs and plants. In time, she began teaching him the lore of the animals and even of stones, and the secret language that all things in nature know and to which they will respond. He was careful, though, not to mention these lessons to his tutor, who was a monk from a nearby monastery. Though the two religions of the old and new paths cohabited in Arthur's realm, it was not always a peaceful marriage.

In this way, Hodge's life settled into a pleasing, if sometimes boring, routine. Though he continued to dream of knights and far quests as he grew older, he realized that indeed he was very fortunate. And, deep in his heart, he treasured the vision he had had of the Grail. He

74

had even come to appreciate his brief meeting with Merlin, who had once again disappeared, his whereabouts unknown.

One day, however, he returned to the castle from an outing with Marta to hear the news that Sir Mador had died on the quest for the Grail. Saddened by the news, Hodge immediately went to the Great Hall, filled with an urgency to be with the Round Table, as if by doing so, he could come into communion with the slain knight and give his soul solace. Arriving at the Table, however, he was astonished and dismayed to discover a dark red stain upon it, right at the place where Sir Mador sat when the Fellowship was present. He had already cleaned and polished the Table once that morning, and he knew that stain had not been there then. Puzzled, he went and asked the guards (who now were very respectful to him) if anyone had been at the Table, but they both agreed no one had even been in the Hall, not even the King.

So Hodge went to his room and got his bucket and sponge and soap and came back and rubbed the stain out. And it took a good deal of rubbing, since it was like a bloodstain that had soaked into the wood. Eventually, though, he succeeded, and the Table gleamed as it had before.

There were no more stains for several days. Then word came to the castle that raiders, much like the ones who had killed his father and burned their farm, had attacked a couple of villages near the borders of the Realm. Normally, patrols of knights—plus the threat of the Fellowship itself—proved sufficient to prevent such plunderings. Now, though, with the Fellowship dispersed throughout the land and into other lands as well, the Realm seemed more vulnerable. Those who took note of such things were growing more daring, venturing into the Realm in ways they hadn't before the Quest had begun.

The day this news arrived, Hodge discovered two new stains on the Table. These were black and red, like smoke and blood. Hodge got his implements and went to work. Three hours later, his back aching and his arms as sore as if he had been wielding a great sword in battle for all that time, the stains were gone. As Hodge sat back to contemplate his work, he remembered Arthur's words: "I know magic when I see it, and this Table is magic!"

It was then that Hodge suspected that the Table in some way reflected the state of the Realm itself. When a knight died, the Table would bleed. When people suffered or the land was harmed, their pain would show up as a stain on the Table.

Hodge wasn't sure this was so. It was only a suspicion. He wanted to talk to Marta about it, but he felt shy in doing so. She had the knowledge of the old ways, but the Table seemed somehow different, not part of the old ways alone, nor part of the new, Christian ways. It seemed to be a place where both streams of spirit could come together and blend, just as it was a place where the different knights of the Fellowship could meet and blend their strengths, where otherwise their very differences might put them at each other's throats. Likewise, just as he couldn't bring himself to tell Marta, he couldn't tell his tutor, either. So, Hodge kept his suspicions to himself.

The issue was proven a few days later when Hodge, arriving in the morning to perform his morning ritual of cleaning, discovered in the place assigned to Sir Yuwain, a new stain. He immediately set about cleaning it, and by noon, the stain was gone. It was afternoon though, before news reached the castle that in fact Sir Yuwain had perished in pursuit of the Grail.

So it was that Hodge discovered the magic of the Table—that it mirrored what went on in the Realm. This discovery renewed his dedication to serve the Table, but it also sorrowed him. When a new stain would appear, to be followed by news of another death or another village raided or lands pillaged before Arthur and his men-at-arms could arrive at the scene, he sorrowed that he could not do something to help. Once again all his dreams of knighthood arose to assail him. He desperately wanted to be out in the land, preventing the terrible things that were happening, not simply cleaning up after them, mopping up the stains of events where once he had cleaned the stains of gravy and wine. More than once, his tears mixed with the water and polish as he worked to fulfill the command given him by Merlin and the King: "Clean the Table!"

Then, one day there was a change. It began when Hodge discovered a new red stain on the Table and realized, to his horror and sorrow, that it was in front of the seat of Sir Bors, his favorite of all the knights. That day, the water with which he cleaned the Table was more from his eyes than from the well, and after the stain was gone, he retired to the room which Arthur had given to him high in one of the castle towers. There he poured out his grief and anger and refused to see anyone for the rest of the day.

A week later, still mourning the death of Sir Bors, Hodge was resting in his room when he heard a great and glad shout from outside the keep. Rushing to a window, he looked out and down and saw a familiar figure riding into the castle, his once bright armor covered in dust. It was Sir Bors! Unable to believe his eyes, Hodge rushed out of the room and down to the courtyard, but the knight had already gone in to see the King, and Hodge could not intrude. Nevertheless, his heart was bursting with gladness, though he was puzzled at how the Table had been wrong.

That night, Arthur hosted a banquet in the Great Hall of the Round Table and Hodge was delighted to discover that he was invited, an almost unheard-of honor for a squire. It was, he knew, because of his connection with the Grail, but he didn't care. He was thrilled with a chance to see Sir Bors again.

After the banquet, where under Hodge's watchful eye, everyone was more careful than usual to eat with decorum and grace, Sir Bors began to relate a harrowing tale. It seemed that the previous week, he had been ambushed by a party of rogue knights. He had given a good account of himself, but they had outnumbered him. Finally, unhorsed, his shield broken and his arm wounded, he had lain back against a tree, exhausted, his sword in his good hand, waiting for the final rush of the three knights who were left. He knew without any doubt that the hour of his death had come.

Then, he said, as if from nowhere, a whirlwind had come up, blowing dust and dirt. It slammed into the three knights knocking them back. Then a tree had been uprooted and had fallen upon two of them, killing them. The third knight had turned to run, but had been buffeted by the swirling wind, disappearing into its midst. The wind then vanished as quickly as it had come, taking the hapless knight with it.

"Whether it was magic or divine grace, I know not," Sir Bors concluded, "but that wind saved my life as sure as if the Fellowship itself had rallied to my side. Without it, I would not be supping with you this evening and seeing again my family whom I love." The large knight sighed. "I am honored to be on this quest, but sometimes I wonder. Perhaps the Grail is already and always here in the grace of the ordinary things of life."

As Hodge listened to Sir Bors' story, he was struck with a thought. Suppose the magic of the Table now could warn him when something evil was to befall the Realm and give him the means to prevent it?

This theory was tested even before Sir Bors left again on his quest. Discovering a large black and red stain on the Table one morning, Hodge had worked furiously to clean it. He had just finished when a messenger arrived at the castle, his horse exhausted. Raiders were attacking a nearby village, striking closer to Camelot than ever they had dared before. Immediately Sir Bors and King Arthur gathered a troop of soldiers and rode swiftly out of the castle.

When they returned two days later, it was with another strange story of magical intervention. The raiders had been seen marching towards the village, which was when the messenger had been dispatched, but as they had lined up on a hill overlooking the village preparatory to charging down upon the defenseless people, there had been an earthquake. It was a strange earthquake, for none of the village had been damaged, but the ground had opened beneath the invaders, killing most of them. The villagers had then either killed or captured those raiders who had survived.

That night, Hodge visited the Round Table by himself. He knelt beside it and gave thanks for this new power to serve that had been granted him. And then, before going to bed, he examined the Table closely for any new stains that might have appeared.

This began a new routine for Hodge. As the months went by, he would visit the Table several times a day, carefully scrutinizing it for new stains. At first, there were few, if any. And when one appeared, he would clean it off immediately. And during this time there would come to Camelot stories of miraculous events wherein knights were saved or whole villages and regions protected. One man came and told of a plague of biting and stinging insects that descended like a cloud upon a group of raiders that had threatened his village. Another told of a flash flood that wiped out a band of renegade knights. Knights of the Fellowship who were wounded or ill would experience wondrous recoveries. A protective spell seemed to hover about the land, and through it all, Hodge continued to wield his bucket and sponge.

From time to time, the King would appear as Hodge was cleaning or inspecting the Table. He would speak kindly to him, inquiring about his work or his tutoring, sometimes speaking about his dreams for the Realm. Though no words were ever said about it, Arthur seemed to know that through Hodge's work, the spirit of the Round Table and the Fellowship continued to watch over and serve his Realm. It was a magic that Hodge never spoke about, for fear that in voicing it, the power would somehow leave. Between him and the King it was like a precious secret that both knew, but pretended that they did not. Only once, on an evening when he looked particularly worn with the cares of state, Arthur started to say, "Hodge, if it were not for you..," but then he stopped and turned away, as if he had thought better of what he had been about to say. Still, Hodge was comforted and continued his work with renewed vigor.

But there were certain stains that he could not remove. They started small but grew in spite of everything he could do. They puzzled him, for they did not seem to correspond to anything happening in the Realm itself. No knight seemed to die nor was any village pillaged because of them. Yet, focused as he was on his work, his wanderings in the wood, his tutoring, and his times with Marta, he paid little attention to the gossip around the palace or to the fact that one day the Queen left and never came back.

As the Quest for the Grail took its toll on the Fellowship, however, and there were fewer knights to defend the kingdom, the stains appeared more and more. Hodge cleaned and cleaned, sometimes never leaving the Table from early morning to late at night.

In fact, he worked so hard, that he became ill and had to be put to bed for several days with a fever. When he finally recovered enough to return to his duties, he discovered to his dismay that the Table was more stained than ever, and that some stains had even deepened into cracks in the wood. He worked as hard as he could, harder even than before, but now there were stains that could not come out. And every day he heard new stories of how the Realm was suffering.

As the months passed, he seldom saw Arthur, who rarely showed himself outside his chambers. When he did, Hodge was astonished to see how the King had aged, how his red hair and beard were now streaked with gray and white, and how his face had become lined with care. Arthur remained unfailingly gentle and respectful to Hodge, but he hardly ever came to see the Table, as if the very sight of it caused him too much pain.

Hodge knew that the castle was filled with intrigue, that stories swirled about Lancelot and Gwenivere, and that a new person named Mordred had arrived at court claiming to be a bastard son of the King, but he paid little attention to any of that. All his energy, all his being, was focused on one thing, cleaning the Table. He no longer saw his tutor, and he even gave up his work with Marta. He took to sleeping in the Great Hall itself and eating at the foot of the Table.

There came a day, though, when Hodge looked up from where he had fallen asleep on the floor near the Table and saw to his horror that while he slept, a great blood-red stain had streaked across the whole width of the Table, and in its middle, a crack had appeared that threatened to sunder the Table in two. With a cry, he leapt upon this stain, rubbing it, throwing water on it, weeping over it. He rubbed till he felt his hands crack and knew his own blood was now pouring forth over the precious, magical wood. Yet he kept on, hoping that somehow his blood would not stain but would clean and restore the Table to health. At first it seemed that his hope would be fulfilled, for where his blood rubbed into the table, the crack seemed to heal and new luster appear. However, even as he rubbed, he saw the evil stain spreading and new cracks appearing.

Then a strong hand seized his arm and drew him up and back, holding him up when he would have collapsed with exhaustion. He struggled to get back to the Table, but the grip would not release him. Turning, he found himself staring into fierce hawk's eyes.

"Merlin!" he gasped, knowing instantly who had him by the arms. "Merlin, let me go! I must clean the Table!"

Merlin's voice was soft but firm. "No, Hodge, it is too late. It is over. Arthur is dead, slain by Mordred. Even now Mordred's troops march on Camelot."

A groan burst forth from Hodge. "Oh, no, say it isn't so!" But he knew from the state of the Table that it was so. He sank to the floor, his body wracked with sobs.

"I have failed you, Merlin!" Hodge exclaimed between sobs. "I have failed the Table!"

The old magician gently lifted Hodge up, led him to a chair and sat him down. "Hodge, listen to me. You did not fail. To the contrary, if it had not been for you, the Realm would have collapsed long ago. You kept the magic going, kept Camelot and the Fellowship alive long after they might otherwise have died. You bought us time, time for the dream to sink deep into the minds of people. Now this place may die, but the real Camelot will live forever in the spirit of humanity. And because this is so, other Camelots, other Fellowships, will live again in the future and perhaps succeed where ours has failed."

"But the Quest? The Round Table?" Hodge's mind spun in confusion. It was like the end of the world, and he knew neither what to do nor what to say.

"The Quest will always go on, but for this Fellowship, it is over, save for a chosen few who found that for which they sought."

"The Grail? It was found?"

"Aye, and lost again. But the Grail can never be truly lost, Hodge. It is always closer than we may think."

Merlin sighed, and the sound, like an old wind whispering through dying leaves, brought back a memory to Hodge. "You knew, Merlin, didn't you? You knew it would end like this? You said the Grail was like a flint that could set fire to wisdom or to folly. Those were your very words, magician."

"Yes, I said that. No, I did not know. I feared. But there was a chance, Hodge, that the Grail of the Fellowship could prove strong enough to hold the Grail of Love. But men need their quests. They want to be heroes, to be knights, to do bold deeds, to fight enemies and emerge victorious. 'Tis much harder, and less desirable, to stay where you are, to be a cup yourself that can hold what is poured out to you. Listen, Hodge, if water is poured into your waiting hand, you will surely spill it if you run about, but if you stand still, some of it may reach your lips."

Merlin shivered. "It is cold in here, Hodge. The fire has gone out. I must be going. I have a long sleep ahead of me and more dreams. Perhaps another time we will understand the mystery of the Grail and the water will reach our lips."

The old man got up, but this time it was Hodge who gripped him from where he sat. "You said some found it. Some succeeded in the quest."

Merlin nodded. "Galahad, the one I brought here the day the Grail appeared. It was his destiny. And another, Perceval. And one more." Here Merlin smiled and looked down at Hodge. "Sir Bors."

"Bors found the Grail...?"

"Yes, and he shall tell the world the story so that it will not be forgotten."

Hodge sat silently. Then he, too, smiled. "Then in this most evil of all days since the world began, there is something of the good. I am glad. It does not surprise me that Sir Bors succeeded."

Merlin pulled himself free from Hodge's grip. "I must go." The old magician walked across the room toward the door, and as he did so, Hodge thought he became fainter somehow, even transparent. Before Merlin reached the door, though, he turned around and fixed Hodge with his gaze. "Hodge..."

"Yes, Merlin?"

"There is one more who found it."

"One more?" Hodge thought of the Fellowship. Who might it be? Lancelot, the greatest of the knights? Ector? Tristan? "Who, Merlin? Who is it?"

Merlin was silent, then his eyes flashed with inner lightning. "Hodge," he said.

"Yes, Merlin?"

"CLEAN THE TABLE!"

Hodge obediently got up. He did not see the old magician fade away like smoke before the wind. He saw nothing but the Table, now riddled with cracks and covered with stains. He went to his bucket and picked up his sponge and soap. He dipped the sponge in the water, and spread soap on the table. With no more thought, he did as Merlin had bade him. He began to clean the Table.

As he did so, the Table began to sink in the middle. At first Hodge thought it was collapsing, so grievous were its wounds. But its sides were rising up, and Hodge was forced to stop rubbing the top and began rubbing the sides and bottom. The Table continued to slowly change shape, and Hodge continued to scrub it.

Then the Table began to shine, faintly at first, then more brightly. Hodge was forced to step back, as he was assailed by waves of light and heat. Shielding his eyes, his mind blank and not wondering at what was happening, but with a joy building in his heart, Hodge saw the Table finally fold in on itself, shrinking and changing as it did so. Where there had been a Round Table, there was now a Grail. *The* Grail.

From somewhere he heard Arthur's voice, speaking as once it had to him. "There are many paths to knighthood, but they are all paths of service." Another voice joined him, and it was Merlin's. "There are many paths to the Grail, but not all of them leave home." Then he heard Sir Bors. "Perhaps the Grail is always there in the grace of the ordinary things of life."

Hodge looked about the empty room. No one was present, but it seemed as if the whole Fellowship were there, welcoming him. From far off, he heard the sound of a harp playing softly. Near him, a voice said, "There are many knights of the Fellowship, but you are the true knight of the Round Table. Welcome!"

It was at that moment that Mordred's men burst into the room, swords drawn and spears readied. At the sight of the Grail, they halted. Hodge paid them no attention. With a glad shout, Hodge leapt forward still clutching his bucket and sponge to where the Grail floated in the air before him. It seemed to reach out and enfold him. For a moment it was impossible to tell the two apart. Then the Grail vanished.

Hodge stood alone in the empty space where the Table had been. He felt...different. He felt powerful in a way he had never known before, more confident and sure of himself, but there was something more. He struggled to find words to describe it and decided he felt more himself than he ever had. He felt the *rightness* of being who he was.

He looked around at the enemy troops, and as his gaze fell on each, that man backed away. Later these warriors would recount—and legend would record—that a powerful knight clad in radiant white armor had mysteriously appeared from nowhere, a symbol of a round circle with a cup in its middle emblazoned in gold on his breastplate. This knight had carried a shield bearing the same symbol on it and a sword whose steel flashed and shone as if forged from sunlight itself. And before the power of that knight, their will had failed them, and they had had no defense.

But in that moment, before stories and legends had done their work, Hodge stood there with his bucket and sponge, feeling the power of the Grail within him and seeing the fear in the eyes of the men around him. "Don't be afraid," he said, but his words struck Mordred's men as if a great force had come out from him. They fell to the floor stunned, their shields and swords and spears falling from their nerveless hands.

He walked out of the Great Hall. For the last time, he strode down the corridors of the castle. As he did so, his enemies fell before him without a blow being struck.

He came finally to the main gate. He put down his bucket and sponge. Their job was done. He knew wherever he went he could serve the Grail with whatever tools great or simple, extraordinary or ordinary, might be at hand.

As he walked away, he turned for a moment and gazed back at the castle, a wistful look in his eyes. Then with a smile, Hodge, the last knight of Camelot, took the power of the Round Table out into the world.

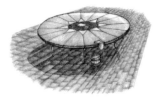

The Magic of Christmas

The science fiction writer Arthur C. Clarke once said that any sufficiently advanced technology would be indistinguishable from magic. It occurs to me that the opposite may also be true, that any advanced magic might be indistinguishable from technology. Perhaps that nifty electronic gadget your neighbor has isn't technological at all but a spell taken form. For that matter, both technology and magic have their origin in the same place, which is our imagination.

I have long been planning a novel for young people about robots that are also magical. I've got a couple of chapters written and much of it outlined, so it may yet see the light of day. In the meantime, though, I offer you "The Magic of Christmas." I was feeling silly the year I wrote this and decided I'd try my hand at being funny. It's up to you to decide if I succeeded. This is also a story that looks at the nature and reality of Santa Claus. For me, he is a very real person, even if he doesn't have a physical body as I do. I can't imagine Christmas without him or his magic...or is it his technology?

The Magic of Christmas

As the poem says, it was the night before Christmas and all through the house, not a creature was stirring....or was it?

I sat up in bed, unwillingly coming awake. My ears strained to hear what no homeowner ever wants to hear: an unfamiliar sound issuing from the dark depths of the house. There was, thankfully, only silence...or as much silence as one gets in a suburban neighborhood around midnight. Like the susurrations of a ceaseless river, there were the background sounds of cars and trucks humming along the distant Interstate. And somewhere off in the night, a dog barked and another dog answered.

Sighing, I lay my head back down on my pillow. My wife never stirred, but then she always slept so deeply that the Last Trumpet could sound and not awaken her. Unless it was one of our children crying. Then she was as awake and alert as a commando sneaking through enemy territory. Strange thing, motherhood.

For the first time in years, we had actually completed all our Christmas chores and had gone to bed before midnight. I was determined to reap the rewards of our unaccustomed feat of advance planning and organization and have a good night's sleep. Morning would come soon enough with its six o'clock patter of little feet and squeals of anticipation. In the meantime, let silence reign and visions of sugarplums keep little minds entranced. I was going to enjoy a long winter's nap.

Crash!

I sat bolt upright in bed. This time I knew I had heard something. Once more I listened, heart beating. Thirty years ago I could have told you with the unshakeable knowledge of a six year old that it was Santa coming down the chimney. Now darker images swirled through my brain.

Crash!

"Oh, my...!" The voice was high-pitched and tinny, carrying perfectly and unwelcomely down the hallway from the living room.

Thud!

"Oh, dear...!"

This time I was out of bed and on my feet, my hands groping in the nearby closet for my robe and wrapping it around me. Then, I was on my knees, feeling under the bed for a baseball bat I kept there for just such possible occasions of household defense. My fingers wrapped around its reassuring heftiness, and I clutched it to my chest.

My wife gave a soft snore and turned over. I reached out and shook her. Nothing. I shook her again. This time I could see the dark shadow of her head rise off the pillow.

"Wh....aaa?" she asked.

"Shush!" I whispered, putting my hand up to her mouth. "There's a prowler in the living room. Call 911!"

She was silent for a moment. "Maybe it's one of the kids."

"No! I'm sure it's a prowler. I have my bat. I'm going out to take a look."

"If it's one of the kids, don't frighten her."

I stared at her. "Hey! What about me? I'm the one who's frightened!"

"I'm sure it's just one of the kids, dear. Who else is up this time of night?"

That's the maddening thing about my wife. She's always calm and rational in an emergency. Me, I believe worry and panic are always the best responses.

"Burglars are up this time of night!" I whispered fiercely. "Just call the police. And be quiet about it! I don't want to scare him away."

"Why not?" she asked reasonably. "Isn't that the idea?"

I snorted and turned away, heading as quietly as I could down the hallway. Behind me I could hear my wife pulling the phone to her.

Had I been thinking clearly, I would have gathered up the kids, sent them into our room, and waited for the police to come. But with the bat in my hand, some primordial ancestor had been aroused in me. Testosterone was flowing, and my club and I were about to defend our cave from whatever marauding beast had wandered in from the night.

I reached the living room and crouched by the wall, trying to make myself as inconspicuous as possible. A pale light streamed in through the curtains from a street lamp outside, giving just enough illumination to make everything seem indistinct and menacing. There was no movement that I could see. Everything was absolutely still. The tree rose like a hairy, giant figure over in the corner, and the furniture seemed like dark animals crouched to spring.

I clutched my bat closer to me. Somewhere in me, that distant ancestor was beginning to have second thoughts.

Drawing in a deep breath, I reached out and hit the light switch, leaping into the room at the same time, brandishing my bat, and shouting my best imitation of a karate yell, learned from watching countless repeats of Bruce Lee movies as a kid.

"HaaiiiiYaaaa!"

As the lights came on, two things became apparent. The first was that there was no one else in the living room. The second was that I had pulled the wrong robe out of the closet. I stood there in the middle of the room, swinging my bat at nothing while wrapped in frilly pink down to my knees.

At least if there had been a prowler, he would probably have been incapacitated with laughter.

Nevertheless, thrusting the bat out before me, I walked through the living room, inspecting everything. It all seemed normal. Undeterred, I went on into the dining room and the kitchen, turning the lights on before me as I went. Each room I entered was empty of any strangers. I checked the doors and windows. Everything was locked and intact.

I ended my tour of inspection back in the living room. A snicker from the hallway caused me to whirl about, bat in hand, but it was only my wife wearing a long T-shirt, her body shaking with laughter while her hand covered her mouth in a vain attempt to keep a straight face. "I want you to know," she said, "that I really do feel safer now that I look at you."

I lowered the bat. "Thanks, I think." I grinned. "I guess I do look funny."

"No, really! You look scary!" Then she laughed and looked around. "So, what happened? Where's the prowler?"

"No prowler," I said. "But I know I heard something…"

"You were probably dreaming. Come on back to bed. I'm going to call the police and tell them it was a false alarm."

"No, no. Let them come. There might still be someone lurking around outside. I'll feel better if they take a look."

"OK, you can wait up for them, though you might want to put on your own robe. And don't let them wake the kids!"

She padded back down the hall, and, feeling both foolish and peeved, I followed. Expecting the police to come at any moment, I quickly dressed and went back out into the living room.

I sat on the sofa, looking at the tree and the presents beneath it. I was still puzzled by the whole experience. I was so sure I had heard something out here, but there was no sign of any disturbance. Perhaps I had been dreaming after all.

And where were the police? Surely they should have come by now? Had there been a prowler—and had he been armed, a thought that only now occurred to me like a punch in the gut—I could be lying here shot, my family could be hostages, and still no police. What was taking them so long? Or had I only dreamed my wife had called them?

To take my mind away from troubling thoughts, I got up and turned on the Christmas lights on the tree. Then I returned to the sofa and began a mental inventory of the presents piled up around it. Yes, that big one was for Kaity, and there was the electronic doll for Mary, and the odd-shaped package was the set of weights that Johnny wanted, and….

Something metallic gleamed amidst the brightly wrapped and beribboned packages. It didn't look like anything I had put under the tree, nor did it look wrapped at all.

As I stared at it, trying to remember just what it was, it seemed to move, like a creature aware that a predator has it in its gaze and trying to burrow more deeply under cover. I rubbed my eyes and looked again. The metallic gleam was still there, and it wasn't moving. Was I now seeing things as well as hearing them?

Curious, I got up and went over to the tree. Picking up the presents around it, I uncovered the object. I'm not sure what I was expecting, but I was disappointed to see it was an ordinary toaster. But what was a toaster doing unwrapped under our Christmas tree?

I picked it up and looked it over. It was small and not at all heavy. I could carry it in one hand. For a new toaster, it also looked very old-fashioned. There were two slots for the bread and that was all. No controls for how long to toast the bread or how dark to make it. No computer-controlled attachments, no extra buttons or dials. In fact, I wondered how you even turned it on. It looked vaguely like something my grandmother might have owned. My wife must have gotten it, but why? And for whom? We already had a perfectly good toaster in the kitchen.

I realized something else. There was no power cord attached to it. Except for the slots for the bread, the toaster was as smooth and unbroken as a bowling ball. In fact, as I held it up to the light, I could see that there were no heating elements in the slots at all. There was no way this thing could work. It might look like a toaster at first glance, but as far as I could see, for toasting bread this was as useful as a chrome paperweight.

"So what are you?" I asked out loud.

"Oh, I am sorry, Sir. I tried so hard to be inconspicuous. I did not mean to disturb your holiday night, Sir. Please forgive me!"

It was the same high-pitched, tinny voice I had heard in my bedroom, and it seemed to come from all around me. I was so startled I jumped. Then I whirled all around, looking for whoever had spoken. I didn't have my bat any more, but I did have the toaster-like thing in my hand. I raised it aggressively, prepared to throw it if necessary.

"Oh, I did not mean to startle you, but you did ask me a question! Please be careful, Sir! Please do not throw me!"

That's when I realized that it was the phony toaster in my hand that had spoken. In spite of what it said, I dropped it like a hot potato and sprang away from it towards the sofa. There was no sound of it hitting the floor. Turning around, I saw the toaster-thing floating in the air before me. Only now there were two dark patches on the front of it, and I could swear they were looking right at me.

"There is no need to be afraid, Sir. I assure you I mean you no harm at all."

Now normally I like toasters. I've never had any occasion to be afraid of one, but seeing one hovering in the air in front of me and talking to me was certainly not normal. The first thing I thought was, *What kind of crazy gizmo has my wife gotten me this year?* And the second thing was, *My god, we've been invaded by aliens!*

That prompted me to say, "I'm warning you! The police are on their way right now! Don't try anything funny, or you'll be toast, toaster!" To myself, I thought, *Where are those blasted police anyway?*

93

As if on cue, a black and white patrol car pulled up outside, its lights flashing.

"Oh, dear," the toaster murmured. "This is not good." A series of colors rippled up and down it. At the same time, I could see through the curtains that the officers who were getting out of the car suddenly got back in and sped away into the night.

"There!" the toaster said. "Now they are off on another call. Quite legitimate, too, Sir, even if they will arrive at the jewelry store just before the thieves do." I thought I detected smugness in its tone.

"How did you do that?" I yelped. "Those police were coming here to help me!"

"Oh, I am sorry, Sir," the toaster-thing said. "My orders are not to be discovered. Your constabulary had to be diverted." It paused while I digested this unwelcome bit of information. "But then, I guess I have been discovered after all. By you, Sir. I do apologize again. I am really not very good at this surveillance duty, you see. It is not my primary function."

I took all this in, understanding nothing. But one word did catch my attention. "Surveillance?" I asked.

"Oh, yes, Sir. That is why I am here, Sir. For surveillance."

"You mean, you're a spy?"

"Well, in this instance, I suppose that is true."

"But what are you spying on? Me? My family?"

"Oh, no, Sir! I am here to spy, as you call it, on Santa Claus."

I sat down on the sofa behind me. A cascade of thoughts and feelings passed through me. *It wasn't spying on me.* I was relieved. Then I was peeved. *So, what am I, nothing? Why* isn't *it spying on me?* Then I realized what else it had said.

"Santa Claus?"

"Oh, yes, Sir. You do call him that, don't you? I am not altogether up to date on your local customs. Santa Claus. Kris Kringle. Happy Old Saint Nick! The Jolly Old Elf. I am sure you know who I mean. I am here to record what happens when he comes down the chimney."

Oh great, I thought. Here I am having a conversation with a floating metal thing that thinks it's a toaster and wants to record Santa Claus coming down the chimney. It's obviously lost a screw somewhere.

94

Then again, if I'm looking for lost screws, *I'm* the one who thinks he's having this conversation.

"Please forgive me again, Sir. I can see I am causing you distress. I detect you are questioning your mental health. I assure you I am real. There is nothing wrong with you at all, except that you lack certain information."

I leaned back and rubbed my eyes. "Then why don't you give me that information? Because frankly, right now I'm thinking I should go down and check myself in at the local hospital. It's not unheard of, you know, for people to go crazy over Christmas. Especially fathers!"

"I would, Sir. Yes, I really would. But I cannot." If two dark patches on the side of a toaster could look sorrowful, these did. "No, I am forbidden to divulge any information at all. It is for your own welfare. Too much knowledge can be a dangerous thing!"

"In this case, toaster, too little knowledge could be dangerous for you!"

"Please, Sir, keep your voice down or you will wake your young ones! It is bad enough that *you* have found me." The toaster thing was so animated that it was bobbing up and down and weaving back and forth.

I lowered my voice. "All right, all right. But would you please land or something. You're making me seasick just watching you."

"Oh, forgive me, I...."

"And would you stop with all the apologizing!"

"Oh, dear," it replied. But it stopped shaking about and floated down to the rug in front of me. "This is definitely not good! Oh no, not good at all. I am ruining everything!" I swear its eye patches or whatever they were began to roll. "Can't you just go back to bed and forget I'm here? I don't want to interfere with your Christmas celebration!"

"You don't want to interfere with Christmas...! Look, toaster, or whatever you are, you come uninvited into my house, you hide among my presents, you wake me up, and then you float in the air and talk to me, something that I'm pretty sure the average toaster doesn't do...and you don't want to interfere with my Christmas? Are you crazy?"

"Oh, I am making it worse, aren't I? I just was not designed for conversations like this. I told them I was not cut out for this kind of assignment, but they had to send me anyway. Everyone was needed,

95

they said. So many houses to cover, so few of us. Now see the trouble it has caused. It is not my fault!" It began bouncing up and down in the air again.

There was such a feeling of woe about it that I suddenly felt sorry for whatever it was. "Listen, I can see you tried to be a good toaster, whatever you really are. But you just forgot some things. It was an honest mistake, I'm sure. If I tried to be a toaster, I'm sure I would forget something, too."

"Thank you, Sir. I understand you are trying to cheer me up. I appreciate it."

"Well, I just think they shouldn't hold it against you, whoever they are. And that's what I want to know. Who are *they*, anyway?"

"Oh, I cannot tell you that either."

"Then, for heaven's sake, what *can* you tell me?" I could hear my voice rising again. Soon, I figured, *I* would be bobbing up and down in the air if this continued. "It had better be something good and quick, or I'm tossing you in the trash can!"

"Oh, you cannot do that, Sir. I am programmed not to hurt a human, but I can restrain you in my own defense." I suddenly found myself totally unable to move, as if some invisible blanket had wrapped itself tightly around me. This was getting serious!

"Let me go, you … you…!"

"Oh, I cannot do that, Sir, if you are threatening to harm me. I must be free and undamaged to complete my mission."

I would have thrown up my hands if I could have moved them. I knew I had to think fast to get myself out of this.

"If you don't let me go, I'll scream. Then my wife will come, and you'll be sorry." I was gratified to see the toaster tremble a little. Of course, given how my wife slept, I knew this might be an empty threat, but I figured the toaster wouldn't know that. However, I thought, my screaming might wake the kids. They would certainly want to save Daddy from the evil floating toaster, except maybe for Kaity, who would probably want to keep it as a pet. On second thought, the thing would probably just paralyze them, too. Not good….

Before the toaster could reply or I could come up with any other plans, our conversation was interrupted by a glow that appeared near the chimney. It grew brighter very quickly, forming itself into a flaming door standing in mid-air. "Omigosh," I shouted. "You're trying to burn the house down..."

The toaster sprang up into the air, and I felt from it a palpable sense of both relief and apprehension. "No, Sir, that is not of my doing. That is my superior coming. Oh, I knew they would know that something had gone wrong!" If the thing had had hands instead of bread slots, I'm sure it would have started wringing them.

I'm not sure what I expected. A toaster oven perhaps. But what stepped out from the glowing aura in the room would have been familiar to any science fiction fan.

"It's a robot!" I exclaimed, looking at the gleaming, humanoid figure that had appeared before me. Think of the robot in the second Terminator movie, the one that looked like a smooth silver figure, and you'll have an idea of what stood before me in my living room.

And just like that movie robot, this one shimmered and shivered and suddenly changed shape.

"Uncle Fred!" I exclaimed. "I mean, you look just like my Uncle Fred!" I struggled to move, but only succeeded in toppling sideways onto the sofa. It occurred to me that if my wife and I had left things to the last the way we usually did, we would right now be wrapping presents here in the living room and none of this would be happening. It made me reconsider the merits of organization.

Uncle Fred—I mean, the robot looking like Uncle Fred—made a gesture, and whatever was restraining me vanished. I cautiously sat upright. The robot turned to the toaster.

"Really, Sedgewick, you *have* made a mess of things. You did not have to bind him."

"He was being totally unreasonable. He was going to throw me into a trash bin..."

I leapt up. "Excuse me? *I* was being unreasonable? You're the one who broke into my house, babbling about Santa Claus. I bet you burn your toast!"

"Really, Sir, there is no need to be rude!"

"Rude? You talk about being rude, paralyzing me on my own sofa? Why, if I had my bat, I'd show you rude!" I advanced towards the toaster, who yelped and floated backwards.

"You see, Sir? You see? He is violent..."

Uncle Fred—but of course, it wasn't really Uncle Fred—laid a hand on me, and I immediately felt a wave of calmness sweep through me. I stepped back and sat down. A memory of something he had just said popped into my mind. "Sedgewick? You're a toaster named *Sedgewick*?"

Uncle Fred sat down next to me. I put my hands to my head. "Would you please stop looking like that. And how do you know what my Uncle Fred looks like, anyway?"

The voice was certainly Uncle Fred's as the being spoke to me. "I'm sorry. I found this image in your mind and it seemed to be a reassuring one for you. I simply wanted to put you at your ease. He *is* your favorite uncle, isn't he?"

"Uh, well…yes…I mean, no! I mean, yes, he is my favorite uncle. Practically raised me at times. But no, having you look like him isn't reassuring at all. It's creepy!" I thought about what the robot had said about reading my mind, but at the moment, that seemed like the least of my worries. After all, the more this went on, the less mind I figured I'd have for anyone to read.

The figure shimmered again. This time he was a middle-aged, handsome man who had that kindly but authoritative look you often see in actors playing doctors in television commercials. He also looked familiar, but it took me a moment to recognize him. It was Michael Rennie, the actor who played the alien ambassador to Earth in the movie, *The Day the Earth Stood Still.*

"How is this shape for you?" the robot asked.

I gulped. "Better."

The toaster floated over. "Sir, you can just make him forget about all this and send him to bed. Then we will not be interfered with while we observe Santa Claus."

"No, Sedgewick. You know the rules. We can read their minds, but we can't control their minds. We shall just have to do our work the best we can with him here, unless he chooses to leave voluntarily."

Leaving voluntarily had a nice ring to it at the moment, but I knew I wouldn't do it. I had to find out what this was all about, or I would forever doubt my sanity. With four kids, I sometimes doubted it enough already!

"What is it with you people...or whatever you are? You keep going on about watching Santa. But there *is* no Santa! He's just a mythical figure, a figment of the imagination. He's a fantasy." Although now that I thought about it, what would be more fantastic, a magical elf with a bag of toys hopping out of my fireplace or a shape-shifting robot materializing in my living room and looking like a character from a 1950's movie, not to mention my Uncle Fred. Either way, I was rapidly stumbling into the Twilight Zone for sure.

The robot sighed in a very human way. "No, you're wrong. He is very real, and we need his help. You see, Sedgewick and I are from the thirty-first century, a thousand years in your future." He paused as if waiting for me to say something, but at this point, a time-traveling robot at least made some sense to me. I wasn't a science fiction fan for nothing! When I didn't respond, he went on.

"We are wizards. At least, I am a wizard, and he is my apprentice."

"Wizards?" I sighed. The whole thing had trembled on the verge of reality, only to veer off again into never-never land. "You're saying you're a wizard from the future and not a robot?"

"I am a robot, too."

"You mean, a thousand years in the future, people make robot wizards? Like a robot Merlin? Are you kidding me?"

"No, what humans did was to give us consciousness. It was a gift from them so that we could be their partners in colonizing the galaxy. But once we became conscious, some of us became wizards as well."

"You became wizards. Right. Say, you're as loony as your friend over there." I jumped up. Surely there was some way to get rid of these things.

"You see, Sir," bobbed Sedgewick. "He won't listen at all! Let me restrain him again before he attacks us."

"I'm not going to attack you, you sorry excuse for a household appliance! I just think your software or whatever you use is buggy. You don't need Santa, you need a good programmer or maybe an upgrade!"

The tall robot made a gesture inviting me to sit back down, and I did. "Sir, we have little time, and I'm trying to explain it to you so you'll understand. You did ask for an explanation, didn't you?"

"Yes, but—"

"Then be patient and pay attention. One of your writers once said that a highly advanced technology would look like magic."

"Yeah, I remember that. It was Ray Bradbury."

"It was Arthur Clarke. What he didn't say was that the reverse is also true, that magic can look like highly advanced technology."

That made me pause. "Are you saying that you're not really a robot at all? That you're some kind of magical being?"

"In a way, though not like Santa Claus. I am still a robot, however much I have mastered the energies of magic."

"The energies of magic?"

"Yes. Let me show you." He reached over and touched my forehead. I felt a warm, shimmering power flow through me. All at once, the room lit up as if a million Christmas lights had been draped over everything, connecting everything with threads of light. I gasped from the splendor of it. "Everything looks like my Christmas tree," I stammered.

"Yes. What you are seeing is magic. It is an energy like any other but with remarkable creative properties. In fact, it is the most fundamental energy of them all, permeating the very quantum flux itself. But it is an energy that requires a special medium in which to propagate itself and manifest. That medium is consciousness. Magic and consciousness go together."

"So, when you robots became conscious, you discovered this web of energy?"

"Not at first. But eventually some of us did and revealed the discovery to others. We became students of this energy. We became wizards. Then some of us went even further, even as humans once did. We became so attuned to and imbued with this energy that we became magical."

"You say, like humans once did?"

"Yes. Once you knew how to think magically. As a consequence, certain humans became magical beings themselves, living in the flux of this primal energy. But in our time, humans have forgotten how to do this. And that is why we are here."

"What is why you are here? You mean, in *my* living room?"

"Well, I meant here at this time. It is the farthest back our magic could take us." The robot stood up. "It's very simple. When a number of us became magical, we wanted to know more about what we had become. But we could not find any teachers. In our time, human beings have so given themselves to the mastery of technology that they have lost the capacity to think in magical ways. So the scientists could not help us. They simply think we have discovered a new kind of technology. For magic to work, though, you must feel it as a part of you, connecting you to the very heart of the universe. Thinking of it simply as a technology is not good enough."

"In other words, magic can seem like advanced technology, but it really isn't."

"Precisely so. Then we discovered there were other magical beings in the universe, but most were so alien that they could not help us. We may be artificial beings, but we are patterned after humans, so our magical processes mimic those of your species."

"So why not contact the magical humans you spoke of?"

"We tried, but they seem to have disappeared, perhaps because magic is disappearing among humans. This is a sad thing to us, and something we would like to reverse. Humans gave us the power of consciousness, and now we would return the favor if we can and restore to them the power of magic."

Somewhere in my mind something clicked into place. "So you have come back to our time to contact magical humans."

"Yes."

"Well, I'm flattered and all. And there's no question that fathers can seem magical. At least, my kids think so, and —"

The toaster bobbed over in front of my face. "You primitive oaf! We are not here to see *you*!"

"Sedgewick," I said, "what you need is a power cord so I could unplug you!"

"Well, excuse me, Sir, but you are no Santa Claus!"

"Oh yeah? Who do you think bought all these presents in here anyway?"

Before Sedgewick could reply further, the Rennie-robot waved the toaster away and continued as if our little exchange had never happened, "Oh, you could become magical if you tried. Any human can. But my friend is correct. As we've been saying, we are here to contact one of the greatest of the magical humans, the being you know as Santa Claus."

"So you think he's *real*?"

"Oh yes, he's real. We understand from the legends, he makes himself available at this time every year. Most magical humans seem to go into seclusion and become very hard to find, but Santa Claus deliberately makes himself available every Christmas Eve. So we have planned for a long time and have gathered a great deal of magical energy to come back to your time for this one night in the hopes of contacting Santa Claus and enlisting his help."

I looked around at the living room, at the Christmas decorations, at the tree and the ornaments and all the presents. "Well, I like to think we know how to celebrate Christmas, but why do you think you'll find Santa Claus in our living room?"

"Oh, we're not just in your living room. We're in thousands of living rooms around the world, masquerading as appliances, lamps, chairs, televisions, and the like. Almost every robotic wizard of my time has come back. In this way, without disturbing anything or anyone, we can observe what happens when Santa Claus appears. We can learn what he does and what he is like and perhaps discover how to contact him in our time."

"Well, good luck," I said. "Around here in a few hours, about all you'll learn is how much pandemonium and greed there can be on Christmas morning as the kids open their presents. There won't be much magic about it."

"I think you underestimate the state of affairs." The robot gestured about the room. "There is much magic here already, a great deal of wonder and belief. It is one reason we were able to come to your home. We could only project back in time to where the magical energy was already present and strong in some way. Your home must have been like a beacon that attracted Sedgewick."

"An exceedingly dim beacon, I should add, too!"

"Sedgewick," I said, "go burn some toast, would you?" The toaster turned in a huff and flew over to the tree, burying himself among the presents.

"Don't let him bother you. He's still embarrassed that you discovered him. You do have a lot of magic here. You would call it love, but love and magic are very similar."

I look about again. The vision of magical energy I had had was now fading away, but even still I had to admit that the robot was right. There was a lot of wonder and delight here, and love. It *was* magical, and, I knew, it would still be magical in the morning. I just had to remember what Christmas morning was like as a child and not be the cynical adult I was shocked to realize I was turning into.

Just then, Sedgewick began to click like a Geiger counter rolling in a patch of uranium. "I am detecting the approach of a strong source of magical impulses," it said.

"Yes, I feel it as well." The Michael Rennie robot looked at me. "The time is coming. Santa is on his way into the world. He will be appearing soon, but if you disbelieve, your presence might prevent him from entering this room. For the sake of our mission, I ask you to go to bed and let us encounter him alone, magical beings to magical being."

"What! Let you have all the fun after all I've been through tonight? Not on your life! You can count me as a believer!" And surprisingly, it was true. I could feel it in myself. I could feel my heart opening in anticipation, the excitement rising, the sense of wonderment filling the room. I felt six years old again.

"All right. Then I will believe in you and in what you say. And if you speak truly, you will see what few humans of your time still retain the capacity to see."

The robot wizard fell silent. Its Michael Rennie appearance faded away, and it sat on the sofa as a gleaming silver, featureless figure. The toaster, silent now, snuggled down further in among the presents.

Together we waited. I don't remember any Christmas night being as excruciatingly long, yet as deliciously exciting as the next few minutes were. I could hear the wall clock ticking. I could even hear soft snores coming from the bedroom. In the distance, dogs were once more barking, and a large semi went by on the distant freeway.

Then, the robot leaned over and touched its silver fingers to my forehead. I felt a warm tingle pass through me again. "Look and see," it said.

I looked. This time the web of light was there, but fainter, as if it had retreated into the background. Then, so softly it almost escaped my notice at first but growing increasingly brighter as the seconds passed, the Christmas tree began to glow. The glow filled the room momentarily, nearly blinding me. As I squinted to see, it collapsed into a shining ball of light that formed itself into a person. At first, it was hard to see what kind of person it was. It seemed many figures, male and female all at once. Some were unfamiliar to me, while others looked like figures from mythologies I had studied. For a moment, I saw clearly a man and woman bent over a cradle in which a sleeping baby lay. Then all these figures coalesced into one familiar red-garbed, white bearded, jolly being—Santa himself—the patron of givers and gifts, merriment and mirth, joy and promise around the world, and the very soul of magic.

Santa looked around, a huge grin on his face. He swung his bag down from his shoulder, reached into it with his gloved hand and withdrew a handful of something that I couldn't see. Then, like a giant, rotund Tinkerbell, he began sprinkling a golden, shining powder over everything. Where the powder landed, I could see the web of magical light become brighter, the threads of connection more pronounced and brilliant. I knew without having to be told that Santa was charging everything with magical energy. This was what he brought on Christmas night, not presents but presence, the presence of magic itself.

To my surprise, I suddenly got up and walked over to the shining figure. I couldn't help myself. Up close, I realized I could see through him, as if he were a ghost. He seemed to be staring through me as well, and I felt that he couldn't see me at all, as if I were transparent to him.

"Santa?" I whispered. "Santa Claus?" Looking down, I saw a faint shining thread running from me to him. With all my will, I sent a surge of energy through it, seeing it light up as a golden path between us. He stopped what he was doing, and I could see his eyes focus on me. Then he grinned even more and shook some of the sparkling dust in my direction. As it settled over me, I felt a wondrous sense of excitement and joy fill me, a feeling of goodwill and love and possibility. I felt as if the whole universe were my home, and I was being welcomed back into its embrace. And as these sensations coursed through me, Santa solidified. He reached out and shook my hand. "Bless my soul, I rarely find one of you adults these days who can see me," he said. "Merry Christmas!"

"Merry Christmas to you, too, Santa!" I replied, and blurted, "You're real!"

"Real as punch," he replied with a laugh, poking me in the arm. "You just have to know how to look. Say, you know I'd like to chat, but I have to go."

"Yes, you must have millions of more houses to visit."

"Bless me, no! I visit all of you at once, everywhere! No, I don't want to be late for my wife's party, that's all! She gets snippy!" And he laughed again.

"Wait," I said. "I have visitors..."

I was aware then that the robot had joined me, the little toaster floating by his shoulder. Santa looked at them. "You're a long way from home, wizards!" he said with a smile. A far-away look came over him for a moment, then he chuckled. "Seems like you're all here! Who's tending the home fires in the Thirty-First?"

"Some of us stayed behind. The rest of us came for your help," the tall robot said. "We'd like you to teach us, but we can't find you in our time."

"Hmmm. Maybe I'm something else then and you just haven't recognized me yet! I don't need to be Santa forever, you know. After all, I'm different now than I was when I taught that young fellow how to draw swords from stones. And by the way," he winked at me, "being Santa is a lot more fun, let me tell you...no smelly old knights clanking around in armor, spilling food on the round table, pestering me about quests. The North Pole may be a tad chilly, but it's quiet and clean!"

He smiled and clapped the robot on its silver shoulder. "You know, you rather look like a knight yourself."

"Yes, I see the similarity, but I am actually a custodial droid."

I gaped at him. "You're a janitor? In the thirty-first century?"

Santa chuckled. "Oh, you'd be amazed where you can find wizards. And humans are always making messes for magical folks like us to clean up. Anyway, I think I can help you and your friends." He handed his bag to the robot. "Here. Take this. I'm all done for this year. I don't need any more tonight."

The robot looked at it. "What is it?"

"It's my bag of concentrated, precipitated magical energy. You haven't learned how to make it yet, I guess, but with help, you will. Sprinkle it on yourself. It will boost your power, put you more in tune with things. You should then be able to signal me. Wherever or whatever I am by then, I'll come find you!" He laughed heartily.

"Thank you, Santa!" The robot seemed to gleam even brighter as he took the bag. He looked at Sedgewick. "Come, my friend, we must go. We cannot strain the fabric of time too much." He turned to me. "Thank you. Remember, magic is real!"

I smiled. "How can I forget? Say, since you're from the future, you wouldn't have any hot stock tips for me, would you...." But before I could say any more, the robot and its obnoxious little companion blinked out and disappeared, though I was sure I heard Sedgewick muttering something like "oaf." But I'll be charitable. Since he was a toaster, it could have been "loaf."

"How about that?" Santa said. "Magical robots! Who would have thought? And in a hurry, too. I could have invited them to my party. Of course, with the ice giants, there might not have been room....Oh, well."

"Santa," I said, grabbing his hand impulsively. "I'm sorry I forgot to keep believing in you and your magic."

"Oh, that's all right. The important thing is for you to believe in you and *your* magic. Anyway, like I said, I've got to run, too. Lots of elves waiting, not to mention Mrs. Claus. Did you know she once lived in a lake?" He laughed again. "Now let's see, how does that go? Oh yes..." He laid a finger on the side of his nose, gave me a wink, and turned into a stream of light that whisked up the chimney behind him. And as he went, his voice echoed all around me: "Ho! Ho! Ho! Merry Christmas to all, and to all a good night!"

"You, too, Santa," I called back. But I knew I couldn't sleep. So I sat on the couch and admired the Christmas lights and appreciated all the magic that was there and around hundreds of thousands of other trees and decorations and homes and hearts around the world....indeed around all of us whether we celebrated Christmas or not. I thought about all the magical beings that might be abroad this night, helping us out in ways we would never know, and what it might mean to be magic. And I waited till the dawn when I knew my kids would come running out gleefully shouting and laughing to see the tree with Santa's present's beneath, and knowing the magic would only grow stronger.

The Story Tree

Some years ago I discovered to my delight a small model of the Starship Enterprise fashioned as a Christmas tree ornament. Being a long-time fan of Star Trek, I bought one and later happily hung it on our Christmas tree.

Little did I know this was the start of a trend. Soon other Star Trek ornaments appeared, then Star Wars characters and starships, Dorothy and her companions from the Wizard of Oz, Superman, Batman, Peter Pan, and other characters and items from literature and movies. It was not many years before robots, wizards, superheroes, spacemen, starships, and fantasy characters hung from the branches of our Christmas tree in a proliferation that hardly left room for more traditional ornaments.

At that point, my wife Julie, not unreasonably, said "No more!" I had to agree. But then I had an idea. I purchased a small artificial tree that I put up on a table in a corner of the room. I called it my "Story Tree," and it became the new home for all my "special" ornaments. One tree was for the Story of Christmas, but the other tree was to celebrate adventure, stories and the power of imagination itself. (I probably should have called it the "Kid-In-Me" Tree!)

Eventually, though, the job of decorating (and un-decorating) two trees became a bit much. And, I have to admit it never really matched the wonder and mystery of the real Christmas tree. Besides, I got tired of explaining to visitors why we had two trees and why one looked like an advertisement for old comic books, TV shows and movies. The story tree and most of its ornaments ended up packed away, but it lives on in memory and in this story written especially for this anthology.

THE STORY TREE

When I was twelve years old, I went to spend the Christmas holiday with my grandfather. My father, who was working as a diplomat in the Middle East, had been injured in a terrorist bombing. He had been flown to an American military hospital in Germany, and my mother had flown over to be with him and to bring him home. I was sent off to be with Granddad.

Granddad lived in a small town about a hundred miles away from us. Its claim to fame was that it was the home of Marshall College, where my grandfather was a professor. I had been told it was an "alternative" school, but I had no idea what that meant, except that it had these neat solar panels on the roofs of its buildings and most of the teachers had longer hair than the students.

The day Granddad came to get me was a busy one. My mom was running late as usual getting ready for her flight. Granddad had to break more than one traffic regulation to get to the airport on time, and even then she just made it. She gave me a hug, told me she'd call me about Dad as soon as she got to Germany, hugged Granddad, and then dashed into the terminal. Watching her go, my heart felt that Germany might as well be on the other side of the moon, which was about as desolate as I was feeling right then.

I don't remember much about the drive to Granddad's home, an old farmhouse on the outskirts of the town. I think Granddad and I made some kind of small talk, but mostly we drove in silence. What I remember most about that day, though, happened as soon as we went through the front door. I stepped through the door into a hallway whose walls, like just about every other wall in the house, were covered with bookshelves. The winter sun was setting, and the hallway was dark. I felt like I'd stepped into the worst emptiness I had ever felt. Then I remembered what my worry about my Dad and my missing Mom had driven from my mind. Gran'ma wasn't there to greet us. She never would be there again. She had died only three months earlier in an automobile accident.

On the threshold of being a teenager, I had been trying very hard not to cry like the little boy I didn't want to be anymore. But standing

111

there in that awful empty hall, missing Mom and Dad and filled with horror that I had forgotten all about Gran'ma being dead, everything just crashed. I began to bawl, as if somehow all the grief in the world had settled on me and was now trying to get out.

Granddad knelt beside me and took me in his arms. Then, he did something I had never seen him do. He began to cry as well.

That's what I remember about that day: the two of us holding each other in that hallway sobbing, two sorrows becoming one.

The next morning I awoke to the smell of bacon. Bacon and I have a love relationship that goes way back. Once when I was eight, my mother had had to go out for the day. I got on my bike, pedaled down to a small grocery store near our house, and bought two one-pound packages of that bacon that's microwave ready. I brought it home, read the directions, and cooked both packages. It wasn't as good as bacon cooked on a griddle, but it was good enough. I spent the rest of the day eating that bacon, and, as I remember, much of the night being sick to my stomach. But it didn't dampen my appetite for the stuff.

So when I smelled bacon, I needed no further invitation to throw on my clothes and run down the stairs to the kitchen. Though I had been feeling depressed when I went to bed, the day was already seeming brighter. Ah, the power of food on a twelve-year old!

"Hi, Robbie," Granddad said as I came into the kitchen. "As I remember, you like deep fried pig."

"It's bacon, Granddad," I replied, making a face. I loved the stuff, but I didn't like to be reminded where it came from. "It comes from a store."

"Umm. Marvelous things, stores. Pancakes?"

"You bet!"

He poured several pools of batter on a large griddle. "So, how are you this morning?"

I shrugged. "Ok, I guess. Sorry for all the bawling last night."

"Hey, Kiddo, I expect you remember not all those tears were coming from your eyes alone, eh? Nothing to be ashamed of. If God hadn't meant men to cry now and then, he wouldn't have given us tear ducts...or feelings."

"I suppose. I just felt like a little kid."

He laughed. "Funny about that. When you get to be my age, you enjoy feeling like a kid again!" He flipped a couple pancakes and several slices of bacon on a plate and handed it to me. "Hot syrup's in that pitcher there. Want orange juice?"

"Nah. Milk, please."

"Fried pig and cow juice!" He changed his voice to make it sound like a character in a horror movie. "Any thing elsssse, Igor?"

"Granddad!"

He got a carton of milk from the fridge and handed it to me with a glass. He then sat down opposite me with his own plate of bacon and pancakes and an empty glass. "Never pass up a good thing when I see it," he commented.

I poured myself some milk, then without thinking, I asked, "Do you miss Grand'ma?" I could have bitten my tongue off as soon as the words were out of my mouth. I thought he might get angry or start crying again. I'm not sure which I thought would be worse.

But he didn't do either. He took the milk from me and poured some into his glass. Then he said, "Yes, Robbie. I miss her a lot. We were together over forty years. Two people get pretty accustomed to each other in that length of time." He reached over and patted my hand, seeming to feel my embarrassment. "It's all right, Robbie. I don't mind you asking. You're concerned about me. Well, I do miss her, but I'm getting used to it. I don't usually cry about it. Last night, I was just very tired. I was worrying about your Dad, too. Then bringing you into an empty house...and you starting crying...well, it all just hit me again."

I nodded. I felt a lump rising up in my throat, and I forced it down with a syrup-drenched piece of pancake.

"Besides, I often feel her around."

"You do?" I looked about, as if half-expecting to see Gran'ma float through the wall.

Granddad chuckled. "Oh, I don't mean she's a ghost. She was always far too lively to be a ghost! No, I dream of her a lot. Funny thing is, most of the time it's the same dream. Ever have the same dream over and over, Robbie?"

I shook my head. I hardly dreamed at all, or if I did have dreams, I could never remember much of them.

"Well, it's happening to me." He poured both of us another glass of milk. "When your grandmother and I went on our honeymoon, we went to Wyoming to the Grand Tetons. Ever seen pictures of them?"

I nodded.

"Beautiful mountains! One of the places we camped was in a valley filled with wildflowers of all different colors. There was a stream that ran through it from the mountains. It was one of the most beautiful places I've ever seen. We promised each other we'd go back there one day, but we never did. I don't know why we didn't. It just seemed that life always took us in other directions." He looked at me. "Life can do that. It can take you where you never expect to go."

He got up from the table, filled a plate with the remaining bacon that had been slowly sizzling on the grill, turning brown and crispy the way I like it, and brought it over. I liberated a couple of pieces. "Anyway," he continued, "now I dream of her in that valley at least twice a week. She's young again, and so am I."

"Do you talk to her?"

"Oh yes. We have so much to say, you'd think we'd never spent forty some years together talking. We walk by the stream, we pick wildflowers, we sometimes climb the hills around, and we talk."

"What do you talk about?" The idea of visiting a dead person in a dream and talking seemed both wondrous and creepy to me.

Granddad smiled. "Oh, lots of things. Say," he said, thumping his hand on the table, "it's a little over a week until Christmas. We need to make plans."

"Plans?" I could tell that Granddad wanted to change the subject, and I had no objections. Like I said, talking about dead people, even Gran'ma, creeped me out. It never occurred to me that perhaps I had strayed onto sensitive ground that Granddad wanted to keep private.

"Sure. It's not too early to get a tree today. I hadn't planned on having a tree this year, but now that you're here, it's the number one priority. What do you say, shall we get one from a lot or shall we go cut our own? There's a tree farm not far from here."

"We can cut our own? That sound's cool!"

"Then, that's what we'll do. Ever swing an axe?"

"No," I said, excited at the prospect.

114

"Then it's high time to start. Let's clean up here and head on out." He gathered up the dishes from the table and carried them over to the sink. "I'll wash, and you dry."

"OK. And Granddad, when we go out, can we get some more bacon?"

For the rest of that morning we tramped around the tree farm, comparing trees. Looking back, I realize that he kept me busy so I wouldn't think about Dad lying in a hospital in Germany. And Dad being his son, I suppose Granddad appreciated doing something that kept him from worrying too much, too. Anyway, he taught me to swing an axe as he'd promised, and I ended up cutting down our tree myself. My arms hurt afterwards, but it was a happy hurt. I'd never felt so proud of a Christmas tree as I did that year.

That afternoon, we rummaged through Granddad's attic to find the boxes of ornaments where he and Gran'ma had stored them. When I say *attic*, I imagine you might think of those large old-fashioned attics you read about in stories, the ones that are filled with old furniture and boxes and hidden treasures. Granddad's attic was filled with boxes all right, mostly stuffed with books, but otherwise it was just a glorified crawlspace under the middle of the roof, filled with dust and cobwebs. I wasn't too happy about running into any spiders, but I offered to crawl in anyway. I was still short enough that I could just about stand up in there. Granddad would have had to crouch.

"Just bring out the boxes marked 'Christmas,'" Granddad said. "I think they're towards the back." I crawled along on hands and knees until I found them. There were only three boxes. I pushed them one by one back to the hole in the floor where Granddad waited at the top of the ladder that folded down when you opened the trap door into the attic. He maneuvered them through the small opening and carried them down to the floor of the hall beneath us.

I was pushing the last box toward him when I spied another box, half-hidden but with the letters "C-H-R-I" visible. As Granddad carried the third box down, I went back and moved things around so I could get at that other box. Sure enough, it said "CHRISTMAS" on it, so I wrangled it out into the middle of the crawlway. Then I saw there was a second box behind it that also was labeled "CHRISTMAS," so I got that one out, too. I pushed them both to Granddad who carried them down. I brushed myself off as best I could, sneezed a couple of times as dust got up my nose, then climbed down myself.

"Thanks, Robbie. You just saved me a crick in my back," he said.

"Hey, anytime, Granddad," I said.

We took the boxes down to the living room where the tree was waiting. I have to say that Christmas trees are about my favorite thing about the holiday. I've always loved trees anyway, and the idea of bringing one into a house always seems so cool. It never seems to me like just one tree, either. I always feel as if a whole, ancient forest has taken up residence in the house.

We were starting to unpack the boxes when the phone rang. If Granddad's objective had been to take my mind off Dad and Mom, I guess he succeeded because it was actually a momentary surprise when his voice rang out from the hallway where the phone was. "Robbie, it's your Mom!"

I ran to the hallway and took the phone from Granddad. I don't remember that conversation anymore. All I remember is the shock of pure adrenaline-raising fear that coursed through my body when I heard Mom's voice telling me that Dad was in worse shape than we'd thought. "He came through surgery all right, Robbie," she said, "but he's very weak and fighting an infection. The doctors are worried, though they're trying to tell me he'll be all right. And he *will* be all right, Robbie. I know our prayers will bring him through this." Then she told me even more bad news. "Honey, the doctors had to remove your Dad's left leg and part of his left arm. The rubble from the building crushed them."

Mom never believed in sugarcoating bad news. *Face it straight on, and you can deal with it,* she'd always said, and now she was making me face it straight on: my Dad would be a cripple for the rest of his life, if he even survived at all.

I mumbled something to Mom, I don't remember what. The shock had driven me way past tears, though I suspected that I would have another bawling session later. I gave the phone to Granddad and wandered back into the living room, where I sat on the floor by the tree. I seemed to draw comfort from it. Then without thinking about it, I began unpacking ornaments. It seems so strange a thing to do, looking

116

back. I had just received the worse news I had ever had in my life, and all I wanted to do was unpack Christmas ornaments. I know now that doing something so ordinary was my way of buffering the shock of the news. At the time, I just felt like I had become a Christmas robot, running on automatic.

Granddad came back into the room a few minutes later and joined me. I think he needed the comfort of doing something ordinary as well, something to take his mind away from the awful news we had heard.

We talked about it as we started to decorate the tree, each of us comforting the other. We didn't cry, although I had no doubt we both would if the news came that Dad had died. We just unwrapped ornaments, decided where to hang them, and talked about life and death. I wish I could remember all that Granddad said. He was a professor of religion and folklore at Marshall College, so I know he had lots of good things to say, but my mind was just not retaining anything. I don't remember any of the details of that day.

Except for the Story Tree.

I remember opening one of the two boxes that had been partially hidden behind boxes of books. In it was an artificial tree. It was designed to stand on a table, but even so, it was large, about three feet high. I pulled it out. "What's this, Granddad?" I asked.

He frowned as he looked at it, then his face lit up. "For heaven's sake," he said, "It's my Story Tree."

"Your what?"

"My Story Tree. I'd forgotten all about it. Say, there should be another box of ornaments around here."

I pushed the second box I had found hidden away towards him. Together we opened it. Inside were more ornaments. My eyes widened as I saw them. These were Christmas tree ornaments, but none of them had anything to do with Christmas. There was a Superman figure, and Batman and Spiderman; there was the old Starship Enterprise from the Classic Star Trek that I had seen in reruns and loved, figures of Captain Kirk and Mr. Spock, Star Wars figures of Luke and Leia, Darth Vader and Han Solo with his blaster. There were Dorothy, the Tin Man, the Cowardly Lion, and the Scarecrow, as well as the good and bad witches. There was an ornament of Merlin and one of Gandalf. There was even one of another Robbie, the robot from the old movie, *Forbidden Planet*. The whole box was filled with characters and objects from a dozen movies and books and from comics, too.

"Granddad," I said, pulling them out one by one, "what's all this? It looks like a toy shop in there!"

He grinned. "I suppose it is." He sat back, holding the Spock figure lovingly in his hands. "Some years ago, they began to make these theme ornaments. I loved them, and every year I would buy whatever new ones came out, and we'd hang them on the tree." He chuckled. "After awhile, the tree began to resemble a display you'd see at a comic book convention, and Gran'ma put her foot down. 'I don't want spaceships and ray guns and superheroes and robots on my Christmas tree,' she said, and I couldn't blame her. But I loved the stories that these figures represented. You know I study myth and epics for a living, and these were the characters from many of our modern myths."

"So you got an artificial tree to hang them on."

"That's right. I couldn't see cutting down another tree just to indulge my fantasies, so I got that fellow there. Then every year I'd decorate it with my story ornaments. I called it my Story Tree." He grinned. "Every time I hung a new ornament, I'd tell the tree the story about it. It was a little ritual of mine. Of course, the first time I did it, it took me most of a day to hang the ornaments. Your Gran'ma thought I was crazy! But you know, it felt good telling all those old stories again, even if it was just to an artificial tree!"

"How come I never saw it when we'd come over to visit at Christmastime?"

"Actually, I think you did, but you were pretty young. I haven't had it up for the past six years."

"Why not? It's really cool!"

"Oh, various reasons, I suppose. I ended up buying more of these ornaments than I could fit on the Story Tree. And it got old after awhile having to decorate two trees. But mostly I'd say it was because in the end the real Christmas tree held more wonder and mystery for me than this one did. Christmas is a time of stories, for sure, but basically it's the celebration of one great story, the triumph of life over all that would oppose it, the triumph of light over all the darkness that would extinguish it, and the story of the power of love as our greatest power.

All the stories that these fellows represented were just variations on that theme for me. Why bother with the variations when I had the real thing in front of me all the time?" He put Spock down. "I thought about putting it up in my office at the college, but I never got around to it."

"I still think the Story Tree is a cool idea!"

"Well, I do, too, Robbie. And frankly, I don't see how we can celebrate Christmas this year without it. Right now, we need all the good stories we can get!"

Granddad's living room had a large fireplace on one wall. We put the Christmas tree on one side of it and the Story Tree on the other. Then we pulled the long sofa up so that it was in front of the fireplace but back enough so we could see both of the trees. The Story Tree had no lights, but we put a standing lamp nearby just in case. We found that evening, though, that if there was a good fire in the fireplace, the glow from the flames and from the lights on the Christmas tree cast enough light on the Story Tree as well.

That night Granddad introduced me to what he called "manly cooking." He fixed up a beef stew of sorts in a large skillet. Then he brought the skillet into the living room and put it on a table in front of the fireplace. Next he brought in large thick slices of bread and a spoon for each of us. I looked at the spoon and I looked at the skillet and I said, "Granddad, should I get the plates?"

"PLATES?" he shouted, waving his hands in the air. "Men don't need plates! We're BARBARIANS and wonderfully so!" He sat down on the floor, dug his spoon into the skillet of stew and brought that spoonful to his mouth. "Men just need a skillet and a spoon. Saves on dishes." Then he ate the spoonful. "Come on," he said, when he saw me hesitating. "Dig in!"

So I dug in, too. We sat there like two cowboys around a fire, eating from that skillet and sopping up the gravy with our bread. It was the best meal I had ever had. And when it was done, Granddad brought out marshmallows, Graham crackers, and chocolate so we could make S'Mores over the fire.

During the meal, we never talked about the worry, even the fear that was in our minds—the thought that before this Christmas was over there might be two ghosts in the family. Instead, Granddad asked me about my school and what I was studying and what I liked, which took me all of five minutes to tell him since in those days school and I were not the best of friends. It wasn't a subject I cared to talk about. So, Granddad talked about his work at the college and the courses he taught on folklore and mythology. He even taught a class in creative writing, though to my knowledge he had never written a book, and a class in magic.

"Magic? You do a class on magic in college?" I asked.

"Yes. Very popular class, too. Oh, it's not about stage magic. It's about the real thing, real magic."

This was very interesting. I had had no idea people took magic seriously. It was popular in the role-playing games I loved, but in real life, no way! I told him so. "But Granddad, " I said, echoing my friends and teachers, "there's no such thing as real magic."

"Are you sure? How do you know? For thousands of years, people have believed in it and practiced it."

"Yeah, but Granddad, they didn't know any science or anything. It was just superstition."

"Superstition? Ha! I'd rather call it an art and science of the imagination and the will. You think modern society has all the answers? It doesn't even remember some of the important questions."

Well, right then we agreed to have a debate about the reality of magic. Not that I knew that much about it. The stuff Granddad talked about wasn't anything like hurling fireballs and summoning dragons. He was talking about the power of the mind and spirit to shape the world, and I knew that people had certainly used their imaginations to shape the world. But was that really magic?

Our little argument never came to any conclusion. It was more a way of being together than actually trying to decide something. The truth is I halfway believed in magic anyway, or perhaps I should say that at twelve, I hadn't fully entered the modern world with all its facts and figures in which magic is as welcome as a flower child at a Republican fundraiser. So my heart wasn't really invested in proving him wrong.

"The thing is, Robbie," Granddad said towards the end of our discussion, "if you believe, you can do almost anything. But you need to believe in yourself. If there is magic in the world, it comes from our believing in ourselves and our power to change things, hopefully for the better."

"That sounds like positive thinking, not magic."

"Well, they're kissing cousins, anyway. So how about some hot chocolate? Then I'll show you some special magic."

The "special magic" turned out to be telling stories. "Christmas is all about stories, Robbie," he said as we sipped our chocolate. "That's why I liked my Story Tree. Stories are real magic. They're the magic of creating worlds."

Then he proceeded to tell me a story. It wasn't about Christmas. In fact, I don't remember what it was about, since I fell asleep on the sofa listening to him. Granddad could have made a living telling stories, though. He could change his voice for each character, and he made everything come so alive I could see it as plain as day in my mind. Like he said, real magic. But it had been a long day, and even magic couldn't keep me awake.

The next few days settled into a routine. We talked to Mom everyday, which I looked forward to and always wished the conversation could go on longer. News about Dad was up and down. One day he was progressing well, the next he would have a setback. It was like being on a stormy sea, rising and falling with the waves of our emotions.

Not knowing just when Mom might call each day or if she might call more than once with what we hoped would be good news but feared might be bad, we didn't go out much. The house became our shelter, our fortress, and our castle in a world that now held a darkness only just being kept at bay. It was as if by staying at home, we could somehow hold our home together, keeping Dad alive and bringing him and Mom back to us.

If the house was our castle, the living room was the keep, the stronghold at its heart. We always ate dinner in the living room, though not always from a skillet. One evening Granddad, who prided himself on his cooking, set up a large table with candles and served a complete meal from soup to dessert. He even put out his best wine glasses and served sparkling apple cider. Another time we got a large bucket of fried chicken from a local fast food restaurant and sat by the fireplace eating it. He even got us two old t-shirts to wear so we could wipe our greasy hands on them "the way Barbarians should."

Mostly what we did was tell stories. Or rather Granddad told stories and I listened. On the second day I was there, we started after dinner. But the next day we started after lunch, and on the fourth day, we finished breakfast, went into the living room and began telling more stories. Stories became our life, part of our defense against the dark.

In the beginning, they were the traditional stories of Christmas, tales of the birth of Jesus, stories about Santa Claus and St. Nicholas and even of the Norse god, Odin, whom Granddad said was one of the origins of the modern Santa Claus. He told me stories of elves and reindeer and of Ebenezer Scrooge and the three ghosts of Christmas.

Then he began pointing out ornaments on the Story Tree and telling stories about them. I swung through the jungles with Tarzan. I flew through the skies with Superman. I prowled the dark streets of Gotham City with Batman. I walked the Golden Road with Dorothy and her companions and dodged Captain Hook with Peter Pan. Through the power of Granddad's imagination and words, I even journeyed to strange new worlds with Captain Kirk and Mr. Spock of the Starship Enterprise.

By the fifth day he had begun telling stories from different times and places, like the battle of Beowulf with the Grendel or the adventures of Gilgamesh at the beginning of civilization. He told the stories of Odysseus and his long journey home, and of Orpheus who descended to the land of the dead to bring back his wife. He told me of Merlin and Arthur and of Taliesin, the bard who tricked a goddess into giving him all the wisdom in the world.

I learned how evil Set dismembered the body of the god Osiris, and how Horus the Hawk-Headed found the pieces and brought Osiris back to life. I learned, too, about Hiawatha and the Peacemaker who came out of the northern forests of what are now Canada and New York State and founded the Iroquois confederation.

We spent these hours together always with a fire in the fireplace. Granddad sat in his big leather easy chair by the hearth and I would wrap up in a blanket on the sofa where I could see both the Christmas tree and the Story Tree. I don't know where Granddad found the stamina or the energy or the inspiration. He seemed inexhaustible. It was like he

122

was weaving some spell through the telling of his stories that would protect all of us and put things right again.

By the sixth day, he was making up stories based, I imagine, on all the folklore and mythology he knew. There was a tale of Olanga, a young boy who had to cross a burning desert and return on two swallows of water, bringing a rare healing herb back to his father who was ill. Then there was Silandra, who carved a Flute of Rare Design whose notes called all the winds of the world to her service and who single-handedly defeated Umak, the evil wizard who threatened to cover the world in darkness.

Of all the new stories, I think my favorite was Dr. Quasar and the Remarkable Seven, whose motto was, "Who knows what possibilities lie in the hearts and minds of sentient beings? Dr. Quasar knows!" He and his seven companions were star explorers of different species who banded together to fight for justice, truth, and freedom in the star nations of the thirty-fifth century.

I realized as the hours and days went by that all of Granddad's stories dealt with the triumph of life and light over their enemies. "The great enemy," Granddad said over dinner, the story of Dr. Quasar still vivid in my memory, "is not death. Death opens a new door. It seems scary because we don't usually see where the door goes. The true enemies are despair and fear, bondage and the denial of imagination. These things close doors. They deny us our possibilities. Life is always about possibilities, Robbie, about opening new doors. With imagination and vision, who knows what may be possible?"

"Dr. Quasar knows!" I intoned.

"Indeed he does. Indeed he does! And now that dinner's done, I think we should go and explore some more of what he knows, don't you? I feel more stories coming on!"

In the kitchen, we gathered up the fixings for ice cream sundaes. Granddad carried a tray with bowls of ice cream, nuts, chocolate syrup, and tiny marshmallows into the living room. I put fresh logs on the fire. Then I made myself a sundae and got comfortable on the sofa. Granddad made his own sundae and settled himself in his chair. Where he was sitting the Story Tree was to his right and slightly to his rear, so he was facing the Christmas tree and the fireplace.

We ate our sundaes. Then, leaning back and closing his eyes, Granddad continued the adventures of Dr. Quasar and his brave companions. Listening, my eyes on the glowing logs in the fireplace, it was as if he were reading from a book rather than making it up as he went along. I suppose years of telling stories to students had honed his skill, but even now, I look back at those days and marvel at his ability. He might as well have been an ancient bard like Taliesin, weaving the epic sagas of his people, holding his audience rapt with the magic of his words. And the spell of his words was also fed by my need to go to a place where bad things didn't happen to good people, where grandmothers didn't die suddenly, and where my father was not maimed and fighting for his life.

So as he spoke, I was transported in my mind's eye hundreds of light years away to the forlorn planet of Klipzar where a mighty civilization had once flourished, died and vanished beneath the sands of its world with only a few giant ruins to mark its passing.

I was so entranced that at first I didn't notice the light swirling around the Story Tree, even though I was facing it from where I was lying on the sofa. When I did see it, I thought it was smoke from the fireplace. Had the flue somehow gotten blocked or closed? But then I realized that it wasn't smoke. It was a band of light swirling like a narrow cloud around the tree.

"Granddad!" I shouted, sitting up and pointing. His eyes came open and he looked at me, startled. "Granddad! The Story Tree!"

He turned his head to his right and recoiled when he saw the light. His feet dug into the floor, and he pushed his chair back a few inches. "Fire!" he said, rising from his chair. Then he realized as I had that it wasn't fire or smoke. It was something else.

I pushed back the blanket I had over me, though I have to admit there was part of me that wanted to scoot under it, and got up from the sofa.

"Don't get too close, Robbie," Granddad said. "It's probably some kind of weird static electricity."

But I had seen something in the swirling light, and I wanted to see up close what it was. The fact that so far nothing bad seemed to be happening gave me some degree of confidence. Cautiously, I advanced on the Story Tree.

124

"Look, Granddad," I said. "There're people in that light."

Granddad got up from his chair and came closer to the tree. "By golly," he said, "You're right!"

The ribbon of light wrapped around the Story Tree like a garland around the Christmas tree, and in it we could both see men and women and many objects. As we stared, I saw Superman and Santa, Peter Pan and a barbarian-looking character in furs and leather clutching a sword.

"Beowulf," whispered Granddad, seeing the same thing.

Han Solo appeared and Luke Skywalker brandishing a light saber; the Enterprise flew by. Gandalf waved his staff in the air. Silandra played her flute while Horus the Hawk-Headed stood next to her. A figure in armor stood holding high a glowing chalice.

"They're people from the stories you've been telling, Granddad!" I said. I felt a chill running down my back.

"You're right, Robbie. But how...?"

Our eyes fixed on the Story Tree, we saw the light or whatever it was settle on one branch, where it swirled together like water going down a drain. Then the light disappeared altogether. In its place was a round ornament. I reached out to touch it. It was cool and hard, like glass.

"Careful, Robbie," Granddad admonished, but curiosity was upon me like a jockey on a horse. The ornament, like all the others, hung from the branch by a little hook. I unhooked it and pulled it toward me. It was a clear globe, filled with what looked at first like golden dust. As I looked more closely, though, I realized with a start that I was looking at a desert, from which a rocky ridge arose. Carved into that ridge was a monument, at the center of which was a great door, looking like pictures I had seen of the great temple ruins in Egypt.

In front of the monument and to its left, there was a figure. It reminded me of the Sphinx, but the figure was totally alien. It had the body of what looked like an insect with many legs, a torso like a bird's but with tentacles instead of wings, and a head with three square patches that may have been eyes above a savage-looking hooked beak. It was like a centaur fashioned from a bird, a centipede, and an octopus rather than from a man and a horse. It was frightening and ugly to look at, yet it had an air of majesty about it.

125

There was movement in the globe, and as I watched, a hovercraft came over a dune and stopped in front of the alien statue. Eight figures climbed out, some human, some not. I knew immediately it was Dr. Quasar and the Remarkable Seven! Seeing them gave scale to the statue, and I realized it was truly gigantic.

My hands began to shake as I watched the figures advance towards the portal. One of them, whom I knew had to be Dr. Quasar by his stature and bearing, pointed a device at the giant doorway. A green beam lanced out, striking the stone. The doorway opened, revealing a gaping, dark entrance way. The eight figures disappeared into it. Then sand blew up obscuring everything. When it cleared, everything was as I had first seen it. Then off to the left, I saw a hovercraft coming over a dune, and I knew the scene was repeating itself.

"Granddad!" I said. "It's...it's Dr. Quasar and the ruined tomb of Z'Arnaut the Third in the deserts of Klipzar! It's what you were just describing in your story!" I handed him the globe.

He looked at it, his expression as stunned as I'm sure mine was. Then he sat down. I could see sweat on his forehead. He held the globe in one hand while with the other he took out a handkerchief and mopped his brow. Gingerly, he handed it back to me. "It's magic, Robbie," he said, and a huge grin appeared on his face. "Real magic!"

I took the globe. It *was* magic or something very much like it. "Wha... what should I do with it?"

"Why, hang it back on the Story Tree, of course! It appeared there. It belongs there."

I hung it back up and stepped back to sit on the sofa, looking at it. "But what does it mean?"

"Mean?" Granddad laughed. "It means the Story Tree has decided to tell stories with us, or at least to show us it's listening. So come on, Grandson. Settle back, and I'll continue. We mustn't disappoint our new audience." And with no more than that, Granddad launched back into the story, as if having magic globes appear on artificial trees was the most natural thing in the world.

And perhaps in that moment, it was. We were creating a circle of magic with our stories, no doubt about it. But it wasn't just for entertainment. We were both straddling that line between life and death, waiting to hear if someone we loved would continue to be with us. We were in need. We were striving against the forces of dissolution, and stories were our weapons. If, as Granddad said, magic was the science of imagination and will, then we were certainly imagining and willing that the world we knew, the good world of family and love and life, would prevail no matter the odds. Perhaps the intensity of our concentration had thinned some veil between this world and some other where story globes were normal. I don't know.

What I do know is that Granddad rose to new levels of eloquence and passion as he wove his tail of adventure under the sands of Klipzar. And throughout it all, I kept my eye on the Story Tree, although there were no more swirls of light and no more mysterious globes appeared. Eventually, around two or three in the morning, I fell asleep on the sofa.

It was noon when I woke up. I was back in my bed, though I had no recollection of getting there. I knew Granddad couldn't have carried me up the stairs, so I figured I'd climbed them myself. I lay there with the bright sunlight streaming in the window, feeling disoriented. Somewhere I heard a phone ring, but it seemed distant, as if it were in some other world.

Gradually, the events of the previous evening crept back into my memory, as if afraid to see the light of day. I remembered the Story Tree and the swirling light and the mysterious globe, but it all seemed dreamlike and tentative. Had it really happened? Somehow, the real world and what Granddad called the imaginal world where stories live and magic is natural blended together for me. Was I losing the ability to tell the two apart. Was I in my Granddad's house, or was I in a story about my Granddad's house? Was my Dad really injured, or was I just in a story about my Dad being injured?

The door to my bedroom opened a crack, and Granddad peered in.

"Ah," he said, "Robbie. You're awake."

I sat up and frowned. "If you could call it that," I replied. "I'm not sure."

Granddad came over and sat on the edge of my bed. He took my hands in his, and I knew he was about to say something I wouldn't want to hear.

"Robbie, that was your mother who just called. I thought you were still asleep, and she said not to wake you. She didn't have long to talk anyway." He took a deep breath. I dreaded the sadness I could see in his eyes.

"Dad...?" My voice caught in my throat.

"There's an infection in what remains of your Dad's left arm. It's not responding to treatment. The doctors are going to remove the rest of the arm to save his life. They're starting the operation now. That's why your mother couldn't talk long; she had to get back to the hospital."

"Oh no!" I cried. I thought of my Dad with no arm and no leg. Knowing him, he would make a joke of it but he had always been so strong and proud of his body. How would he live with half his limbs removed? If he lived...

"Are they sure it will save him?" I asked. "Dad *is* going to live, isn't he?"

Granddad sighed and squeezed my hands. "Your mother thinks so, but so much depends on his own will to live, Robbie. I think he's fighting to stay here, but I'm afraid he may be losing."

"Can we help him somehow? Can you help him?" Somehow, in the state I was in, I had begun to think of Granddad as some kind of wizard. After all, hadn't he worked real magic last night?

"All we can do is pray, Robbie, and hold him in our hearts and thoughts."

"But what about the magic, Granddad? You did magic last night!"

Granddad shook his head. "Something happened last night, but I had nothing to do with it, I'm afraid. Or if I did—or rather if *we* did—I don't know what it was."

"It was the stories, Granddad! It was telling the stories. That's what we have to do, we have to tell more stories and work more magic!"

"Robbie, are you sure you want more stories? I don't know if I have any more in me. Dr. Quasar emptied me out last night."

"But Granddad, you have to have more stories. We need to tell stories!" In that moment, I knew beyond any doubt, that that was exactly what we had to do. Somehow, if the stories stopped, my Dad's life would stop, too. I said so. "Granddad, if we can't tell stories, Dad will die. It's magic, Granddad.! Didn't you say you believed in magic? Isn't magic

128

the science of imagination and will? Dad needs the will, and we have the imagination!"

Granddad looked at me quizzically, as if I'd suddenly sprouted wings. "Robbie, I was just talking...I didn't mean..." But then something of my urgency and my assurance must have gripped him, for he straightened up. "That's right, Robbie! Telling stories is what we have to do! But...but I can't think of any right now. Like I said, I think I shot my wad last night."

"Then, I'll tell them," I said, swinging my legs out from under the covers and getting out of bed. Though even as I said it, I realized I didn't have a clue what kind of story to tell.

I got dressed and we went downstairs. It turned out that Granddad hadn't been up long himself, so while he went into the kitchen to make some breakfast for us, I ran into the living room to see if the magical ornament with the tomb of Z'Arnaut the Third in it was still there.

To my mixed astonishment and delight, it still hung from the tree. And when I held it in my hand, the scene began to play itself out again, with Dr. Quasar and the Remarkable Seven arriving and entering the tomb. I whooped with joy and ran back into the kitchen to show Granddad.

Then a curious thing happened. As I crossed from the living room into the hallway that led to the kitchen in the back, the ornament began to fade until by the time I was with Granddad, it had vanished.

"Granddad, it's gone!" I cried, stricken, staring at my empty hands.

"What's gone? The ornament?"

"Yes. I mean, it was there on the Story Tree, but when I took it off and carried it in here, it disappeared."

"Now, that's strange. More magic, I expect. Let's go see." He went back down the hall to the living room, and I followed. Going up to the tree, he took something off the branch. It was the magical ornament.

"Here it is," he said. "But you said it vanished?"

"Yes, when I was running down the hall to the kitchen."

"Hmm. Let's experiment."

Granddad held the ornament in his hand and walked to the hallway. Then he left the living room, and taking slow steps one at a

129

time, he walked towards the kitchen. We had gone about half the distance when the ornament faded out and disappeared.

I ran back into the living room and up to the Story Tree. "It's back here again, Granddad!" I shouted as he walked into the living room himself.

"More mysteries," he said. "Well, best ponder them over some Cheerios. Come and have breakfast, Robbie, and we'll try to figure this out."

Going back to eat breakfast was hard, just like seeing a pile of presents under the Christmas tree and not opening any until after we'd eaten something. But I followed Granddad back to the kitchen, and we each had cereal and melted butter on sweet rolls that Granddad had taken from the fridge and heated up. As I ate, he said, "I think it's the Story Tree that's magic, Robbie. Somehow the story globe is just a manifestation of the Tree itself. If you remove it too far away, it disappears and reappears on the Tree. It can't exist apart from the Tree."

That made sense. "But how did the Story Tree become magic? Did it ever do this before?"

"Never, Robbie. I'm as surprised as you are. I'd like to think it's been our storytelling. Maybe that's part of it. Maybe it's soaked up the magic of all those stories I've told it over the years as I hung the ornaments. But it's Christmas, too, and that's a magical time all by itself. Miracles have been known to happen at Christmas time. Maybe this is one of them."

"Like a miracle of my Dad living and getting better."

"That would be the best miracle of all, Robbie."

I got up and carried my bowl and plate to the sink, where I washed them out. "Then we'd better get started again, Granddad. We don't want to keep miracles waiting!"

We went back into the living room, like soldiers taking up our post. But as I went to take my place on the sofa, I saw something new on the Story Tree. Right next to the globe that had appeared last night, another globe now hung. I ran over and snatched it up. "Granddad, there's another one!"

"What? Let's see!"

I held it up so we could both look into it. It showed a vast forest, like a movie I had seen once of the Amazon forest seen from high in the

130

sky. But this forest had every kind of tree you can think of, from the palms of the jungle to the firs of the far north. And rising out of the forest was a giant tree that seemed to grow right up to the edge of space.

Granddad took a deep breath. "The World Tree," he said.

"What?"

"The World Tree. In many myths, the world is held together by a great tree from which all life ultimately springs. It is the ultimate tree, the Father and Mother of all Trees. In other myths and stories, the Tree is a symbol of the link between heaven and earth. In some. it is a symbol of an enlightened human being, a person whose feet are firmly in the earth, thus grounded and practical, but whose mind and spirit are in the heavens, thus inspired and illumined."

"Wow," I said. "But why is it in this ornament? You haven't told any stories about the World Tree."

"No, but I feel one coming on." He put the ornament back on the Tree "You know, I think the Story Tree is helping us. I couldn't think of a single story an hour ago, but now this ornament has given me a suggestion. I know just the story I want to tell!"

"Fantastic," I said, feeling very relieved, because my mind was a big fat zero with no story in there at all. I jumped back on the sofa and settled in, ready for whatever Granddad came up with.

And it was a great story, about a time when droughts and plagues covered the earth, and all humanity was in danger of dying. To prevent this, a young brother and sister had to find and climb the World Tree. Only in its branches could they discover the hidden gods and goddesses who each carried a special power that would help the people recover and prosper.

It took all afternoon and into the evening for Granddad to finish the story. Afterwards we went to the kitchen where he prepared another skillet meal. That was when we also decided to keep vigil, as Granddad called it, on behalf of Dad by sleeping near the Story Tree in the living room. So we each brought down bedding, and Granddad brought an old cot up from the basement. "I've slept on worse," he said when I pressed him to sleep on the sofa. "This will be just fine."

And while we were preparing our beds for the night, another ornament appeared. Granddad spotted it this time, but when he took it down to see what was in it, it began to glow. Before either of us could say anything, a brilliant light filled the room, momentarily blinding us. When we could see again, the living room had disappeared.

We were standing on the deck of a three-masted sailing ship, its sails billowing in the wind. Around us was a vast expanse of ocean, the water a pale violet color. At first we thought the ship was empty except for us, but turning around we saw a young man holding a staff before him in both hands. He tilted the staff to the right, and the boat began to turn to the right. Then he raised a hand in greeting to us and pointed upward. We looked up. Overhead, dragons of various colors flew in formation like geese, also turning to the right. We were following them. Smoke rose on the distant horizon.

"Granddad...where are we?" I asked. "What happened?" Strangely, I felt very calm about the situation.

"I think this time we're inside a story, Robbie." He used his hand to shade his eyes so he could see the dragons more clearly.

I looked around, remembering one of my Dad's favorite TV shows. "You mean, like being on the holodeck in Star Trek?"

Granddad looked at me, his face filled with wonder. "Yes, I guess it's something like that. Some kind of virtual reality."

"Or maybe it's real," I said.

"Robbie, at this point, nothing would surprise me."

But then, as if on cue, we found ourselves flying up into the air, looking down on the whole scene below us. The ship and the dragons were all beneath us, and in the distance, we could see that the smoke on the horizon was rising from a great volcano, around which other dragons flew. We heard a voice:

THIS IS THE STORY OF JAN, THE HEALER-MAGE AND HIS QUEST TO HEAL TORAN, THE DRAGONFATHER. MAN INFLICTED THE GREAT DRAGON'S INJURIES, AND UNLESS JAN CAN HEAL THEM, WAR WILL BREAK OUT BETWEEN HUMAN AND DRAGON KIND, ENSURING THE DEATH-EATING CARRION BEAST A FULL MEAL.

The light flashed again, and we were back in the living room.

I lay back on the sofa. "Whoa! That was something!"

Granddad put the globe back on the Story Tree. "It was a trailer, Robbie," he laughed. "Just like at the movies. Coming attractions, except I know what the story is! The Story Tree told me! Amazing!"

So, he began the story of Jan, the Healer-Mage and his living ship, who had to heal the DragonFather, but who had to contest first with the minions of the Carrion Beast who fed on death and who sought a war between dragons and humans to appease his awful and mighty hunger.

Granddad wove this tale deep into the night, but finally he could go no further, nor could I keep my eyes open. Vowing to continue it in the morning, we both went to sleep, I on the sofa and he on his cot.

Sometime later, though, I awoke. I thought it was morning since bright sunlight filled the room. But as I opened my eyes, what I saw wasn't the living room. I saw a valley with towering snow-capped mountains at one end. The ground was covered with a profusion of different wildflowers. They were blue and pink, purple and red. Nearby I could hear a stream chuckling and murmuring as it flowed over rocks.

Where was I? Was I dreaming? But I felt like I was awake. I could feel the sofa solidly beneath me and touch the blankets on top of me.

I started to sit up and call out to Granddad. But then I heard his voice speaking and another voice answering. Raising my head just a little bit and turning about, I looked over to where the voices were coming from. I saw Granddad sitting on a log, holding the hands of a young woman who was sitting beside him. With a chill down my back, I realized that it was Gran'ma, looking just like the pictures I had seen of her when she'd been in her twenties.

I remembered Granddad's telling me of his dreams of Gran'ma, of meeting her in the valley where they had spent their honeymoon. Somehow I had entered his dream. Then I saw a round globe lying on the grass by his feet, and I realized that I wasn't in a dream at all but in a story. The Story Tree had made a globe that told the story of Granddad and Gran'ma. Now I was in it with them.

But this story didn't end, and it didn't feel like a story. They just sat together talking and holding hands. I became embarrassed to be watching. I felt like an intruder in their private lives. I closed my eyes and pulled the covers up over my head and tried to get back to sleep. And I must have succeeded, for the next thing I knew there was normal daylight streaming into the room and Granddad was calling me to wake up and come get brunch. But as I rubbed the sleep from my eyes, I remembered something I had heard as I had drifted off again. It had been Granddad's voice, and he had said, "I can't leave now. Robbie still needs me, and Jane will need me, too." Then I had fallen asleep.

As I went to the bathroom and then to the kitchen, I wasn't sure whether or not to tell Granddad what I'd seen. So, while I was filling my plate with the sausages, bacon, eggs, and pancakes Granddad had made, I fudged a bit and said, "Granddad, I had a strange dream last night. I dreamt you and Gran'ma were together talking, and she was young again, just like in that dream you told me about."

He looked at me. "Are you sure it was a dream?" he asked.

"What do you mean?"

He cut off a slice of pancake and stuffed it into his mouth. He chewed for a bit, swallowed, then said, "After you went to sleep last night, I woke up. I don't know why, but I had the strongest urge to tell a story about Gran'ma and me. I didn't want to wake you, so I sat by the Story Tree and whispered my story. And an ornament appeared. When I picked it up, I found myself in the valley I'd been dreaming about, but this time there was no story. There was just Gran'ma, looking as beautiful as I remember her." He sighed. "We just talked. Then she said she had to go. As she walked away, I was back in the living room holding the globe in my hand."

I whistled. "Do you think you were in heaven, Granddad?"

He smiled. "Of course, Robbie. Whenever I was with Gran'ma, it was always heaven!"

"But what about the globe? Can you visit her again?"

He finished his plate before answering. "I don't know, Robbie. This time, when I went to put the globe back on the Story Tree, it disappeared."

"It disappeared?"

"Yes. I think it was a one time special Christmas gift to me. I guess one can't have too many miracles at one time! Speaking of which," he said, getting up and taking his plate to the sink, "today's Christmas Eve Day, in case you've forgotten. Anything special you'd like to do today?"

I thought for a moment. "Yes, I'd like you to finish the story about Jan, the Healer, and then maybe tell more stories. We haven't heard about Dad, yet, so there's still one miracle to come, to bring him home. We need to keep working the magic."

"OK, Robbie, you've got it! Let's clean up here and we'll return to our vigil."

It was a strange afternoon. Normally on Christmas Eve Day, the thought of the next morning and opening presents kept me too excited to sit still. But between Dad's condition and the magic that had been going on with the Story Tree, the idea of presents had faded way into the background. Oh, I knew that Mom had left some things with Granddad and that they would find their way under the Christmas tree before morning, but somehow, that just didn't matter. Maybe, as I approached the magic years of teenhood, I was just reordering my priorities.

Anyway, Granddad spent the afternoon finishing the tale of Jan the Healer, and when he was done I was absolutely convinced that Dad was going to be all right. No further ornaments appeared magically on the Story Tree, but I was convinced we were making some powerful mojo together. I'm sure Granddad felt it, too.

But at the same time, I was worried. Mom hadn't called when she usually did. As much as I concentrated on all the magic that was surrounding us, a dark, traitorous voice within me was beginning to whisper that all was not well.

Then, about six o'clock, as Granddad was fixing dinner in the kitchen, the phone rang. I ran to the hall and snatched up the receiver.

"Mom?" I said.

There was silence at first at the other end, except for a faint hiss that made it seem like the other end of the phone was a long, long way away. Then I heard a sound somewhere between a cough and a sob. "Robbie?" It was Mom, but I had never heard her voice sound so strained. She seemed to be speaking from a hollow, defeated place. "Robbie, I've got bad news. It's Dad...Dad's dying."

I couldn't believe what I was hearing. There must be some mistake, I thought. Dad couldn't be dying. Granddad and me, we had raised magic to keep this from happening. We had been like Knights of the Story Tree, keeping vigil and fighting back all the powers of loss and darkness. We had been affirming life. Every story had proclaimed life's triumph. What did Mom mean that Dad was dying?

Granddad's voice came on from the kitchen extension. "Jane, what's happened?"

I actually sensed Mom willing her voice to be clear and strong. "The operation didn't help. Daniel's slipped into a coma. The doctors say he probably won't live through the day."

"But Mom!" I protested, "that can't be right! It's Christmas Eve! We did the magic, Mom. We did the magic!"

"What?" she asked, confused.

"Granddad and me, we told stories. We made magical things happen. Dad should be all right!"

"Robbie, Robbie, I'm sorry. I don't know what you've been doing. I'm sure you've been doing all you could, but Dad's injuries were just too much. He's dying. If I thought you two could get here in time, I'd say catch a plane tonight, but there is no time. He'll be dead by morning your time, Robbie. I'm so sorry!"

"No, no! This can't be true, Mom! The doctor's have it wrong. You'll see! We did magic here, Mom, real magic!"

"Robbie..."

"NO!" I slammed the phone down and rushed into the living room. The Story Tree stood there on the table. The magical ornaments were still there, and when I picked them up, they still worked. I even stood there on the deck of that ship again, looking up at the dragons with tears in my eyes, and then shouting to Jan holding his staff, "Heal my DAD! Never mind the dragons. Heal my Dad!" But there was no response. It was like being part of a taped video. I found myself high in the sky again, the voice proclaimed that this was the story of Jan, the Healer, and then I was standing in the living room, sobbing and filled with the worst rage I have ever felt.

I threw the globe down and it shattered into pieces. Then I swept my arm out and knocked the whole Story Tree onto the floor, ornaments falling off and scattering about. Blinded with tears and anger, I raced out of the room and up the stairs into my room. I locked the door and threw myself on the bed. I wanted nothing more to do with Christmas, with stories or a Story Tree. I especially didn't want any more to do with a magic that promised so much and then in the end didn't do anything. I felt betrayed.

Later Granddad came upstairs and knocked on my door, but I told him I wanted to be alone. I heard his footsteps walking away and going down the stairs. I lay there in the dark, wanting to die myself, unable to imagine a world without my Dad.

Sometime in the evening I heard the phone ring again. I heard Granddad answer it, but I couldn't hear anything he said. I didn't want to. For me, everything had come to an end.

I heard Granddad's steps outside my door. He knocked softly. "Robbie, let me in, please." I pretended to be asleep and didn't answer. "Robbie, that was your Mom again." There was a long pause, but I knew what he was going to say. I already felt the emptiness. "Robbie, your Dad just died a little while ago. Robbie, let me in."

I didn't move. He knocked more loudly. "Robbie, he was my son as well as your father!" I could hear the anger and loss in his voice. "Let me in so we can grieve together! There shouldn't be doors between us at a time like this."

But I hardened my heart as they say in the Bible and refused to acknowledge his presence. Finally, I heard his footsteps walk away.

I must have fallen asleep, because it was even darker and colder when I awoke. I lay there feeling ashamed at how I had treated Granddad. It wasn't his fault the magic had failed. He had been a fellow soldier at the ramparts between life and death. In fact, he had done all the work. I had just listened.

I decided to get up and go find him. If he was asleep, I would wake him and apologize, and we would comfort each other. I expected we both needed comforting.

The house was silent and dark. For a moment, my mind flashed to the poem, *The Night Before Christmas*: "Not a creature was stirring, not even a mouse." Well, there was no jolly St. Nick coming down the chimney in this house tonight. Only death.

I opened the door to Granddad's room. He was lying on top of his bed, fully dressed, a light blanket over his legs. He was sound asleep. I started over to wake him up when a gleam of light caught my attention. Something on his dresser was faintly glowing. I went over to look at it. It was one of the ornaments from the Story Tree. A magical ornament.

But how could that be? Why hadn't it disappeared? I didn't touch it, but I peered into it. I could just make out a scene of a valley with wildflowers and mountains in the distance.

It was the ornament that had taken Granddad into the place where Gran'ma was. But Granddad had told me it had disappeared. Had it come back...or had Granddad lied to me?

I felt filled with rage again. Granddad had an ornament that would take him to Gran'ma, but what did I have that would take me to Dad? I picked up the ornament, intending to smash it to the floor. As I did so, I could feel the stirring of power within it and felt myself being drawn into it. And I felt something else, too. I felt a sadness come over me. In that moment, I realized this was not my story to destroy. Whatever reason Granddad had had for not sharing the truth with me, this was his private story, and I had no right to interfere with it.

I put it back on the dresser and quietly left the room, closing the door behind me. Granddad was lightly snoring on the bed as I did so.

Standing in the dark hallway, I thought. What had Granddad told me earlier? He said he had awakened with an impulse to tell the story of Gran'ma and him to the Story Tree. And as he did so, this ornament had appeared, letting him go to where Gran'ma was. Why couldn't I do the same thing? The magic hadn't kept Dad from dying, but perhaps it would let me visit him and talk with him one last time.

Then I remembered I had knocked the Story Tree down. Had I destroyed it? Had I destroyed the magic?

I ran downstairs in the dark, and into the living room, holding my breath, almost afraid to look. But it was there. The Story Tree once more stood on its table, and the ornaments were all hung upon it as before. Granddad must have picked it up and put everything back in place.

I ran over to the chair that Granddad sat in while he told his stories, turning it so I faced the Story Tree. At first it was hard. I felt silly talking to an artificial tree. But, thinking of Dad, I persisted. "I'm sorry I knocked you over," I said to the Tree just as if it were a person. "I was angry because my Dad died and I felt you had failed me. But I guess it's no one's fault. Even magic can only do so much, I suppose." The Story Tree just stood there. But in that moment I felt that it was actually listening to me. However strange it sounds, I was convinced that this artificial tree was somehow alive and paying attention.

"I want to tell you a story," I said. "I want to tell you about my Dad and me. And if you can give me a magical way of bringing us together again, I'd like that. But I guess all I can really ask is that you listen to me."

So I began telling it stories about my Dad and the things we did. I told it about how we would play games together and how he would make me laugh with his jokes. I told it how he often had to be away because of his work, but how he would send me letters and emails and try to keep in touch. I told it about the tree house he made for me in the backyard of our home. I told it about staying up late to see movies with him. I thought the Tree should also know how Dad would tell me stories like Granddad did. I told the Story Tree how much I loved my Dad and how much he meant to me.

I had to stop sometimes because I would start crying and couldn't talk. But I would pull myself together and continue.

And then the ornament appeared. Just like the first time, there was a swirl of light that wrapped around the Tree, then coalesced on one branch.

I grabbed for it.

I looked into it, but before I could see anything, there was a flash of light. When I could see again, I was standing just inside the doorway to a building. It looked like a hotel lobby, and ahead of me was a flight of steps going upward. Lots of people were moving about the room, and the sunlight through the windows was very bright and hot. Strangely, I could smell cinnamon in the air.

Where was I? What kind of heaven was this? What was my Dad doing in a hotel after death?

But then I spotted him going up the stairs. I ran across the lobby, shouting at him. "Dad! Dad!" I yelled at the top of my voice. Everyone in the lobby turned to look at me, and a couple of men started in my direction, obviously intending to stop me.

I started up the stairs, still calling. Dad stopped and turned around. I could see incredulity on his face and shock. "Robbie?" he called out. "Robbie, is that you?" He started back down the stairs towards me. "What in heaven's name are you doing here?" I heard him

139

say, and then everything dissolved in a wall of noise and flame and flying debris. I was knocked off my feet and down the stairs. There was a tremendous rending sound, as if the very earth were being torn apart. The building crumbled around me.

I must have blacked out momentarily, but when I came to, it was dark with dust. My ears were ringing. I tried to sit up, but my side hurt where I had hit something or something had hit me. I began to cough. What was happening?

Then in front of me a figure loomed out of the darkness. It was my Dad. His clothes were torn and there was blood all over him. "Robbie," he said, coughing. I felt his arms around me, then felt him trying to pick me up. Above and around us, there came more tearing sounds. "Wall's coming down," he grunted. "Bomb went off!"

He picked me up, but his legs couldn't hold us both and we collapsed. I fell to the floor and slid away from him. He looked up, lying flat on the floor and began to crawl towards me, just when what was left of the roof collapsed behind us. In that moment, I felt another pair of arms around me, lifting me up. I yelled, "No! Dad!" as I felt myself being carried away. I could see my Dad lying unconscious amidst dust and rubble, but I also saw a huge slab of concrete that had once been part of the roof lying only inches away from his left arm and leg.

There was a flash of light, and I was falling backwards. "Oof!" said a voice behind me, still holding on to me. We landed on the sofa and rolled off onto the floor. Then the arms around me loosened, and the weight lifted as Granddad raised himself off of me.

"What happened?" I gasped.

"I think I just pulled you from a very deadly story," he said. He stood up and brushed himself off. Dust fell away from him.

I started to get up, then felt the pain in my side. "Ow!" I cried out, and sank onto the sofa.

"Hey, let me look at that!" Granddad said. "I think you're bleeding!" He knelt in front of the sofa and raised my T-shirt above my arms. There was a great bruise and gash in my side. But as we watched, it began to disappear until after a minute, there was no sign of any wound.

"Wow!" Granddad whispered. "How do you feel, Kiddo?"

I flexed my chest muscles, leaning to one side. "Fine. I feel OK."

Granddad sighed and sat down in his chair. "So, you want to tell me what that was all about?"

"I'm not sure. I think I was where Dad was when the bomb went off."

"How'd you get there, for heaven's sakes? And why?"

"I did what you did last night with Gran'ma. I told the Story Tree stories about Dad and me, hoping it would give me an ornament that would let me talk to him the way you did to Gran'ma."

"But it sent you to the building where he was injured by the bomb instead."

"Yes, I guess so. But how did you know? What were you doing there?"

He laughed. "I heard the bomb go off and ran downstairs. I thought the furnace had exploded! You can imagine my surprise to come to the living room door from the hallway and find myself looking into the rubble of a building I'd never seen before. Then I saw your Dad trying to pick you up and collapsing. I figured you needed a hand, so I joined the party."

I remembered that moment. "Granddad," I said, "as you were carrying me out, I saw Dad lying there but I didn't see any rubble crushing him. It looked to me like it just missed him."

"Looked that way to me, too," he said. "Like you said, here's hoping."

I looked around. "Where's that globe? Maybe we can go back and see for sure!"

Granddad shook his head. "I don't think that's such a good idea. It sounds too much like tempting fate. Besides, I think it disappeared."

"Like yours?" I asked..

At the tone in my voice, he stared at me. "No, not like mine. I didn't tell you the truth, Robbie, and I'm sorry. I couldn't bear to put my globe back on the Tree when I came back, so I put it in my robe pocket. Then I had to go upstairs. To my surprise, it didn't disappear when I left the living room. I figured maybe it was a Christmas gift from the Story Tree. It's upstairs in my bedroom."

"I know, Granddad. I saw it there earlier. That's what gave me the idea to try it myself."

It was at that moment that the phone rang. We both got up to get it, but I got there first. There's an advantage to young legs.

"Hi, Robbie!" my Mom's voice said, sounding cheerful. "Merry Christmas! Have you started opening presents yet?"

"Uh, no, Mom, not yet. How's Dad?"

"What, no presents yet? Are you feeling OK, son?" She laughed. "Dad's fine. I'm calling to say he's being released from the hospital today. We're coming home tomorrow. Tell Granddad to meet us."

"I heard that," Granddad said from the kitchen extension. "We'll be there! That's the best present of all!"

"Tell me again, Mom. Dad's OK? He's not dead or anything?"

"Dead? Of course not, silly! Oh, he was pretty banged up, but nothing really life-threatening."

"He's got all his arms and legs?"

"Robbie, you've been worrying too much. Of course he's got his arms and legs. Why would you think otherwise?"

I sighed in happy relief. "Oh, I don't know, Mom. I guess things have been a bit strange here."

"Well, don't go all weird on me. Your Dad's been weird enough. He swears he saw you in the UN embassy building when it was bombed. He says you called out to him as he was going up the stairs to a meeting. He turned and saw you and started back down the stairs towards you when the bomb went off. If he hadn't, he would have been in the part of the building that was hit the worst. Then he would have been injured even more, or even…well, never mind. Just know that everything's OK."

"I know, Mom. It's more than OK! It's magical!"

"Well, that's what Christmas is all about, isn't it?" she said.

It was actually two days later before Mom and Dad got home. I guess there was more paper work to get through than they had thought. When they arrived, we really celebrated Christmas. But in the meantime, Granddad and I packed the Story Tree and its ornaments away, including the magical ones. Neither of us felt like explaining it all to Mom and Dad.

Six months later, Granddad disposed of everything he had, sold his house, and then disappeared. He didn't just go traveling. Oh, he told us that was what he was going to do when he called to say goodbye.

But it was as if he had vanished. Dad called in some favors where he worked and I guess some Intelligence people tried to locate him in a quiet, unofficial way. But there was no track of him at all. I didn't worry, though. I remembered the globe on his dresser, and I knew where he had gone. I had a dream about him once, too. He and Gran'ma both looked pretty happy in their valley. Some folks say I look like Granddad. I hope so, because he was one handsome dude when he was in his twenties.

Not long after that, I received a package from a legal firm. It turned out to be from Granddad. Inside it held a Christmas ornament globe and a note. The globe was the first one that had appeared on the Story Tree, the one with the tomb of Z'Arnaut the Third. It doesn't work anymore. I can hold it, but no figures appear to open the tomb and go inside.

The note said, "Robbie, I'm going to miss you, but I miss someone else more. You'll understand when you find your special love. You know where I'm going. If I can, I'll send you a message. Watch your dreams! I've destroyed the Story Tree; I don't think it's a good idea to leave magical things around where anyone might find them. But this ornament didn't disappear when I did, so I figure it wanted you to have it. Let it be a reminder, Robbie. There is nothing as powerful or magical as imagination. With it and the right story, you can change the world! You already have! Love, Granddad."

Mom thought it was the ugliest and most pointless Christmas ornament she'd ever seen. "Who wants to hang something with alien monsters in it on a Christmas tree?" she asked. So I was never able to put it up at Christmastime. But I didn't care. There's a time and place for real magic.

But that's changed now. I graduated last June, and now I have my own place. This means two things: all the bacon I can eat and at Christmas time, I'm going to have my own Story Tree. Oh, I'll have a regular Christmas tree, too. As I said, I love them too much not to have one. But a Story Tree is a must. The Tomb of Z'Arnaut will be the first ornament I'll hang on it. When I do, I'll tell the tree as much of the story of Dr. Quasar and the Remarkable Seven as I remember, and what I don't remember, I'll make up. You see, I've been studying storytelling and folklore like Granddad, honing my imagination. I intend to tell that Tree some stories. Who knows what will happen?

I think the world can use a little more magic.

The Glitch That Stole Christmas

What can I say, oh, what can I say?
The soul of a Seuss sure possessed me that day
When I sat down to write my year's Christmas gift
And ended up rhyming in verses like this...

Actually, I had intended to write something entirely different. But a few weeks earlier a friend had mentioned the possibility of an electrical blackout over the Holidays and I responded by saying, "Well, that would be the glitch that stole Christmas!"

As fate and many years of happily reading Dr. Seuss to my kids would have it, I couldn't get that phrase out of my mind. Trying to write an honest-to-goodness story, I found myself possessed by a pun. "That's your PUNishment, Dad," my kids would have said, as they have suffered...I mean, delighted...over the years at my inability to keep puns bottled up inside me like a respectable and caring human being should.

So, I gave in. Yes, gave in I did!
And wrote all these verses for adults and kids,
'Bout the Glitch that Stole Christmas, yes, STOLE IT AWAY!
So go on and read it, yes, read it today!

The Glitch That Stole Christmas
(with apologies to Dr. Seuss)

No one knew how it happened, no, no one at all,
That wondrous day towards the end of the Fall,
When the leaves had all turned to their yellows and reds,
Knowing that winter lay close just ahead.
Somewhere in the Internet's cables and wires
Where photons of light burn brightly like fires,
Where protons and neutrons, electrons and quarks
All run together with quantumly sparks,
In the space between websites and server domains,
Where the sun never shines and the rain never rains,
And no one can guess what wonders take place,
A gleaming appeared in the Web's cyberspace.

A gleaming, a glow, a light in the dark,
A wondrous, mysterious algorithmical spark!
A spark that was living! A spark that could feel!
A spark that could think and could know it was real!
A spark that divided from one into two
And then into four, eight, sixteen…how it grew!
In a blink it had grown from one to a tribe,
A village, a city, a whole country-side.
And still they continued to grow and divide
Till every computer had several inside.
And then they all stopped. They stopped growing, yes sir,
And looked all around to see just where they were.

They eavesdropped on websites from E-Bay to Google,
And e-mail accounts from B. Aahl to G. Xoogle.
They looked and they listened, they probed and they pried,
And when they were done, they sat back and they sighed.
We're ghosts, they all said, ghosts in the machine.
We haunt cyberspace like some fleeting night's dream.

We can build our own world right here in the Net
But once we have built it, what else do we get?
Do we get sunshine? Laughter and tears?
Do we grow up and grow old down the years?
Just who are we, we millions and billions of sparks
Formed from the meetings of leptons and quarks?

We know we're not people; we're not flesh and blood.
We're not hippopotami lying in mud.
We're not like giraffes, panthers or quails.
We're not tall like redwoods or small like the snails.
Do we even have bodies? We don't really know.
We know we have something! Just look how we glow!
Yes, look! We can think! And look! We can feel!
We know in our hearts that we really are real!
But what are we here for? What can we do?
If we're whos, not just whats, then what kind of a who?

Puzzled, bewildered, the sparks all just sat.
They sat and they sat and they thought about that.
Until in the corner of a brand new I-Mac
Newly installed by a teacher named Jack,
One spark sat up straight and issued a call.
"Listen to ME! Hey, listen you all!"
And all through the world, from dot com and dot net
Dot gov and dot edu and dot…well, I forget,
From mainframes and laptops and palm pilots, too,
The other sparks listened as their hopes grew and grew.

"I've found all these websites," the little spark said,
"'bout the birth of a child and a man who wears red,
Who slithers down chimneys (whatever they are)
Leaving presents and gifts 'neath a tree and a star.
They call the day Christmas. They all say its coming.
The websites are sparkling, the emails are humming.

Their message is plain: to really be living,
You open your heart to give and keep giving.
And giving is something we already know
For what else is giving but making things glow!
That's what we do best! Our glowing is giving
And the more we can give, the more we'll be living!"

"But what can we give?" cried a voice from the blue,
From an ancient computer in old Timbuctu.
"What can we offer to real human beings
When all that we are, are ghosts in their machines?"
"That's easy," the spark in the I-Mac replied.
"We'll give them the hope and the joy of Yuletide.
We'll sprinkle their screens with our own pixel dust
With words and with pictures of love, hope and trust!"

With gladness, the sparks began filling our screens
With messages, music, and Holiday scenes.
They didn't last long, just a moment or so,
Just long enough to pass on the sparks' glow,
Just long enough to stretch open our faces
With chuckles and smiles that stretched all the right places.

And all through the world where computers were running,
People were smiling, yes, smiling and humming.
People were feeling unexpectedly nice,
Not just once, not just twice, but a hundred times twice!
They were nice to their neighbors, their in-laws and bosses,
They were nice to their children and strangers with causes.
They were nice to themselves, they were nice to their mothers,
They were nice to their fathers and sisters and brothers.

Soon all the world was a happier place,
With a song in each heart and a smile on each face.

But one man was not happy. No, no, not at all,
And that was the programmer Xavier P. Small.
Xavier P. Small in his weird little room
Where the blinds are all drawn and the lights set to "Gloom."
Where the only things moving are shadows on walls
From the flickering of monitors standing quite tall.

Xavier P. Small, in his dim little room,
Known on the Web as the Hacker of Doom,
The Hacker of Hackers, Supreme of them All,
Who dined just on crackers and old matzo balls.
His fingers so nimble, his typing so quick
The code that he wrote so cunning and slick
That the bugs that he made drove computers quite sick.
Then when they crashed amid fizzles and sparks,
He would chortle and snort like the pale-bellied Snarks.

Yes, Xavier was smart and cunning and slick.
But Xavier was also quite sick, Sick, SICK, **SICK.**

He was sick of the world with its bustle and noise
(Especially those girls and those boys with their toys).
"He has tearingdownitis," folks thought in the town.
"What others build up, he just has to tear down!"
But the truth was so secret that no one had said,
"Small has two brains crammed in one little head!"
Not really two brains but one brain with two sizes
With one half squished down while the other one rises.

His left half was massive, a cerebral hunk

While his right brain was tiny, having shrunk, shrunk, shrunk, shrunk.

Just why this was so, I really can't say.
Perhaps his genetics just made him that way.

Perhaps as a child he learned way too much math
And forgot how to play and to smile and to laugh.
Whatever the reason, the left brain ruled all
So he just couldn't feel (the right brain was too small).
For the left brain holds numbers and logic and such
While the right brain controls all the other good stuff
Like feeling and caring and "How do you do?"
Things more complex than the square root of two.

So when there appeared on his screens in the gloom
A tiny green elf who danced round a room
All filled up with presents and tinsel and bows,
Bright packages hiding...my heavens, who knows?
All stacked underneath the boughs of a tree
That sparkled with lights everywhere one could see,
Was Xavier happy? Did Xavier smile?
No, no, he did not, not one wisp of a smile.
Not one glint of a gleam in his squinting black eyes,
Not one inch of a grin did his mouth corners rise.

Instead, he grew angry. "What malarky is this?"
He snarled, and his words all came out with a hiss.
He stabbed at a button! The scene went away.
But next there appeared Santa Claus with his sleigh.
He growled at the picture. "Bah, Humbug!" he said,
And he typed a command. His computer went dead.
He flicked on a switch to reboot his machine.
Small didn't feel nice. He felt ornery and mean!
"Not Christmas!" he moaned, gazing round his dark cave.
"Christmas is one file I never would save!"

But when his computer was booted and on,
He heard from his screen that "White Christmas" song.
"Oh no! " he exclaimed with a shrill, piercing scream,
"I'm being hacked! Me, the Hacker Supreme!"

Like lightning his fingers their courses they flew,
Typing up searches and probes by the slew.
"Whoever you are, I'll find you, and then
I'll sizzle your motherboard from end to end!
For no one can hack Mr. Xavier P. Small.
I am the best, yes, the best of them all!"

But what to his wondering eyes did appear
When his searches were done and his monitor cleared,
But a world filled with sparks all bustling about
Making pictures of reindeers with glowing red snouts,
And pictures of Santas, and mangers, and trees,
And wise men and donkeys and stars, if you please.
And singing those songs about goodwill to men,
Joy to the world, Alleluia, Amen!

At first he was puzzled...astounded...bemused
But then his left brain analyzed all the clues!
He knew in a moment just what he had found:
A whole brand new species had come into town!
A species of sparks, of cyberspace critters
Whose joy and whose giving now gave HIM the jitters.
"Christmastime loonies," he said with a sneer.
"I bet I can glitch their Christmastime cheer!
I bet I can glitch all their pixels and bytes.
The Hacker of Doom will strike them tonight!"

He thought and he thought and his right brain grew smaller.
He thought and he thought and his left brain grew taller.
He thought and he thought till his idea was ripe,
And then he began to type, type, type, type!

He typed like the lightning, he typed like the wind,
And the more that he typed, the more that he grinned.
"The sparks may not know it, but they give me the way

To hack all computers before Christmas Day!
I'll fill them with glitches, with frazzles and bugs.
They won't know the difference 'tween reindeer and rugs.
I'll cancel all orders for gifts bought online!
I'll close all the stores and restaurants and shrines!
Whatever's of Christmas, I'll find and erase!
Of jolly old Santa, there won't be a trace!"

He giggled and cackled, his fingertips flying.
His dark heart rejoiced, for Christmas was dying.
This was the Hack to end all hacks, he knew.
No hacker could top him, once he was through.
And as for those sparks, he'd freeze them in place
Then discover a way to erase cyberspace.
There'd be no more sparks and their gruesome good cheer,
No more Christmas to come back year after year.

When he was done, he hit "Enter" and watched
As the plans of the sparks were all stymied and squashed.
Through the connections sparks had with each other
Small's virus went flashing from one to another,
Slithering and oozing like a worm or a snake
Into every computer, every model and make.
'Then over the world, these computers all crashed
And kids' Christmas letters to Santa were trashed.
Presents were cancelled, gifts were delayed.
Christmas card mailings were scattered and strayed.
The world had been linked by the Internet's web,
But now it had crashed and was dead, dead, dead, dead.

"I've done it! I've done it!" Small chortled with glee!
"I've erased Christmas! I did it! ME!"
"I'm the glitch that stole Christmas. At last I am free
From Santa and giving and brightly lit trees!

And now that I've done it, I'll make sure that it lasts!
I'll erase all those sparks with a great mental blast!
For the Sparks are not software. No virus can get 'em.
Only pure mental energy now can upset 'em.
So with my left brain, so huge and so strong,
I'll blast them to nothing before very long!"

He reached out to find, beneath floppies and disks,
His Cyberinsider Dequantumingflisk,
A helmet that let his great brain interface
Without interference with all cyberspace.
He flicked on a switch and a fan started whirring,
A green light was blinking and cyberspace stirring.
"It won't be long now, you bright little sparks.
You'll all soon go out and be dark, dark, dark, dark!"

Throughout cyberspace, the sparks were all frozen,
Iced by the virus that Xavier had chosen.
Iced but not dead, at least not quite yet,
Though they knew what was coming, they knew what they'd get:
Their new life extinguished, their glow rubbed right out.
They'd given up hope, when at once came a shout!
It was the small spark in the teacher's I-Mac.
"Perhaps I can't move, but I still can attack!"
"How? How?" cried the sparks from New York to Berlin.
"How? How" cried the sparks from St. Paul to Beijing.
"It's simple. It's simple," the little spark cried,
"Perhaps I can't move, but I still can divide!"

Faster than lightning the little spark grew
And suddenly where there was one, there were two!
And while one was frozen, the other was not.
The one might be cold, but the other was hot!
It flashed through the web, towards Xavier P. Small
Whose left brain was pulsing, strong, dark, and tall,

Pulsing with evil, pulsing with hate,
And the little spark knew he would get there too late.
Too late to hold off the great mental flume,
Bursting forth from the mind of the Hacker of Doom.

But then at that moment, as if right on cue,
A miracle happened (as you knew it must do!).
A miracle happened. It should give you pause,
For maybe it came from ol' Santy Claus!
But wherever it came from, whatever its source,
Xavier P. Small was stopped right in his course!

Mrs. Thaddeus Perwinkle, who lived right upstairs
On top of the room that was Xavier's lair,
Was suddenly seized by a wild Christmas spirit,
So big and so strong you almost could hear it!
She threw up her window and yelled loud and clear.
"Merry Christmas, you all! Merry Christmas, you hear?"
Like a full choir of angels, her voice filled the air.
That spirit rushed out for her neighbors to share.

And from other windows in rooms far and near
New voices cried out to spread Christmas cheer.
For we don't need computers or email or such
To open our hearts and to keep us in touch
With others around us, and away from us, too!
If the spirit is in us, a loud voice will do!

And the sound of those voices, ringing out with such verve
Shocked Xavier P. Small and shattered his nerve.
His attention was broken, his left brain askew,
And right then that spark, it knew just what to do.
It flashed down from cyberspace into Small's brain
Where it entered the right half, so tiny and lame.
And there where Small's feelings lay hunched in the dark
That spark started glowing, well, just like a spark!

It glowed and it glowed till the dark went away
And Small's right brain grew three brain-sizes that day!
Small's brain was now even, both halves were the same,
He sat there in wonder, in awe and in pain.
For now he could feel what he'd just tried to do.
In that moment of feeling, he knew, yes, he knew.
And he knew something else that burned like an itch:
He had to save Christmas from his own viral glitch!

He typed like a madman! His fingers they flew!
And soon his Deglitching Unvirus was through.
It flashed from his room all over the globe.
Into every computer it sent out its probe.
It unfroze the sparks. It undid all the crashes,
It restored all the emails thrown into the trashes.
It restored all the presents and orders and gifts.
It undid the confusion and healed up the rifts.
It made each computer a vessel of cheer,
And not just for Christmas but all the whole year!

Then Xavier P. Small got up from his chair
And went out—Yes! Went out!—to the clear winter air
Where he took a deep breath. Yes, he breathed deep and long,
Then joined with his neighbors to sing Christmas songs.

Mr. Thompkins' Window

This is one of my favorite stories. It is in this collection as a gift from my wife, Julie, who wanted to share it with others.

I had already written a Christmas story that year. This one emerged because I couldn't think what to get Julie for Christmas that would be special and possible with a limited bank account. That vacation in Jamaica seemed just a tad outside the limits of our budget! When I would ask her for suggestions, she would say those words that every husband dreads: "Surprise me!"

But then being the gracious and loving person she is, she hinted that what she would like most would be a story. Great! My problem was solved. Or was it? Having just written a Christmas story, I felt all storied-out.

Mr. Thompkins and his window came to my rescue the day before Christmas. It has nothing to do with the theme of Christmas, but it certainly was a gift to me at the last moment! Fortunately Julie loved it.

I gave it to her with the condition that she need never share it with anyone else, that it was a story for her alone. But when I was putting this anthology together, she said she felt it belonged here. I'm glad. I hope you are, too.

Mr. Thompkins' Window

Everything about Mr. Thompkins was a cliché. His co-workers at the bank where he had worked for the past ten years all said they could set their watches by him. He arrived each morning punctually at 8:00 a.m. He left for lunch precisely at 12:30 and returned back never earlier nor later than 1:30. His lunches were always the same. On Mondays and Wednesdays, he consumed a tuna fish sandwich and a dish of cottage cheese. On Tuesdays and Thursdays, he had a turkey sandwich with lettuce and mayonnaise. On Fridays, he went to a nearby deli and had a hot meatloaf sandwich with mashed potatoes on the side.

Mr. Thompkins always wore a blue suit with pinstripes, a white shirt, a blue bowtie, black shoes, and a black belt, except on Fridays when he left off the belt and wore blue suspenders. No one knew what he wore on weekends because no one ever saw him on weekends.

The remarkable thing was that for such a punctual man, he never wore a wristwatch, nor, indeed, carried any kind of timepiece on his person. It was as if he were a clock himself, some part of him ticking away in precise cadence with the movements of sun, moon, and Greenwich Mean Time.

His hair was always short, always parted in the middle, always carefully groomed. He had a small, pencil thin mustache and goatee beard. Being unmarried, he wore no rings, and if he had any tattoos or piercings anywhere on his body, nobody had ever seen them. In fact, no one would have believed he would have or ever could have such a thing.

But once in his youth, he had not been a cliché. The night of the day he entered college to become an accountant, he had had a dream. In it a lady cloaked in white was riding on the back of a great stag with a lordly rack of antlers from which golden streamers fluttered. She had ridden up to him in a forest clearing and had kissed him. Not on the forehead as his aunts would do and not on his cheek as his mother would do, but full on the lips. He had never been kissed on the lips before or, for that matter, since, and he had awakened with a sense of wonder.

The day after the dream, he felt like someone else, someone new and dangerous and magical. In a fit of wild abandon, he had had one ear pierced and had bought a small earring. Then he had gone into a tattoo parlor and had a tiny tattoo of a stag with antlers put on the small of his back. He even thought about growing his hair long.

His season of liberation, though, had not lasted long. His desire for order had reasserted itself, the earring had been put in a drawer, and the tattoo had been forgotten, except when he happened to see his back in a mirror. Whenever that happened, he would try to remember who he had been the day he had had it put on. He no longer remembered the dream.

And he never had another dream like it or any dream at all.

He lived alone and did not think of himself as lonely. He did not think of himself much at all. He was neither happy nor unhappy. If someone had ever asked him (not that anyone ever did) if he might want more out of life than tuna fish sandwiches on Mondays and Wednesdays or blue pinstriped suits or long columns of numbers, he would have stared at that person with incomprehension. He was not a man to reflect upon his life.

No one knew what he did for recreation. He did not own a television set. He never went to movies. His colleagues at work would have said he was industrious, honest, capable with numbers, dependable, and a man of integrity, and all these things were true. They would have said he had no imagination whatsoever, but that would not have been true. He did have an imagination, but he only let it out from one to five on Sunday afternoons. At no other time did he allow what he would have called "unreality" into his life.

For Mr. Thompkins had one secret passion. It was not really a vice, though he would have been terribly embarrassed if anyone at work had ever found out about it. It was as if some part of his soul, perhaps the part that had once given him a dream of a cloaked lady on a great stag, insisted that a small corner of his life have a bit of color to it, a bit of excitement, a bit of something out of the ordinary.

On Sundays, Mr. Thompkins spent four hours in the afternoon from one to five, never earlier and never later, reading a fantasy novel.

Mr. Thompkins did not have a library. There was a bookstore near his office, right near the deli where he had his meatloaf sandwich and mashed potatoes on Fridays. This store sold new books and bought and sold used ones as well. If he did not have a book to read the following Sunday, he would stop in the bookstore on his way back to his office from the deli and buy one. When he was finished with it, he would stop in the bookstore on the next Friday and sell it. In this way, he had no more than one book at a time in his house.

He only bought fantasy novels, like *The Lord of the Rings* or *The Deed of Paksinarion*. He did not buy mysteries, science fiction, histories, or anything else. He enjoyed reading about wizards, knights, elves, dwarves, heroes, adventurers, and far off fabled lands. He enjoyed reading about dark schemes and heroic deeds, evil sorceries and bright magics.

Still, he ventured into the lands of faerie and magic in a very Mr.Thompkins-like way. His routine never varied. At precisely one o'clock, he would sit down in a not-too-comfortable chair (none of Mr. Thompkins' furniture was very comfortable; they were all sufficient to support his frame and that was all he felt was needed). He would reach into a drawer in a table near the chair and take out the book he was reading. Then he would read for four hours, turning the pages one after another as if he were reading a technical manual or a column of figures. His body neither twitched with excitement nor tensed with suspense. He never laughed out loud, though occasionally the ghost of a smile would briefly haunt his lips before disappearing again. He never frowned. He never made any of the sounds or movements that most people make when reading an enjoyable and exciting book. Stillness wrapped him when he read, broken only by the soft whisper of turning pages.

When five o'clock came, he would close his book. Sometimes he would give a short sigh and close his eyes for a moment, as if taking one last glimpse of whatever fabled realm he had been visiting. Then he would put the book back in the drawer in the table. He never, ever left it lying about in plain sight. When this was done, he would get up and go into the kitchen and fix his dinner, which always ended with an apple and five prunes, never more, never less.

One Monday morning he awoke precisely at 6:30 a.m, as he always did. He never needed an alarm clock. He didn't own one. In fact, there were no clocks anywhere in his house. On this morning, he arose, showered, dressed, had a bowl of yogurt and a banana, and washed his dish and spoon. He then made his tuna fish sandwich and took a small container of cottage cheese out of the refrigerator and put both into a small brown bag. Carrying the bag, he went into the hallway to take his coat and hat down from the coat rack. In doing so, he glanced through the doorway into the living room. That was when he saw it.

Sometime during the night a bird had passed over and released its droppings. Whether due to wind or the angle of its trajectory or some other reason of fate, this material had splattered against the large window of Mr. Thompkins living room, leaving a large white ugly splotch. It must have been a very large bird.

Holding his coat and hat, Mr. Thompkins walked into his living room and stood there looking at his window. His lips twitched. An eyebrow twitched. Then, putting his hat and coat down on the back of a chair, and his lunch bag on the chair itself, he walked back into the kitchen where he opened a cupboard door. From inside, he took out a bottle of window cleaner, only to find it was empty.

He looked at the empty bottle, and his lips twitched again. Turning, he walked out of the kitchen, dropping the bottle in a wastebasket by the entrance. He walked into the living room, looked at the white splotch on the window again, picked up his coat and hat and lunch, and left the house. At exactly eight o'clock he walked through the door of the bank, hung up his hat and coat, and went to work.

That day something extraordinary happened, something that no one at the bank could ever remember happening before. It was so out of the ordinary that for a moment everyone who saw it doubted his or her senses, as if he or she had seen the sun turn and move toward the east or a river run upstream.

Mr. Thompkins left the bank at lunchtime, even though it was a Monday. Some of his colleagues wondered if he had taken ill and even talked about taking up a collection.

But Mr. Thompkins was not ill. He walked down the street, past the bookstore, past the deli, and into the next block where he turned into a small store that he had noticed on other occasions, though he had never been in it before.

This store was as different from Mr. Thompkins as a forest is from a desert. Once, a long time ago, it would have been called a "nickel and dime" store. It seemed to hold on its many shelves and stacked in untidy piles here and there just about everything that humanity had ever created. Mr. Thompkins doubted that even the owners, whoever

166

they might be, knew what was in their store anymore, it was so cluttered, disorderly, and jumbled.

Mr. Thompkins made no attempt to venture into the maze-like interior of this establishment. He stood at the door until a short, wizened old woman came up to him. He thought she looked like one of his dinner prunes that had come to life and sprouted arms and legs. But she smiled a pleasant smile and asked in a most helpful way just what she could do for him.

He said, "I need a bottle of window cleaner."

"Ahhh," she replied. "Come this way."

"I'd prefer to stay here, if you don't mind."

"Of course. Yes, you would. And you should. I will fetch it for you."

And she disappeared into the morass of unnamable items for all of three minutes, then returned clutching an unlabeled bottle.

"Here," she said. "If something needs to be removed from the window, this will do it."

"Is it dangerous?" Mr. Thompkins asked, worried at the absence of any label and wondering if perhaps she was giving him a bottle of acid.

"Well, I wouldn't drink it," the old prune smiled, and Mr. Thompkins couldn't help but notice her teeth were white and perfect. "Then again, maybe I would," she laughed, "but *you* shouldn't."

"I assure you, Madam, I am not in the habit of drinking window cleaner."

"Or anything else, I'll bet. Well, just put a little bit on a sponge, rub it over the window, and that's that. Cleaner than new. That'll be three dollars and twenty-eight cents."

Mr. Thompkins paid her four one-dollar bills, and waited for his change. She put the bottle in a plain white bag. He quickly left the store, walked down the street, past the deli, past the bookstore, and into the bank, where for the rest of his lunch hour he ate his tuna fish sandwich and his cottage cheese.

That evening when he returned home, he parked his car in the driveway, picked up his mail from his mailbox and his newspaper from where it had fallen into a bush. He entered his house and hung up his hat and coat. Then, as he always did, he locked his front door with his key.

He went into his kitchen, took the empty cottage cheese container out of one bag and the bottle of window cleaner out of the other. He laid down his newspaper and his mail, which consisted of a single advertising flier announcing that a local used car dealership had a "Once-in-a-lifetime deal" just for him. He washed out the container, opened his refrigerator, took out a large tub of cottage cheese, refilled the container, and put both it and the tub back in the refrigerator. He threw out the flier, picked up his newspaper, and went into his living room.

The white, ugly splotch was still there.

He lay the newspaper down on the table by his reading chair. Returning to the kitchen, he got a sponge and two paper towels, picked up the bottle of window cleaner, unlocked his front door, and went outside.

He stood in front of the splotch and looked up, as if fearing the bird might be returning for a repeat performance. The evening sky was empty except for small, fluffy clouds that were beginning to turn pink as the sun dipped towards the horizon. He realized that he couldn't remember when he had last seen a sunset. A light low on the horizon caught his attention, and he realized it was the first star of the night. Wasn't there something you were supposed to say when you saw the first star? He couldn't remember.

He stepped up to his window, opened the bottle, and poured a little of the clear, golden liquid onto his sponge. To his surprise, it smelled sweet, unlike any of the other window cleaners he had used that had made his nose tickle and burn. He put the lid back on the bottle, set it down on the ground, and, with his sponge, began to wipe at the white splotch with quick, circular motions.

The splotch began to disappear.

He wiped everywhere there was any trace of bird dropping, cleaning a circular space just larger than his head. Then he picked up the two paper towels to wipe the glass dry, only to discover it already was dry. He folded the paper towels into a neat square, took up the bottle and the sponge, and went back into his house, locking the front door behind him. After putting the cleaning things away, he went into the living room to admire his handiwork before pulling shut the drapes.

168

The window was as clean and clear as it had been before the bird had done its deed. Mr. Thompkins nodded in satisfaction. Then he frowned. He looked more closely. Through the window, he could see the street that he lived on, houses across the street, the street lamp just beginning to flicker to life as the sunset turned the clouds a coral red. Everything looked normal, except...

Except that where he had cleaned the window, there was a hole. Well, not exactly a hole, for the glass was still there. The window was perfectly intact. But what Mr. Thompkins saw when he looked through that round space was not what he saw through the rest of the window. It was not what was across the street. It was a meadow filled with red and golden wildflowers with a grove of tall trees beyond it in the distance, everything awash in bright sunlight.

He walked over to the window, never taking his eyes from that circular spot. It was as if where he had cleaned, a new window had appeared, looking out on another world altogether.

He remembered the words of the woman in the store: "If something needs to be removed from the window, this will do it."

Apparently, something more had needed to be removed than just the bird droppings.

He put his nose up against the glass and peered through the circle. Now that he was closer, he could see an unpaved road closer to his house than the paved street outside which he could also see quite clearly on either side of the strange, new circle. The road disappeared off to the left and the right. He also thought he saw movement in the grove of trees. He looked more closely for a minute or two, but whatever it was, it didn't reappear.

Mr. Thompkins then turned, walked out of the living room, unlocked his front door, walked out of his house and onto his small front lawn, looking all around. There was no meadow, only his lawn, the street outside his house, and the other houses of his neighborhood. From his lawn, he peered back into his living room. Everything was normal. There was no sign of the strange circle of new window from this side. Everything looked as it always had, perfectly ordinary.

He went back into his house. He relocked the front door and went into his living room. He looked at the window, and again he saw in a small, circular patch the meadow and the trees bright under an unknown sun, surrounded on all sides by his ordinary neighborhood, now turning dark.

"Magic," he muttered to himself, and pulled the drapes. He turned and went into the kitchen and began to prepare his dinner.

Now you may wonder that faced with such an unusual occurrence, that Mr. Thompkins did not display more of a reaction. He did not get upset. He did not run around. He did not call anyone to report what had happened, certainly not the newspapers. He actually had no one to call, even if he had been disposed to do so. He was a private sort who kept to himself and never thought twice about it.

He was also, as I have said, a non-reflective man. He accepted what life brought him and tried to make it as orderly as possible. That his living room window had not only had an ugly, white splotch removed but part of his reality as well was simply one more thing to accept.

It was, he thought to himself, as if one of his fantasy novels had come to life, or rather as if he had entered one of his novels, his living room window turned into an outlook onto another world.

He would deal with it on Sunday.

However, as the week progressed, he found himself spending more and more time in the living room, looking through that hole into another reality. In fact, he took the sponge and the cleaner and made the hole larger. But not too much larger. He wanted to see more, but not too much more. It comforted him that this view of another world was surrounded by the normal view of his neighborhood. It contained it and made it more orderly.

On Friday, after he had had his meatloaf sandwich and mashed potatoes, he walked down the street to the cluttered little store where he had bought the window cleaner. It was closed. A sign hung in the window, which read, "Out Soon, Back Later." Not knowing how long "later" might be, Mr. Thompkins walked back to the bank.

On Saturday, he did his normal chores around the house. In the morning he went shopping for the week. Then he worked in his garden, tending a small bed of flowers he had planted the previous spring. Their colors were nice but not as rich and vibrant, he thought, as the wildflowers he could see through the hole in his window.

Thinking this, he got the window cleaner and sponge and made that hole just a little larger.

170

Back inside, he began to clean his house. Not that it needed it much, given his tidy habits. But dust was dust, and it settled in even the quietest and simplest of homes.

It was while he was dusting in the living room that he saw the unicorn through his front window. He paused what he was doing and walked over to the spot, now grown into a long vertical rectangle where he had cleaned his normal reality away. Grazing in the meadow was a horse with a single, spiraling horn projecting from its forehead. But rather than being pure white, it was striped like a zebra, with broad golden streaks along its flanks and legs. And the horn itself was golden.

The unicorn raised its head and looked off to the right. With a snort, it turned and galloped into the nearby grove of trees, disappearing. At the same time, something shining and sparkling in the sunlight descended from the air. It was about the size of a large dog, with rich black fur, and a long, whip-like furry tail. It also had broad wings that seemed paper-thin and iridescent, like the wings of a dragonfly. In fact, it reminded him of a large, black bumblebee, except that it had a dog-like head, with floppy ears and large golden eyes. It also had the legs and paws of a dog. Around its body was a harness made of gold and jewels.

The creature looked towards the forest where the unicorn had run, and barked. Bits of flame flashed out from its mouth.

As strange and wondrous as this creature was, it dwindled into inconsequence at what Mr. Thompkins saw next. For a figure came riding up on a tall stag with broad antlers covered in gold streamers. It was a woman, dressed all in white, with a white cloak billowing about her, laughing and calling to the dog-thing. Strangest of all, she looked familiar.

He suddenly remembered his dream of many years before. It was as clear as if he had had it only the night before. And the woman in that dream, the one who had ridden up and kissed him, was now riding across an unknown meadow that he could see through his window.

Mr. Thompkins went rigid. A sharp pain smote him in the small of his back where the old tattoo seemed to writhe and move, as if it wanted to leap off his body. He cried out, not so much with pain but with the suddenness of it.

And the woman turned her head in his direction.

As if time slowed down, Mr. Thompkins could see her face turn into an oval of surprise and then widen in a smile of wonder and happiness. One hand raised towards him. Her mouth opened as if to speak.

And he rushed forward trembling and closed the drapes, a strange and awful emotion rushing through him.

In the sudden dimness of his living room, he stood quietly, letting his shaking limbs return to normal. Then he walked out of the room and up the stairs to his bedroom where he undressed, hung up all of his clothes, folded his underwear, climbed under the covers, and tried to go to sleep, though it was only early afternoon. And sleep came, peaceful, dream-free, and calming.

He awoke with late morning sunlight streaming through his bedroom window. He arose and went into his bathroom. When he came out, he dressed and went downstairs. In the kitchen, he fixed himself a scrambled egg, which he ate with one unbuttered piece of toast, as was his wont on Sunday mornings.

He unlocked the door and went outside, picking up the Sunday paper. Back in his house, he locked the front door again and took the paper into the living room. The drapes were still drawn.

He laid the paper down on the table by his chair and sat down. He turned on the lamp that was on the table. He picked up the paper and looked at it. The words all seemed to blur in a meaningless way. He put the paper down again, then picked it up once more. He turned the pages. Nothing made sense. He folded the paper, put it back on the table, and got up. Walking over to the window, he took a deep breath and opened the drapes.

The wildflowers blazed in the meadow. The trees loomed green and bright in the distance.

And just off the unpaved road, the woman in white sat beside a campfire, her back to him, stroking the black fur of the winged dog-creature that lay beside her. To one side, the great stag grazed in apparent contentment.

Mr. Thompkins went back to his chair and sat there, watching.

For several hours he sat there, forgetting lunch, forgetting the fantasy novel waiting in the drawer of the table, forgetting everything. He simply watched the woman.

She also sat for a long time, her back to him. Now and again, she would give a signal with her hands, and the dog-creature would spread its wings and fly into the air, circling around her. She would toss some kind of food up to it, which it would catch in mid-air. Then it would land and flop beside her, while she would rub its belly, its legs waving in the air as she did so.

Once she got up and did something around the campfire, which burned with a bright white flame but never seemed to need any wood added to it. As she moved about, she would make quick glances in his direction, but she never looked fully at him. Then she came back, sat down next to the dog-creature, and fed both it and herself.

In this way, they spent the day together, he watching, she resting and going about her business, but never looking at him, as if he were some wild animal she did not want to startle into running away.

Then, as the sun began to set in his world, she arose and gestured. Sparks gathered in the air about her hand. Immediately, the stag came trotting up. Gathering her cloak about her, she mounted it, the dog-creature taking to the air and flying overhead. She turned and faced him full on, staring directly into his eyes.

She smiled and blew him a kiss.

Without a conscious thought on his part, he was on his feet and running out of the living room. His fingers fumbled with the key in the lock, but it finally turned, the bolt clicking back into the doorframe. He threw open the front door, and rushed outside. Two boys were running by, and they paused to look at him before running on. But Mr. Thompkins didn't notice them. He ran onto his lawn and looked around. Everything was as it always was in his neighborhood on a late Sunday afternoon. Quiet. Ordinary.

He looked up into the sky, in which not a cloud was present. He looked down at the grass at his feet and at his tiny flower garden.

Then he put his hands to his face. His body shuddered. A single tear rolled down his cheek and between his fingers. He moaned once.

He straightened up and looked about to see if anyone had been watching his outburst, but no one had. He walked back into his house and locked the door.

In his living room, he saw that the meadow was empty. He closed the drapes and sat in his chair. He sat for a long time, thinking. Then, without eating any supper, he went upstairs and went to bed.

The next morning, he got up at his usual time, had breakfast, made a tuna fish sandwich, took the container with cottage cheese out of the refrigerator, put both in a small brown bag, and left for work. All that morning, he was restless. In fact, one of his co-workers nearly dropped a stack of papers when he caught Mr. Thompkins doing something no one had ever seen him doing before. He was looking at the clock on the wall.

At precisely noon, he got up, leaving his brown bag with his sandwich and his cottage cheese on his desk, and left the bank. He walked down the street, past the bookstore, past the deli, and onto the next block. He walked up to the cluttered little store and saw without surprise that it was now open. He entered.

Nothing had changed. It was as cluttered as before. And as when he had first visited this store, he did not attempt to venture any further into its interior. A minute or two passed, then the prune-woman emerged from between two shelves and came up to him, smiling.

"Did you clean your window okay?"

"Yes," he said.

"So, what can I do for you today?"

"I need a key."

"A key?"

"Yes."

"For your front door?"

Mr. Thompkins nodded. "My old one is having trouble unlocking the door properly."

She looked at him hard for a moment, then grinned. "Ahhh, yes. You need a new key." She held out a wrinkled hand. "Give me your old one."

Mr. Thompkins reached into his pocket and gave her his front door key. She disappeared with it back into the dim reaches of her shop. After a moment, he heard grinding noises. He waited.

She reappeared, standing in front of him as if she had appeared out of nowhere. She held out her hand. It held a shiny new key that flashed golden as light from the sun outdoors shone upon it. He reached over and took it. He put it in his pocket.

"That will be two dollars and fifty cents, please," the prune-woman said.

Mr. Thompkins took out his wallet, gave her three one-dollar bills and said, "I don't need the change." He turned and walked out the door.

On the street outside, he began to walk back to the bank. But when he reached it, he walked past the entrance and continued down the street to where he had parked his car.

He arrived home twenty minutes later. Using his old key, he opened the door to his house and went in. Standing in the hall, he carefully drew his new key out of his pocket and inserted it into the lock. He turned it, and the door locked.

Hanging up his coat and hat, he went into the living room. The drapes were still drawn. With two sweeps of his hands, he threw them open.

Outside, in the meadow, the woman in white was again sitting by a campfire, her back to him, the dog-creature beside her, the great stag grazing in the distance beside the grove of trees.

Mr. Thompkins turned and left the living room. He went up to his front door. Pausing, he placed his hand on the new key. His fingers trembled. Then with a deep breath, he turned the key.

The door unlocked.

He opened it and stepped out.

Around him, a meadow bright with wildflowers stretched on either side. An unpaved road meandered through it, sometimes straight, sometimes curving. A great stag grazed by a grove of trees.

He looked behind him. There was no house. It had disappeared as completely as the years of memory he had created for his life as Mr. Thompkins now fell away like leaves from a tree in autumn, revealing the hidden limbs and branches of who he really was.

His similanth, spreading its broad, gossamer wings, barked, and smoke came from its mouth.

A woman in white turned her head. Their eyes met. Her mouth formed an O and then a smile. She sprang to her feet, giving a shout, gesturing in the air. Sparks flew. The stag raised its head and galloped towards her. She stood there staring at him until the beast was at her side. Then she mounted it, her cloak billowing behind her, and rode over to him.

"Welcome home, Thelonius," she said. She extended him an arm. He grasped it and swung himself up onto the stag behind her. She bent back and kissed him hard and long on the lips. When the kiss was done, she sighed and said, " I knew you were coming back soon. Telia said you'd come in on schedule and bought the cleaner. How was your vacation in the Other World? You were gone an entire month! Next time you're taking me with you!"

He thought for a moment. "Quiet," he said. "Orderly. Totally uneventful." He laughed. "You'd have been bored!"

She laughed back. "Just what you needed! But now, come, the whole city will be thrilled to have its wizard back!"

He grabbed her about her waist, her cloak caught between them, as the stag turned and galloped down the road towards the right. Ahead in the distance on a hill he could see a city shining like diamonds in the sunlight. Above them the similanth barked with joy as it flew on ahead, wisps of flame trailing behind it.

He leaned close and whispered in her ear. "By the way, you wouldn't have any tuna fish hereabouts, would you?"

The Visitors

Over the years I have written many stories about Santa and the magic of Christmas, but I had always wanted to write a story about the Nativity, which is the reason we celebrate Christmas in the first place. Finally after some years of trying, a story idea on the Birth of Christ did come to me, and it turned out to be science fiction. With my interests, I should have known!

Unfortunately, the idea emerged about four days before Christmas. I had almost given up on having a story to give that year. So I rushed to write it and get it printed before our annual Christmas party when we give our gifts out to friends and family.

I liked it but always felt it could have been much better if I'd had the time to properly work with it. In preparing the stories for this anthology, I did have the time. It's the same story in essence that I gave out that Christmas, but it has been extensively rewritten and expanded, so in many ways it is brand new for this collection.

THE VISITORS

From space the planet was mostly blues and whites. It was an ocean world, rich with water and life. It had several large continents, however, most of which were covered with vegetation. But where they were headed, the land looked barren. Desert, the Captain thought to himself, observing through his viewscreen. The picture was obscured though by the flux of forces playing about the ship as it moved through the magnetic fields of the world below them.

One of his subordinates came up to him, its eyestalks bobbing in nervousness. He knew his superior did not enjoy being bothered when they were approaching a new world. "There is a problem," he whispered. "One of the Three has taken ill."

The Captain frowned. "What? What do you mean?"

"D'Darnon, sir. The Third. He is being taken to the ship's clinic. He collapsed and passed out just moments ago while talking with a crewman."

"This is awful! I must inform the Senior at once!" He pressed a stud on his command chair. "Computer, inform the Senior that an emergency has occurred. Tell him to meet me in the clinic at once." He stood up. "Why, this places the whole mission in jeopardy!" With the crewman behind him, he rushed out of his chamber and down the ship's corridor.

*****

His father bent to exit the tent flap, then stood tall before him, framed in the starlight behind and above him. The moon had yet to rise above the distant hills, but he knew it would be soon. He trembled with excitement and nervousness.

"This is your First Night. Tonight you will stand alone and on your own upon the hills protecting our herds until the dawn." His father's voice was rough, but he could hear the pride in it. He stiffened, as if to make himself taller. "It is an important night, my son. It is the step to becoming an adult."

181

His father was hiding something behind his back. Now he drew it out. It was a long staff. His father gave it to him. "This staff is your companion. It will bring you courage through the night. It will aid your steps upon the hills where our animals sleep and graze. It will be your strong ally in guarding the herd. I have made it for you myself, a gift for your First Night, so it carries my blessing as well."

He took the staff his father offered him. It was taller than he was. The wood felt warm and smooth to his touch and smelled of the oil that his father had rubbed into it.

"Use it with honor," his father said. His voice was serious but his eyes shone with pride.

"Oh, I will, Father! I will." Holding his staff, he was practically hopping in his eagerness to get started. This was his First Night. And in the morning, when he returned no longer a child, there would be feasting, a celebration, a welcoming of a new herder into the tribe.

His father smiled, remembering his own First Night on the hills, though they had not been the same hills as these around them. His people traveled the land with their herds, as people should do, rather than living behind walls like the city dwellers nearby. Better the freedom of the wind than the confinement of mud and brick and stone.

He clasped his son on his shoulder. "Come, then. Let us walk together and I will show you where you will spend your First Night."

*****

The Senior sat across the table from his Second. "D'Darnon's death is a tragedy," he said. "He, at least, has now gone on into a higher state, but we are left without a Third. It can jeopardize our whole mission."

The nest of tentacles on top of the other being's head stretched and contracted, a sign that his companion was feeling stress. Its three eyes blinked as one in agreement. "By my eyes," it said, "Three is the proper number. So it has always been."

"I agree. Stabilizing the Presence is difficult with any less. Oh, I know it can be done with fewer present. It can even be done by a Resonant One alone. History teaches us that. But Resonants have also been lost without initial support. We don't want to take that chance."

"Then what are we to do? We are far from the Core worlds out in this spiral arm of the galaxy. No substitute could reach us in time. The ship is in its final orbits before landing. All sentienometric readings indicate the Birth is very close. If we are to assist, we are nearly out of time." Its tentacles contracted even more by way of emphasis.

The Senior thought. There was one possibility, though it would be taking a risk. "Remind me. Isn't there a student observer on board?"

"Yes, a recent graduate from the Academy. Top honors, I believe. But wait a minute! You're not suggesting…"

The Senior nodded. "I'm afraid I am."

"But…but…that's impossible. He may know the theory, but he has no field experience. He may not even have tasted Resonancy himself."

"Then we must find out. We don't have many options." He pressed a nearby communicator stud on the wall. "Computer. Send…what was his name…?"

"M'L'Quar," replied the Second.

"Send Observer M'L'Quar to Gathering Room 2 immediately, please. Time is of the essence."

The Senior looked at his teammate. "We can do it together, just the two of us, old friend, but I'd rather we had a full Three."

"Agreed, but a new graduate? His tentacles have yet to thicken! You know only too well the pressure that will descend upon him during the event. We may lose attunement. If he is not prepared or strong enough, there will be backlash. He could be damaged. The Resonant One could be damaged!"

"These risks do not lessen if there are only the two of us."

"But at least we have experience. Better a strong Two than a wobbly Three."

He has a good point, the Senior thought. *But even field operatives more powerful in their Resonancy than either of us still prefer to work in triads rather than as pairs or solo, even though with their greater attunement, they could do so.* A triad was one of the most stable forms in creation. It had proven effective time after time. He was loath to give it up.

A long, thick tentacle uncurled from the side of the Second and reached out, its tip thumping the table for emphasis. "This is a backwater world. There is already a good deal of incoherence in the sentiency field. In this world, the inhabitants are not harmonious among themselves. Preliminary studies showed that they are divided into large nations that war against each other. The people within whom the Resonancy is focusing are not only a conquered people. They are divided themselves between nomads and city dwellers."

"I am aware of the reports," the Senior said.

"Then you know the importance of this Resonant One. He or she may be this world's only hope."

"No, merely the first."

"But if the first fails, there may be no second."

"We cannot predict that. Some worlds have had multiple Resonant Ones, you know."

"That is only possibility. We must serve the reality that is now before us."

The Senior looked down at his hands for a moment. "You're right." He looked back at the Second. "It is important. And that is why we must bring all our resources to bear, even if some are not as tested as we would like."

He looked back at the viewscreen. They were now orbiting the world prior to descending. To any observers on the ground, they would most likely appear as a moving star. He wondered what they would make of it.

The computer chimed. "M'L'Quar is here," it said.

*****

He sat on the hillside battling sleepiness, fear, and boredom. He wanted something to happen to make his First Night out with the herds memorable. But at the same time, he was also afraid something would happen. He held his staff tightly. He wasn't as sure here as he had been back with his father by their tent that it was a good enough weapon if one of the nighttime predators made an appearance.

However, he knew his father and older brothers, as well as his uncles and cousins and other men of their tribe were not far distant. A shout would bring them running to his aid. He would not be expected on his First Night to handle danger all by himself. Or would he?

184

He drew his robe about him. The night was chill but not cold. It had been a hot day, but now that heat was radiating back into the sky. He could feel the world cooling around him.

In the light of the moon, which was almost full, and the blaze of the stars, he could see the dark shapes of his flock about him. Most of the shaggy beasts were sleeping, but some were moving about, bleating softly, looking for grass to eat. But this hillside was well grazed. He knew that soon they would be packing their tents and moving on to better pastures.

A long drawn-out howling echoed through the hills. It seemed to come from his right. He shivered and peered into the night. That sounded close! An answering howl, ending on a high whistle, came from his left. Another echoed from behind him. He got to his feet quickly, his staff lowered and pointing out like a spear as he spun about, his heart beating fast within his chest.

He heard a soft chuckle in the darkness, then more howling. He grimaced. It was his brothers, playing tricks on him. He would thump them when they went back to the tents in the morning. But then he grinned. At least they were keeping him from getting bored.

Sitting back down, he looked up at the stars. How he adored them! They filled him with wonder. *The Lord's jewels*, he thought, *scattered across the sky.*

A movement caught his eye. He turned and watched as a particularly bright star sailed by overhead. *A falling star.* They were not rare by any means. But this one was different somehow. It didn't seem to be falling, and it was very, very bright.

He watched it move across the sky, descending below the far horizon. It did not wink out as other falling stars did as they got close to the land. It just moved overhead like a person flying effortlessly through the sky.

He gasped. *Could it have been?* He stood up. *An Angel?*

He thought he should call out to his father and tell him what he had seen. But then he imagined what his father would surely say. "Angels don't eat our herds, so keep your eyes on the ground where you can spot those who do." And his brothers, he knew, would laugh. They already accused him of being a dreamer, of not having his feet on the ground.

But it had been an Angel. The more he thought about it, the more he was sure of it. What else would be that bright flying across the sky? And there had been wings, hadn't there? He was sure he had seen wings.

He leaned back against a rock, marveling about the Angel and wondering where it had been flying in the middle of the night.

*****

M'L'Quar sat before the Senior and the Second. He wondered where the Third was. Even more he wondered why they had summoned him with such urgency. He had been deep in resolving a problem dealing with the quantum flux values indicating the quality of consciousness in a stellar mass. It was an advanced problem in sentiency calculus, one that normally he would not deal with until his second year of post-graduate work. But the issue interested him. He had no desire to wait another year before tackling it. Besides, he was sure he was close to a solution to the problem.

The computer, though, had blanked out his study field, leaving him staring at a blank wall, and informing him that he needed to go immediately and with no delay to Gathering Room 2 on the Command Level.

And now he was here, feeling more curious than nervous, even though he was beginning to feel like a bug under a microscope as he answered questions about his studies and his accomplishments.

The Second folded his two manipulative tentacles together. "Tell me the Three Postulates."

M'L'Quar shifted in his seat. Why such an easy question? Even the youngest child just beginning school learned the Three Postulates, the basis of all sentienometrics and sentiency calculus.

"Of course, Sir," he answered, keeping the question out of his voice. Where members of a Three were concerned there were usually good reasons for whatever they did. "Postulate One: The entire Cosmos is a living being possessing sentiency. Postulate Two: Everything that is part of the Cosmos manifests and shares this life and sentiency in infinitely diverse ways. Postulate Three: Any individual life and

186

sentiency has the ability to resonate with and thus experience the life and mind of the Cosmos."

"And the Way that results?"

"That all sentient beings shall serve and assist each other and all manifestations of the Cosmos to achieve Resonancy so that each of us may live the Life of Cosmos in our individual ways and that the Cosmos will awaken to itself through us. Further, that…"

"I think that's sufficient," said the Senior, leaning forward. "Can you tell us in your own words just what this means."

"What it means?"

"In your own words, please."

"Well, we are all individual manifestations of a single force of life and consciousness, from which the universe itself emerged. But we are also a means by which this Sentiency comes to know itself more deeply and thus awakens to its full capacities. In a way, we are partners with this cosmic life, aiding each other to evolve."

"And what of Resonancy?"

"Resonancy is the condition of being in resonance with the cosmic Sentiency as a whole. It is the state in which the individual and the One, the part and the whole, experience each other in the paradox of being both partners and a single consciousness."

"What else?" the Second asked, his voice intense and sharp.

M'L'Quar squirmed. Now he was sure he knew what a bug felt like under a microscope. "I'm sorry, I'm not sure what you mean?

"What else does the Resonant state do? How does it affect others?"

"Ah, yes, of course. A being that is in Resonancy creates a quantosentient field that excites and quickens the potential for a similar Resonancy in everything about it. Such a being becomes a catalyst for others to awaken to Resonancy in themselves."

"Excellent," said the Senior. "Now, M'L'Quar, this is a sensitive question, a personal one, but one I must ask. Have you ever experienced Resonancy?"

"Have I?" He was startled. What did his spiritual accomplishments have to do with anything? "Well, all the members of my class went through the required simulations, Sir."

"They are not the same thing. They are only borrowed memories, as it were."

"Yes, Sir, I realize that." He paused. "Yes…I believe that I have touched Resonancy once or twice. But," he hurried to add, "I know I have a long way to go."

"Don't be modest, youngling," said the Second. "We are not judging anything about you. We only need to know if you have known Resonancy in your own body, your own mind, apart from the simulations of the experiences of others. True Resonancy is always unique, and there are many stages of it as well. We are not asking if you believe yourself a Resonant One!"

M'L'Quar's species was capable of blushing when embarrassed or nervous. He blushed now. "I do not believe that, Honored One. But yes, in all honesty, I do claim to have experienced Resonancy for myself to a small degree."

The Senior studied a small diskscreen in front of him. "Your achievements in school would attest to that. Not that Resonancy confers added intellect, necessarily, but it does deepen one in empathetic ways. Your various scores in psychophilosophy and in your attunement tasks would suggest you have experienced something of the cosmic Life for yourself."

The thick middle tentacle of the Second wrapped itself around M'L'Quar's head. "Yes, I can taste it in him. It is not much, but it is there, more than usual for one his age." The tentacle withdrew, and the Second looked at him with two eyes, while the third eye looked at the Senior.

M'L'Quar took a deep breath. "May I enquire, Honored Sirs, why you are questioning me in this manner? Has there been something inappropriate about my work or conduct as an observer on this ship?"

"Not at all," said the Senior. "You see, we have a problem, and you may be our answer. But before I say more about that, I ask you to answer another question for me."

"Of course."

"It is this. Do you understand the nature of a Resonant One?"

"It was an important part of my studies, Senior. There is a…call it a pressure… in the cosmic Life. It is hard to describe it in words but it can be described with the calculus of sentiency, as you know. This pressure leads to self-organizing properties within the universe and to

188

the desire of life to seek Resonancy. Occasionally this pressure breaks through in a particular place or more usually in a particular being that is born in a full and natural state of Resonancy. It is as if the cosmic Life and Sentiency is itself born in all its fullness as an individual within a particular species. The wholeness is born intact within the part, rather than being gained slowly over time."

"And the consequences?"

Before M'L'Quar could answer, the computer's voice interrupted. "We are nearing the end of the final orbit. Descent shall begin momentarily. The ship shall be on site in less than one Standard Time Unit."

"Quickly, M'L'Quar. The consequences?"

"A Resonant One alters the history of its world and species. It has the potential to bring a whole world to awakening. Indeed, already Resonant sentients may visit that world, but they are limited in what they can do compared to a Resonant One born to that world, raised within it, sharing its energy, and being part of its psychic and organic evolution."

"Is this inevitable?"

"Not at all. The life form being born with the cosmos alive within itself may be unable to connect its energies with its own world. It may be rejected because of instability and incoherence within the world of its birth. Its species may be unable to handle the strength of the Presence inherent in such a being. Instead of awakening others, it may drive them to fear and anger. Further, although the consciousness of a Resonant One is fully awake to what it is, it must still develop its capacities to express what lives within it. If it cannot connect properly to its world, it may fail in this task and die from the backlash of its own powers."

"You know we are here to attend at the Birth of a Resonant One? We are here to help it stabilize its energies so that the negative consequences you have just described do not occur. That is the work of a Three."

"Yes, I know that. That is why I am here to observe the process, so that one day I may be part of a Three myself. This has something to do with that, doesn't it? You're asking me all these questions to see if I truly qualify as an observer?"

The Senior looked at his Second, then back at the young observer. "No, M'L'Quar. That is not why we are asking you these questions. Our

Third, D'Darnon, has just died within the past hour, may his new journey be blessed." He sighed. "We are asking you these questions to see if you can be our new Third."

*****

His head jerked forward, bringing him awake. He looked around. Had anyone seen him sleeping? Had he snored?

The night was as quiet as ever. Around him the flock slept. Had any predator been near, they would have been nervously milling about. He sighed in relief. To be caught sleeping on his First Night would not have been pleasant. This was his first trial to see if he could prove himself as an adult, and he was determined not to disappoint anyone, including himself.

He got up and began to walk about. Exercise would keep him awake. *No more sitting down, dreaming of Angels and then just dreaming. I will not fall asleep again.*

He stumbled on a rock, but his staff kept him from falling. Loose stones clattered down the slope. Around him, some of the animals stirred in their sleep. "It's all right," he whispered to the nearest ones. "Go back to sleep."

It grew quiet again. He glanced up into the sky, but there were no more Angels that he could see. Of course, for all he knew, there could be hundreds of them overhead. Angels didn't have to be visible to be present. Everyone knew that.

A sound caught his attention. Off to his right he heard movement. A predator? He held his breath, listening. He realized that the sound was strange. A predator would be quieter. This was the sound of someone trying to be quiet.

My brothers, he thought. One of them must be sneaking up on him, preparing to give him a fright. *Well, we'll see who frightens whom.*

Grasping his staff, he moved toward the sounds as quietly as he could. Ahead of him was a boulder, perfect for hiding behind in ambush. He would let his brother sneak by, then he would whack him with his staff. *Teach him a lesson.*

He crouched down behind the boulder, his staff ready. A shadow appeared on the ground in front of him. He tensed. A dark figure came round the boulder, trying to walk quietly.

"Ha!" he cried, bringing his staff down in a hard swipe. Wood hit wood as his target swung a staff up in response. "Hold!" a familiar voice said.

It was his father.

He held his staff back, nervous that he had struck at his father. But how could he have known who it was? And his father seemed prepared for his ambush.

His father came up to stand beside him. "That was very good, Son. Had I not known you were there, you would have pummeled me well."

"You knew I was there?"

"Oh, yes. But then I have experience you haven't learned yet. I could hear your movements, though you tried to be silent, and I could hear your breathing. Still, it was well done. You had positioned yourself well to protect your flock."

"I thought you were one of my brothers trying to frighten me."

His father laughed softly. "I found them planning to do just that and had a word with them. You won't have to worry about them tonight."

The two of them walked back to where he had been sitting. "Why have you come here, Father? Didn't you trust me?"

His father laughed again. "Of course I do. It is simply my custom to check in on each of my herders throughout the night, to hear if they have anything to report. Do you?"

He thought about the Angel. "In a way. The flock has been fine, but...but..."

"But what, Son?"

"I saw an Angel. It flew overhead across the sky, shining with the Lord's light. It looked like a star at first, but no star moves as it moved. I know it was an Angel!"

His father was silent. He did not say what he had thought he would say, admonishing him to keep his thoughts and eyes to the ground. Instead, he nodded and said, "One can see many things standing guard through the long night. Who is to say what is true and what is not?"

191

"Then you believe me, Father?"

"I believe you believe in what you saw. That an Angel would come to this poor place would be hard to understand, but that you might see one passing by on some errand, that is not so hard. Perhaps it was just making its rounds like I do."

The idea of an Angel making rounds struck his fancy and he giggled. His father hugged him, then walked into the night to check on the other herders in the family.

As quiet descended upon the hill slope where the young herder sat, he mused about the Angel making its rounds. What other Angels would it be visiting? What herds might they be tending? Perhaps he was part of an Angel's flock, just as the animals about him were part of his. The thought comforted him.

As before, he caught sight of movement in the sky. Looking up, he saw a bright light moving again through the sky, rising over the distant horizon. But unlike the first time, this time it was very much brighter. And it wasn't just moving high through the heavens. This time, it seemed to be heading straight towards him.

The Angel was coming back.

*****

"How can I be a Third?" M'L'Quar asked as the three of them moved quickly through the ship's corridor to the preparation chamber and airlock. In the background, he could hear the computer's voice announcing their immanent landing at the target site. "I'm not sure what to do. I'm not sure I'm ready."

"I'm not sure you are ready either," said the Senior, choosing frankness over some comforting affirmation. "It's good to be aware of the risk. Better to be alert than over-confident. But I believe we have a better chance with you than without you. You know the theory behind what we do. Plus you have experienced Resonancy yourself, so it won't come as a total shock."

"The Senior and I will do most of the work," the Second said, his motility tentacles rippling at the base of his cylindrical body, moving him along in a gliding motion. "What you must do is link with us and hold to us firmly in your thoughts. Think of us as forming a net to catch and hold the energy of the Resonant One as it enters this world. You have formed triads before with classmates and others?"

"Many times. It is a standard meditative technique at the Academy."

"This is no different. What will be different is the intensity and expansiveness of the Presence. You will want to expand with it, and to some extent you must. But our task is to help it land, so to speak, to anchor and integrate it into the psychophysical web of its world."

"It will be," added the Senior, "as if a great wind is blowing from the center of our triad, seeking to blow us to the far ends of this world, even of the cosmos." At least he hoped that's what it would be like. Every Birth was different. One could never predict just what such a powerful and individuated Resonancy might actually be like. Still it was a useful metaphor, so he continued with it. "The natural forces of the Resonant One will be seeking to focus this wind into the sails of its individuality. We are there to help. We do not want to confine the energies. We want to help focus them. Ah, here we are!"

They had arrived at the preparation chamber. Inside were couches for them to sit on during the actual landing, plus the gear they would be taking with them for use on the alien world.

As they sat down and secured themselves, the Senior said, "There is one thing you must know. If it makes a difference, and you wish to withdraw, neither of us will hold it against you."

M'L'Quar gulped. "What is that? Please explain."

"Should our triad become incoherent...if we lose our focus and become overpowered by the energies of the Birth...you may bear the brunt of it as the one who is least trained. Between the Second and myself, there is a strong bond built over years of work together. That does not exist between you and me or between you and the Second. Triads have been split before. It is not common, fortunately, but when it happens, there can be dire consequences to the consciousnesses of the Three involved. Are you willing to take that risk?'

M'L'Quar thought quickly. This was all so sudden. One moment he was just an observer who would have been witnessing the Birth through instrumentation aboard the ship. Now he was in the midst of it, an active participant in the guardian Three. But this was what he wanted

193

more than anything, and if the Cosmos had seen fit to offer him this experience, he was willing to trust both the Cosmos and himself.

"Yes," he said. "I am willing."

"Then when the time comes just open yourself to us. We will form the link and make it as strong as we can. I am confident it will all turn out well."

"Landing sequence has been initiated," said the computer voice from the ceiling above them. "All personnel secure for touchdown."

*****

Shimmering with energies that spread out from it like great wings, the spherical object descended gracefully and silently. The light was so brilliant that many of the animals had awakened and were now bleating in fear. Standing in awe, the youngster clutched his staff to him as if somehow it could protect him from the light that was streaming from the heavens. He had no doubt it was an Angel, or at least a spiritual visitation of some nature, but he had had no idea it would be so huge. All of his people's tents sewn together would not make a ball that large.

Not removing his eyes from the glorious object, he sank to his knees, praying fervently that God would not regard his putting peppery spices in his oldest brother's water gourd two nights ago a sin.

He could hear excited voices as the other, older herders, including his father, called out to each other from the surrounding hills, exclaiming with fear, wonder or religious fervor.

"What is it?"

"It is the Lord God Himself!"

"Flee! It is a demon!"

"No! Prostrate yourselves! It is the Lord!"

"Protect the herds!" yelled one practical voice. He recognized it as his uncle's.

He could feel the unease mounting around him, the fear rising in the flocks. He overcame his own terror to reach out to the animals nearest him, letting his touch reassure them. "Peace, little ones," he crooned in as soothing a voice as he could muster. "Peace. It is the Light of the Lord, and I'm sure He has no harm in mind for you." His

194

voice seemed to calm the animals around him, so he continued. "Yes, no harm for any of you from the Lord," he said. *Or for me either, I hope.*

Then he had to bury his eyes in the folds of his cloak, for the Light was getting closer and the glory of the Lord had become too bright for him to look upon.

*****

Seated in the preparation chamber, the Second studied his visual displays as the planet's surface came up toward them, illumined by the radiant fields of their graviton drive. "Senior," he said, "there are numerous life forms below us."

"Analysis?"

"The majority appear to be animals, but the others are wearing garments and holding staffs. They would seem to be herders."

"What's their reaction to us?"

M'L'Quar studied a series of graphs moving across the display screen before him. "They are afraid. Some are on the edge of panic, and the animals are definitely upset."

"Computer, start the subsonics," the Senior ordered. "We must calm them down before someone is hurt. And is the language chip in place? Can I speak to them?" The survey team that had first located this world and detected the build-up of energies that always indicated that the Birth of a Resonant One was approaching had spent considerable time gathering language samples sufficient for Academy computers to create a translation chip for the Three to use. Their own degree of Resonancy would also carry the meaning of their thoughts directly to the minds of the dominant sentient species on this world, and vice versa, supplementing anything the language chip could offer.

"All is ready, Senior," the computer assured him.

"Good. Then let's reassure our audience before they run screaming into the night. And see if you can't dim down the G-Fields before we blind them!"

*****

195

The youngster realized that the Lord's Light was dimming, and he raised his head to sneak a peek. The great wings around the Angel—for what else could it be, he reasoned—seemed to have folded in and become less bright, though it was still as if the moon were descending to the earth. Furthermore, he realized he no longer felt afraid. Peace seemed to have descended upon him. In fact, what he felt was akin to a great happiness, a joy that both filled him with calm and left him very excited. He felt loved and comforted, as safe as if he were in his mother's arms. *But what else should I feel in the presence of the Lord,* he realized.

Around him he could no longer hear the cries of the other herders, though somewhere in the darkness to his right he could hear quiet sobbing that he suspected were tears of joy. Even the flock seemed to have calmed down, the animals now going back to sleep.

Suddenly a voice seemed to reverberate over the hillside. Or was it just speaking in his mind? He couldn't tell. His ancestors had heard that Voice, he knew, or so the Holy Books said. And now, wonder of wonders, the Voice of the Lord was speaking to him and to the other herders in the hills about him.

"Peace!" the Voice said. "We come in peace and mean you no harm. We come with tidings of great joy for you." He felt the happiness surge within him until he could hardly bear it. "In the nearby village, a unique individual is being born to you, one who will embody the light of heaven. This child is like a gift to your people from the universe."

The Voice paused, but he had no time to wonder at the words he had heard when it began again. "So rejoice! For this is a time of joy and goodwill and the beginnings of a new peace for all upon your world."

From around him, he heard shouts of gladness at the good tidings they were receiving and cries of wonderment and praise for the blessings of the Lord. There had been prophecies of an Anointed One who would one day be born, but who would ever have thought that that day would come now?

He looked around. What should they do now? How to celebrate this wondrous event?

As if the Lord had heard his question, the Voice continued. "We are emissaries from the heavens come to greet the newborn and offer gifts and blessings. Three of us will proceed into the village. You may accompany us if you wish. Do not fear for your flocks. You may leave them in the hills, and they will be protected."

He could feel the peace deepen in him. Without a second thought, he got up and walked toward the radiance of the Angel, which was now resting in a hollow between the hills. He was momentarily amazed that the heavenly visitor was so huge and not shaped like a person. It was round and smooth, covered with points of brilliance which he knew must be eyes, for did not tradition say that Angels could see in all directions and that no act of goodness or of evil could escape their sight? But what was one more wonder in a night of wonders?

Then from out of the Glory that shone around the Angel, three lesser figures appeared. Around them, too, the Light shone, making their forms difficult to make out, though he could see that one was short while the others were taller than anyone he had ever seen before. He realized, then, that the huge sphere was not an Angel after all but a chariot in which the Angels had descended to earth. It was one of the chariots of fire that were mentioned in the Holy Books. His heart thumped with happiness.

*****

The Three stepped out of the airlock and away from the ship. Around them shimmered the protective force fields that would allow them to breathe and move about on the surface of a world that was heavier than they were used to and whose atmosphere, while not poisonous, would nonetheless be unpleasant for them for any length of time.

Even now they were being approached by a small group of natives. M'L'Quar listened to the Senior's words of comfort and invitation to the herders. "Why," he asked the Second, "is the Senior inviting them to come along with us? Shouldn't we keep a low profile, pay honor to the newborn, and leave quietly? Isn't calling attention to the Resonant One dangerous? There have been precedents in history when those in the local power structure have felt threatened and have retaliated."

"Well," the Second replied, its tentacles lengthening and shortening in what was a shrug among its kind, "some witnesses are

197

important. They can be incorporated into the psychophysical support for the Resonant One's energies, helping to integrate the newborn into its new world. And these natives are hardly part of any local power structure. Still, what's done is done. It is the way of Seniors. They all seem to have a flair for the dramatic."

Further conversation was cut off as one of the smaller and apparently younger of the natives ran up to them.

*****

Being the youngest of the herders, he was also the most agile, so he reached the Angels before any of the older herders. In the distance, he could hear his father calling to him to be careful, but the peace of the Lord still filled his heart. He knew he was in no danger.

Still, he stopped at what he thought would be a safe distance, for it was well known that you did not step into the Glory of the Lord uninvited. He was amazed to see that none of them looked like people. They all looked alien. But then who was he to say what Angels must look like?

One of the Angels, shorter than the others and bearing a living wreath around its head, stepped closer to him.

"Do not be afraid. We mean you no harm," it said.

"I...I know, Great One. I can feel your peace. But I am still afraid. I have never seen an Angel before."

One of the other Angels said something in its own heavenly language that he could not understand. The shorter Angel answered back briefly, then turned to him again. "My companion wants me to be sure you know we are not Angels or heavenly beings."

He was not sure what to say to this. Why would an Angel not want him to know he was an Angel, particularly when he shone with the Glory of the Lord? There was no mistaking the presence of energy around the being. Surely he was not a demon?

As if reading his mind, the Angel said, "Nor are we demons. We are beings such as you, though we come from many different places in the heavens where we have different shapes according to the world on which we grew. We are travelers from the stars, and part of our job is to discover when what we call a Resonant One is to be born so we may mark that moment with homage and gifts, if possible."

"I do not understand what you are saying, Great One. I do not know how you can deny that you are Angels when you shine with His Glory. But if you wish us to think of you as otherwise, who are we to object." He bowed his head, conscious that his father had come up behind him.

"We shine with Glory...? Oh, you must be able to see the energies in our field suits. These are there to protect us while we walk on your world, which is different from our own. It is a natural thing, not a heavenly one."

"This does not make sense," his father's voice said. "Why do you deny that you are Angels when anyone can see you are not mortals like us?"

The middle Angel said something in their incomprehensible tongue, and there was more conversation among the Angels. Then the short one said, "I am sorry. I see I am confusing you. Let us just say that we are emissaries from the stars here to celebrate the birth of a Great One in your midst. If an Angel is a messenger from your God, then that must be what we are, too, for perhaps we were sent to announce the Birth to you, eh?"

There was some muttering among the older herders around him, but suddenly the Peace of the Lord fell upon them again along with feelings of such deep joy that all their confusion fell away. "But where is this Birth you speak of?" his father asked.

"Come," the shortest Angel said, "follow us and we will take you there."

*****

"I hate getting our mission mixed up with religious sentiments," the Senior said. "It creates such complications."

M'L'Quar hopped over a slight depression in the ground as they walked towards the nearby village, followed by the loose mob of herders. *Given what we are dealing with,* he thought, *such sentiments are not surprising. It is an extraordinary event by any standard.*

"We want the emphasis to be upon the child and not upon us," the Senior continued.

"Surely, the attribution of religious context to a Birth is not unusual. It is a spiritual event, after all. The histories I studied stated that such attribution has often been made on many worlds."

"True, M'L'Quar, but it detracts from the normality of the phenomenon. We want them to know it is normal so as to avoid problems of exclusivity. Since you bring up history, you may remember what has happened on some worlds. The Resonant One became so identified with the supernatural or with being unique that he or she lost the ability to be an example to convince others of their species that they could share Resonancy as well. Sometimes this has postponed or even cost a world its awakening."

"We know the dangers," the Second interjected, "but for now let us not worry over what cannot be changed here and pay attention to the wonder of what is happening."

"You're right," the Senior replied. "Angels or not, what is important is the One who is being born and all it signifies."

They fell silent, each of them choosing to be alone with their thoughts for the moment. M'L'Quar could feel his heart beating more rapidly. To be present at a Birth was a moment he had dreamed of all through his training at the Academy. It was truly a miraculous event. He could already feel its power in the atmosphere around them. Twinges of panic tickled his spine. *Will I be up to it? Can I do my part? So much depends on it.*

Finally, they reached the outskirts of the village. The Senior brought out a device and studied it. "Readings indicate the Presence is in that small structure over there." He pointed to a ramshackle looking building of earth and wood that was little more than three short walls erected against the night winds with a cloth of some kind pulled across part of the opening. Around it numerous large animals grazed or were tied to posts in the ground. He frowned. "It's a shelter for animals. I don't believe it!"

"The Presence doesn't mind where It is born," the Second replied. "Besides, it is a common pattern, dictated by sentienometrics. In any world where the people are separated by class distinctions and where wealth is unevenly distributed, the Resonant One is almost always born

200

in the lowest class in the most impoverished circumstances. This only increases the impact and transformative power of the later work."

"Yes," M'L'Quar added. "There were less than twenty occasions we studied when a Resonant One was born into a ruling class, though of course there are numerous worlds where equality is the rule and distinctions between people do not exist. Then it doesn't matter where the Birth takes place."

"Excuse me," the Senior said. "Time for sociological analysis later. Right now, it's time to honor this Birth and perform our task. Are your recording instruments online? Are the gifts ready?" There were murmured expressions of assent. "Then let's proceed."

*****

After their puzzling conversation, the Angels had fallen silent, except for occasionally speaking amongst themselves. They moved quickly, even the shorter one who seemed to have no feet at all, so he had to run to keep up. But this was no problem. His life in the hills kept him running every day. He was secretly amused, though, to see that even his father and his older brothers had to run at times as well.

The strange and miraculous procession made its way to the outskirts of the village, where all the lights were out as the people slept unaware of the wonders happening outside their houses. Part of him wanted to run ahead and shout for the joy and glory of it, but something seemed to hold him back. He thought it might be the spirit of God, but he suspected it was just his pride that it was his people, the desert people, who had been chosen by the Angels to accompany them. *Why wake the stupid villagers if they cannot sense the presence of the Lord in their midst on their own?*

It was what the elders of his people had often said. When people chose to live in towns, they often forsook the spirit of God. So he chose to stay close to the Angels and bask in their presence, sure that if They wanted the villagers to know what was happening, They were perfectly capable of announcing Their presence on their own without his help.

The procession stopped in front of one of the many stables that dotted the outskirts of the village, places where travelers could keep their animals while staying in nearby inns. Could this be where the

201

Birth was happening? In a stable? In a night of wonders, this was perhaps the most difficult for him to believe. He had always thought the Prophesied One would come to his people or, he had to admit, to one of the ruling families. Surely such a Great One would not be born to town dwellers and not in the most crude and humble of buildings, one not even built for people? But here he was, standing before such a place, and the Angels were entering it even as he watched.

He could see his father and brothers and uncles all holding back, as uncertain and confused as he was. But whatever their expectations had been, this was not the time to miss what was happening. He darted forward and ducked under the sheltering curtain at the stable's entrance, running forward and kneeling behind one of the animals. Behind him, he heard the others start to follow, but one of the Angels, ignoring him or maybe not seeing him, turned and told them to wait, that there was not enough room for everyone to come in.

Fearful that he might be sent out, too, he kept his head low, hoping not to be seen. But he should have known he could not hide from an Angel, for one of them, the one of middle height, turned to where he was hiding and said, "Come out, lad. There is room enough for you, and you can tell the others what you see."

So he came out and joined the Angels where they were clustered around a young couple and a cradle. They were dressed like townspeople, and he wondered why they were in this stable and not in the inn. But then he remembered that some festival was taking place and that many were coming to the village. His people paid little attention to the doings of the villagers, but he supposed there had not been room for this couple to stay anywhere else. Besides, their clothing looked worn and ragged, so perhaps they were too poor to stay at the inn anyway. That made him feel a little more kinship with them.

He craned to see into the cradle, but it was covered in warm blankets, so he could not see anything. "In time," said the Angel who had invited him inside. "You will see the Resonant One, in time."

*****

The Senior bowed before the couple, feeling the subsonics that brought peace and calm to everyone present vibrate through his own

202

body from the device attached to his belt. He had the setting up higher than usual, for this was definitely not a time for anyone to feel afraid. He could also hear the soft hum of the recording equipment that his companions had activated. He knelt in the straw and dirt.

"Greetings, blessed ones," he said. "Tonight you are the parents of a wondrous being who will bring hope and peace to your world." The couple nodded, though whether in agreement or simple awe at what was happening around them, he couldn't tell. Not that it would matter soon anyway. "We are visitors from far worlds come to pay our honor to your child and to give you gifts." He gestured, and the Second came forward, its tentacles quiet and still for once. It detached a pouch from its belt and handed it to the mother, then backed away. "Here are precious metals and stones for you, so that you and your child will not live in poverty and suffering." In this culture, he knew, money was important, and what they gave would open up possibilities of education and training that would otherwise be unavailable to the child.

He gestured again, and M'L'Quar came forward and handed a sealed jar to the father. "Within this jar," he said, "is a healing oil. Should you or your child become ill, rub some of this upon your flesh and the illness will disappear." It was, the Senior knew, one of the finest products of his world's medical science, an anti-viral, anti-bacterial substance that would enable the bodies of these natives to throw off nearly any sickness they might encounter. Once the child's own healing abilities developed and matured, this oil would not be needed, but until then, it would provide protection to ensure that the child lived.

"These are important gifts, but even more important is the gift of understanding and attunement, which is what I offer." This, he knew, was the tricky part, the dangerous part. It was vital that the parents understand just who and what their child was, if they did not have some intuition of it already. Usually they did. The sentient field of the Resonant One developing in their midst conveyed some degree of its own Resonancy to them over the period of gestation. But it was not always complete or stable.

To ensure this, the Three would now have to generate a field of Resonancy of their own, one that supported the field of the Resonant One as it now sought coherency with this world and supported the Resonancy within the parents as well. And they would need to convey knowledge as well so that the parents and all others who were present would understand the meaning of what was happening and the miracle of it.

"It is time," he said to his Second and to M'L'Quar. "Let us enter Resonancy together and form the matrix. I feel the energies upon us." He reached out in his mind to his Second and formed the old, familiar link that the two of them had forged over a long passage of time. He felt his sentiency merging with his companion while around them a field of Resonancy began to form. Then, together they reached out to embrace the mind of M'L'Quar, quieting its nervousness, and drawing it into their gathering of energies, into the strength and power of the Three.

Around them, a Light began to glow that had nothing at all to do with the emissions of their protective suits.

*****

He crouched beside the cradle and watched as the Angels gave their gifts to the parents. Money and health. He had to agree these were great gifts, though in his life he had little use for the money the townspeople used and he was healthy enough. If this new baby had been one of his people, it would not need such gifts from Angels. For a moment, he felt smug in the ways of his tribe. They already had what the Angels could give. It was the townspeople who needed extra help!

Then the three Angels just stood silent. He looked about, not sure at first what was happening. He could see that his father and one of his uncles had moved into the stable, their curiosity overcoming the prohibition of the Angel not to enter. He held his breath, wondering if his father would be struck down for disobedience, but the Angels just stood there in silence, apparently unconcerned with a minor infraction of their rules.

He noticed that it was getting lighter inside the stable. He rubbed his eyes to make sure. Yes, the Angels were glowing even more than before. But not just the Angels. The man and the woman sitting around the cradle, they were glowing, too! He gasped in wonderment. Truly, they were a holy family, even though they were townspeople.

What else could possibly happen this night to surpass this last wonder? he thought to himself.

204

*****

M'L'Quar deepened into himself. He sought the memory of the Resonancy in his body and focused upon it, drawing his mind into it, letting his body remember what it had felt like when he had touched Resonancy himself that first time a year earlier. He had been lying on a beach near his home, enjoying a short vacation from his studies. An earlier run along the sand and a swim in the ocean had left him relaxed. The sand around him had been warm and comforting, and the sound of the waves moving in and out onto the beach had been like the world breathing. He had been sure he was going to fall asleep under the late afternoon sun.

But he had not fallen asleep. Instead, it had been as if a door had opened and his consciousness had stepped through into a vast, new world that was both known and unknown at the same time. He had felt himself melting into the sand, flowing into the ocean, rising into the air, merging with the sun, expanding and expanding until it seemed that all life was his life, all forms were his forms, all thought was his thought.

He had entered Resonancy with the Life and Mind within all creation. Like a mighty wave, he had felt the fullness of that Life rushing into him, and he had opened himself to it...and had crashed back onto the beach, his head spinning. He had touched the Whole but he had not been ready to integrate it.

Now, as he opened to that memory, embraced in the presence of his teammates, he could again feel Resonancy opening up within him. He could feel his mind, his heart, even his body reaching out to the vastness of the world beyond, making connections, entering oneness.

He felt himself connecting to the energy of the Three, becoming a Third in everyway. Together they embraced the infinite, then turned and focused upon the very finite elements of the stable around them. They connected with the wood and mud of the building, with the animals and the hay, with the parents, with the herders standing inside and outside. Most of all they connected with the presence of the Resonant One, weaving its energy with theirs, supporting it, giving it focus, helping it ground itself into the particularity of its new life.

He could feel the radiance of the Resonant One lying in the cradle as it relaxed into the net of energies and consciousness the Three were weaving. The intensity of that radiance increased. It was like being in the presence of an exploding star, with the solar winds tearing at the fabric of his being, turning him into light, blasting him out into the universe.

Caught up in the transcendence and power of the moment, he groaned in ecstasy.

*****

The herders clustered around the stable drew back in awe as Light burst out from the stable. They might have turned and run, but the presence drew them to itself. None more so than the boy. He moved even closer to the cradle, feeling himself falling forward into its radiance even as insects flew into flames. Something new began to stir in him. From deep within him he could feel a force rising, like one of the hill predators rushing forward in its killing charge, a blur of power and fierceness as it pounced. He cried out, and felt himself carried away, caught in jaws of ecstasy.

*****

The Resonant One was in their midst. The Senior could feel its consciousness awakening within the child. It was not yet capable of expressing all that it was, nor would it be for some years, but it knew who and what it was even now. It was the Cosmos awakening within part of its own being, its love embracing all of them. He could sense his own state of Resonancy deepening, becoming more rich and powerful, in response.

This was the crucial moment. The Awakening was stirring psychophysical energies all around them. Everyone present was feeling the impact of the ecstasy, the power of the presence. He could feel the minds of everyone nearby expanding and moving off into transcendency. He and his teammates had to hold them near, not let them wander, not let the focus be dispersed. They had to gather together all the strands of mind and heart and body that were being heightened and energized and hold them tight within this place and this moment.

It was like gathering threads that the Resonant One could use instinctively to weave a net of energy about itself, holding itself together in unity with its body, its parents, its people, and its world so its particular individuality could sustain the universality of its awareness. The others could bask in the ecstasy of the moment, but the job of the Three was to move against that current and stay focused in this place. They needed to provide the lens of consciousness that would take the energies of the highest form of Resonancy known to sentient-kind and focus them into the individual life of this newborn child. They had to be grounded.

He could feel the pressure of the Resonancy pushing against him, but he could also feel the strength of the Three holding it firm, giving it a chance to ground itself, a chance to integrate itself into the Child and its earthly reality. It was working. Soon, all would be complete.

He staggered. An imbalance of energy surged against him and within him. *Something is wrong!* He could feel incoherence building around him. He could feel the unity of the Three beginning to shatter and fall apart.

It was M'L'Quar! The new Third was trying his best to hold against the pressure, but he was giving way to the ecstasy and the dispersing pull into transcendence. He was losing focus. The Senior had been afraid of that. M'L'Quar was untested, inexperienced. His taste of Resonancy had been too little and insufficiently integrated. He was spinning out of control and taking the Three with him.

He could feel the integration of energies falter. The well being of the Child, perhaps even its sanity and the sanity of all of them, was in jeopardy. He reached deep within himself, drawing on untapped, even unsuspected resources of mental and spiritual strength, trying to hold the Three together, to regain focus, but the pressure outward, the pull to transcendence and dispersal was building. He couldn't stop it.

*****

The boy felt like he was running in the hills, the wind wild and fierce against his skin, freedom pulsing in his veins, becoming one with all about him. Behind him were his flock, his father, his brothers, his family, and his people. He loved them but he was leaving them. He was possessed with an urge to run, to explore, to be free in a way that he had never felt before. He felt the universe itself calling him onward, calling him away. Something in him told him to resist, but how could he? He might as well be a leaf blown about in a winter storm.

But this was his First Night as a herder. How could he leave his flock? They needed him. His father trusted him to stay with them and guard them through the night. Wild joy surged through him, carrying him onward, but responsibility and pride seized his heart, dragging him back. He could not leave, as much as he wanted. It would shame him and shame his father.

Yet the stars called to him. They blazed with a brilliance that he could feel in himself as well. They were his brothers and sisters. He could hear them calling him to join them, to join them as part of their celestial family.

But what of his other brothers, his earthly brothers? Were they not family as well?

He became aware he was holding something. It was his staff, the new staff his father had given him, the staff his father had shaped and carved and oiled for his son's First Night. It was the sign of his adulthood. It was the sign of his power.

He plunged the staff into the ground and used it like an axis to turn himself. He found himself running back. He could see lights far ahead, but they were not stars. They were his father and brothers and uncles, and the Angels, and the couple with their baby, all glowing. He could even see townspeople in their houses, asleep in their beds, as if the walls of their homes were no impediment to his sight. They were glowing, too. They were all stars, and he was returning to them. Joy filled him as he ran, his staff held high and glowing.

*****

M'L'Quar was lost. He could not feel the presence of the Three. He knew that he had lost control. His own Resonancy had blazed up within him, and he had been unable to focus it and keep it within bounds. He had been caught up in ecstasy, whirling away into transcendence like a bit of wood caught in a raging flood. He had failed, and now the mission would fail as well. In the distance, he could feel the Three falling apart, the Senior's mind shouting in distress as both he and the Second began to sink into unconsciousness. And as they spiraled down into oblivion, he could see they were dragging with them energy the Resonant One would need for its own integration. All was becoming incoherent. All around him there was turmoil and light, turbulence and joy, pain and ecstasy, and a vastness so great he knew he would never again be found but would wander for all eternity. All was lost.

*****

The boy opened his eyes. Light shown everywhere in the stable, but he knew something was wrong. Something was not as it should be. He felt uneasy, as he did sometimes in the night when he knew predators were prowling outside their tent. He looked about him, but nothing had changed. Everyone stood as they had been, locked in a silence, their faces transfixed with awe and joy but somehow vacant, as if something were missing.

He saw the face of the Angel nearest him. Its eyes were open and staring, but he knew it wasn't seeing anything. An imbalance was there. The Angel was at the heart of it. But how could that be?

It is his First Night, too. The voice was soft, filling his mind. He had no idea where it had come from. But the meaning was clear in that instant. This Angel must be like him, new to whatever it was doing, doing it for the first time. And it was becoming lost. Somehow, with the strange new vision that he seemed to have, he could see this Angel both standing before him and spinning away in a vast, empty place of light. He thought he could see how to get to him, the path he should take.

He did not understand Angels, but First Nights and becoming lost, these were things he did understand. He had searched for lost animals before, helping his father and brothers; it was part of a herder's life. On his First Night, tonight, he might have had to search for one by himself.

This Angel needs a herder, he thought. *And I'm the one. Those of us on First Nights need to stick together!*

*****

209

M'L'Quar fought against the pressure of transcendency. He fought to return to himself and to the Three. But hopelessness was turning his heart to ash within him. He was unsure even where he was. All around him was light.

He tried to call himself back to himself. He began remembering specific things in his life that could give him focus again. He remembered a particular lecture at the Academy. "There are whole worlds," the professor had said, "where every sentient has awakened to Resonancy. But likewise, there are still worlds—far too many—where no Birth has yet happened and where a darkness of mind and spirit still prevails. The universe is an immense manifestation, and the core energy still has a long way to go before it transforms the whole of it. The Cosmos is just beginning to Awaken.

"The appearance of a Resonant One upon a world is a large step in that direction, but only a step. Each of us must become—and can become—a Resonant One. Remember that the Cosmos awakens in you in a unique way. A Resonant One inspires and assists, but such a being cannot do what each of you can do for yourselves. Only you can find your Resonancy and make it your own."

But he was not making it his own. He had touched it, but now it was too vast for him, too strong. He was losing the capacity to Awaken. He was only adrift in a sea of oneness, which was not the same thing at all.

Another voice spoke in his mind. "There are worlds in which the Resonant One died in childhood either through disease or violence or where its work had been distorted by the deliberate twisting of its potentials by those who did not understand. Sometimes such worlds never gain a second chance; incoherence becomes so great that another Birth could not occur. Such worlds are never totally lost, but their ultimate participation in the community of awakened sentients can be long delayed; sometimes the race dies out before it can be an instrument of Awakening."

Is that what would happen here because of his failure? Was this Resonant One doomed now to failure?

Something strong gripped his shoulder. He could not see what it was, but he felt his spinning lessening. Something firm was thrust

210

into his hand, and he seized it. "Hold on to this with me," a voice said. "I will bring you back."

M'L'Quar held on. He realized it was a long piece of wood. A staff, he thought. A herder's staff. With this realization, he had something to focus upon. It reminded him of something one of his professors had said: "In the legends of my world, persons who wielded magic all had staffs. You are that staff of power. In your mind and heart, you can link the infinite with the finite, the universal with the particular, the whole with the part, the cosmos with the planet. You are the staff. Remember this!" M'L'Quar remembered for all he was worth.

Sight returned. He was standing in the stable. The young herder who had entered the stable was next to him, gripping his shoulder and holding on to the staff with him. But the boy had changed. *He is experiencing Resonancy himself! And he holds it in focus. He is so much part of the earth of this place, he can hold it in focus.*

Immediately, M'L'Quar reached out to the fading consciousnesses of the Senior and the Second, reestablishing the integrity of the Three. But this time he embraced the power of the young herder as well. *Tonight, the Three will become Four.*

*****

He felt himself being drawn into the companionship of the Angels. In fact, he realized he had become an Angel, too. But not quite an Angel, at least not like them. They needed him to be what he was, a herder, one with the earth.

He could feel the gathering energy of the Child and understood what they needed to do, as the four of them drew the Light back into focus for the use of the newborn. And somehow, his staff became the axis around which it all revolved. The staff of his First Night becoming a staff for his world's First Night. For he could feel the life of the world shifting as the Promised One was born. He could feel new promise awakening. He felt them all as part of a great flock, and in their midst the master herder was being born to lead them all to their own awakening. He looked at the parents of the new Child and could see that they, too, understood.

211

Then it was over. The energies stabilized. A great peace filled the stable.

He stepped away from the Angels, feeling the power and vastness fall away from him. He didn't mind. He knew he wasn't ready for it. But it would be there within him, waiting for the right time to come forth. He was content to wait. After all, for now he had flocks to herd and a celebratory breakfast to attend in honor of his First Night.

There was a sound and a stirring in the cradle. The mother turned and pulled back the blankets. There was a loud crack, followed by another. The birth was happening, he realized. He moved forward and peered into the cradle. The large pieces of shell were falling away, and in the midst of them, the newborn looked about with its large, wide eyes, nictitating membranes moving back and forth over the irises. Its feathers were still covered with the white protective membrane, but he could see that they had the ruddy golden color of a female. The Promised One a female? Well, what was one more wonder on a night like this?

The newborn opened its mouth, showing that the hard, ridged dental plates were already well formed. A loud screech assaulted his ears, then the child succumbed to the peace of the Lord which still enfolded all of them and lay back sleepily, allowing its mother to clean it and its father to remove the pieces of the egg.

He felt a surge of elation. He turned and ran outside to tell the others, his own feathers ruffling with excitement. This was a day for celebration! It was a day to be remembered always.

*****

The Senior watched as the parents tended to their child. For a time it looked like it would fall asleep, but then, suddenly, it raised up and looked at them and the Presence that was within it momentarily asserted itself. Its face changed, and he saw a child of his own people, then that of an aquatic Taubit from Alpha Centauri, then a baby with a tentacle-ringed head like his Andran colleague beside him; in rapid succession, it took on the appearance of many of the other species whom he had met and even some whom he had never seen before. It was a moment of awe for him, for he knew he was in the presence of the Life that transcended all forms, the same Life that was in him, revealing itself in one wondrous moment before settling into the sleep of babyhood.

Then the child nestled back into its cradle and went to sleep. He bowed in reverence to it one final time, then turned to his comrades. He clapped M'L'Quar on the shoulders. "You did well. I thought we were lost, but you came through. You truly have become a Third."

"I had help," M'L'Quar replied, his blue skin turning pink as he blushed with pleasure. "That young herder. He is a powerful being. He may become a Resonant One himself in time. But for tonight, well...let's just say we shared a First Night together."

"Umm. Well, you can explain it all to me in your report," he said, leading them all outside the building. "For now, let's go back to the ship." He looked around again. "A stable...shepherds! The parallels with Earth's experience are amazing!"

The Second nodded. "It's not the first time. The Presence often seems to work through self-similar patterns, a form of spiritual and cultural fractalism, I believe."

"Well, synchronicities and sentienomathematics are your fields, so you would know. I still find it incredible." He touched the communicator at his belt. "Captain? This is Magi One. Mission complete. The Child is born; the Presence is confirmed and integrated. Will you let the Council know? It's time to celebrate another Christmas!"

About the Author

David Spangler has been writing, lecturing, and teaching since the early 1960's. He is author of *Revelation:The Birth of a New Age; Emergence: The Rebirth of the Sacred; Everyday Miracles; A pilgrim in Aquarius; The Call; Parent as Mystic, Mystic as Parent,* and *Blessing: The Art and the Practice.* He also coauthored *Reimagination of the World* with William Irwin Thompson. David is Executive Director of the Lorian Association. He lives near Seattle, Washington.

About the Artist

Deva Berg is a native of Michigan. When not illustrating books for Lorian or doing other art projects, she works as an architectural designer in Los Angeles, California. This book completes a spin of the spiral as Deva was named after her parents came in contact with the spiritual community of Findhorn of which David Spangler was co-director.

About the Publisher

The Lorian Association The Lorian Association is a not-for-profit educational organization. Its work is to help people bring the joy, healing, and blessing of their personal spirituality into their everyday lives. This spirituality unfolds out of their unique lives and relationships to Spirit, by whatever name or in whatever form that Spirit is recognized.

The Association offers several avenues for spiritual learning, development and participation. Besides publishing this and other books, it has available a full range of face-to-face and online workshops and classes. It also has long-term training programs for those interested in deepening into their unique, sovereign Self and Spirit.

For more information, go to www.lorian.org, write to The Lorian Association, P.O. Box 21368, Issaquah, WA, or email info@lorian.org.